Say You'll Love

Kiki Archer

Title: Say You'll Love Me Again
ID: 24808895
ISBN: 978-0-244-19041-5

K.A Books *Publishers*

www.kikiarcherbooks.com

Published by K.A Books 2019

Copyright © 2019 Kiki Archer

Editor: Jayne Fereday

Cover: Daniela Di-Benedetto @designbydaniela

Kiki Archer asserts the moral rights
to be identified as the author of this work.
All rights reserved.

Author photograph: **Getty Images**

ISBN: 978-0-244-19041-5

*Ride the journey called life with no regrets.
Thank you all, for everything.*

CHAPTER ONE

The clock ticked quietly in the corner of the room. Steady. Stable. Safe. A comforting heartbeat that filled the silence.

Sophie closed her eyes. Was it comforting? Or was it horrifying? The tick symbolising the present, only there for a split second, before the tock pushed the present into the past.

"Tell me what happened."

Sophie stayed silent. *Happened.* The tock came again. It happened, then it was over, gone. She waited for the tick. How self-indulgent, she thought, to spend the fleeting moments we have in the present, talking about the past.

"It will help. Sophie, I promise."

CHAPTER TWO

"I miss her so much." Sophie felt her nostrils flare. It was that all-too-familiar first stage of her tears. Her jaw would tense next, as her back teeth bit together in the vain hope the control would rise against the quivering onslaught of the rest of her face; her forehead and eyebrows joining in the betrayal with flickers of uncontrollable pain. Sophie closed her eyes, having learnt the only way to regain composure was to keep her jaw clenched, her brow furrowed and her nostrils wide as she drew in a breath which she held for as long as possible whilst shaking her head, as if willing the emotion away. She exhaled slowly.

Her friend's voice coming from the armchair opposite was gentle. "You have to open up to me."

"I know," managed Sophie as her nostrils danced some more. She looked to the wooden floor, her whole face clenched in a scrunched up mess of dying composure. "It's just so hard," she said, as she pulled down on her sweater sleeves, ready to absorb any escaping tears. "No one knows, and I've had no one to talk to." Her words faltered as the tears started to flow. "I'm so lost, Laura, and I'm so alone."

The gentle voice snapped and rose an octave. "I've always been here for you!"

Sophie balled her fists into her sleeves, wiping her cheeks roughly before pushing herself up from the sofa. "I knew this was a bad idea."

"Sorry, sorry, it's not. I'm still learning. Please. Forgive me. Sit down. Let me try again."

"You're judging me. I knew you'd judge me."

"The last thing a life coach does is judge their clients."

"So what was that?"

"That was your friend shocked to find out one of her closest friends hasn't been able to talk to her."

Sophie shook her head. "I didn't plan on talking to you today. You said it would be all about *empowerment* and *identity* but then you went and did that thing where you asked if I was okay."

"And you faltered for that second too long."

"And you didn't say anything."

"Rule number one of the life coach: Use the silences."

Sophie looked down and found the knot in the floorboard she'd befriended earlier. She scuffed it with the toe of her shoe. "Silences don't make me talk."

"You just talked in that silence."

"But I didn't say anything worthwhile."

"You did in the silence before and, anyway, everything you say tells a story. Right now you're deflecting."

Sophie's laugh wasn't intended. "Are you *actually* being serious? You said I was doing you a favour. You said you needed a case study for your certificate: *Realising potential*. But you're just sitting in that armchair like M from James Bond."

"This is a pixie cut. It's not an old-woman's hair style. It's sophisticated and grown up." Laura adjusted the fall of her short fringe. "You've just told me something huge. Let me help you."

"I didn't mean to tell you."

"I know. It came out in one of my tactical silences."

Pulling on her sleeves again, Sophie bit the inside of her lip before shaking her head, trying desperately hard to stop more tears from falling. "Oh, Laura, she's broken my heart into a thousand tiny pieces, but all I want to do is pick them up and place them right back in her hands."

The screech was loud. "You loved her?!"

"I love her."

"Oh god, Sophie, just sit down would you!"

"I can't. Everything reminds me of her which makes it so hard to forget about her. The last thing I need to do is to sit down and talk about her. It's over."

"Why do you have to forget about her?"

"Because she told me to fuck off."

"Oh what a bitch! How dare she? Who is she? Show me a picture! Do I know her? Why haven't you told me about her? About women? Is she your first? Honestly, Sophie, where has this come from? Have you always felt like this? Have you ever felt like this about me?"

"I'm not sure life coaching's meant to go like this."

"Sod the life coaching, I want the gossip!"

"And that's why I've stayed quiet. This is the realest thing that's ever happened to me and I don't want it degraded into something it's not. It's fine, honestly, I'll just figure this out on my own." Sophie sniffed at the reality of the words. "I chose to keep the highs quiet so it's only fair I keep the lows quiet too. Karma I guess, to suffer on my own. To cry."

Stepping around the small coffee table, Laura reached out for her friend's hands. "Crying's how your heart speaks when your lips can't explain the pain you feel."

"Life coaching 101?"

"I saw it on Instagram. But I can do this. I can help you. Let me help you. Please sit down and be my client. We'll do things properly. This fits in with the *Resilience* part of the certificate: *Navigating those inevitable bumps in the road.*"

Sophie pulled her hands out of her friend's, hiding them back in her jumper. "This is so much more than a bump in the road. I honestly don't know if I can recover from this." She shook her head. "If I can return to the person I was before."

"So sit down. Talk about it. Tell me what you mean."

"Honestly, I'd rather not."

"Would it help if I promised to keep our sessions private, even from us? As if you're a stranger who's just walked in? The second you leave the room you're my friend again and I won't mention anything we've discussed in here."

Sophie couldn't swallow her splutter of disbelief. "I know you. There's no way you could do that."

"Confidentiality. It's a big part of life coaching." Laura started to pace behind her armchair. "Imagine I cross paths with a client in town. Now imagine they're with their wife. Imagine that client's been moaning to me about said wife. Let's say he's told me about the kinky shit she likes in bed. The kinky shit he's uncomfortable with. I'll have to say hi to her like I don't know she's into doctors and nurses."

Sophie laughed. "My turn to coach you. Doctors and nurses isn't kinky, and if you're going to be a life coach you can't be judgemental. And why would clients be talking to you about their sex lives anyway? I thought life coaching was all about empowering people to achieve their goals?"

"Their professional goals and their personal goals." Laura returned to her armchair. "Sit down. I can empower you and this mystery woman to play nurses and nurses if you like."

Sophie gave a mirthless laugh before giving in and slumping back on the sofa. "Jazz and I would definitely both be doctors."

"Jazz! This bitch is called Jazz?!"

"Jasmine. She uses Jazz on stage."

"Why does she need a stage name? Is she a showgirl?"

"What do you mean showgirl? Why has your mind automatically gone to showgirl? What is a showgirl anyway?"

"Oh, Sophie, are we doing this or not?"

"I don't know, are we?" Looking around the space, Sophie had to admit that Laura had tried to get the set-up correct. The not-so-small fourth reception room in Laura's parents' not-so-small three-storey house had been redecorated with no expense spared. "Where's your armchair from?" she asked, returning her attention to the plush leather.

"You're deflecting, but it was shipped over from Italy. Look how deep-set these buttons are. It's the finest upholstery money can buy."

"And this sofa?" asked Sophie, stroking the cushion next to her thigh.

"Oh that's just DFS. Top of the range mind. But I felt it important to differentiate between life coach and client."

"And the plants?" Sophie signalled towards the tall topiary framing the French windows and neat garden.

"I had a feng shui expert in. She worked with mum's interior designer. Apparently the best look for a therapist's room is simple, ordered and neutral but with a personalised softness displayed through family photos and children's drawings."

"You're twenty-three, Laura, and you're an only child with no offspring."

"Exactly, so I chose that painting. Dad commissioned an artist. It complements the light green theme of the room."

Sophie followed the nod and twisted to the wall behind her. She hadn't noticed it when she'd walked in. "Okay," she managed, after a long frown. "I can see it's you, but where are you? And where did you get those kids from?"

"I'm working in the paddy fields with some Indian children. Look how they're crowding around me."

"Have you been to India?"

"No, but I went on that gap year to Corfu."

"You were gone for three weeks."

"It's an artist's impression. It's fine. It does the job." Laura waved her hands at their surroundings. "I'm serious about this and I know everyone's probably thinking it's just another venture funded by my deep-pocketed parents but I'm enjoying the course and I want to get my certificate so I can do this properly and, yes, while life coaches don't need qualifications I want something to add to my presentation wall over there to show that I really do mean business."

Sophie peered at the wall. "What's the certificate that's already up?"

"Oh that's my grade one piano. Another personal touch." Laura nodded. "So are you comfortable?"

"Not really."

"Well let's ease ourselves in." Laura smiled. "Hi, I'm Laura and I'm going to be your life coach."

Sophie couldn't help but smile back. "I'm Sophie."

"So. I'm going to provide you with the tools to confidently face any difficult situations in your life. I'm going to help you push past any emotional barriers you may be experiencing. I'm not going to be an agony aunt and I'll never attempt to tell you what to do." The monologue faltered as the laminate sheet that had been resting on the coffee table was lifted. "Life coaching's all about objectivity, structure and empowerment, not instruction or indoctrination." Laura returned her attention and nodded at her friend. "Basically, Sophie, I'm going to give you the power to help yourself. I won't be offering advice, opinions or judgements as that undermines the basic principle behind life coaching: You already have the answers. You just need a little help in finding them." She nodded again. "It's like this. I won't be controlling the JCB, I'll simply be by your side with a shovel. Happy?"

"As I'll ever be."

"Was that good? Did you like that analogy? We were told to think of one that would illustrate our role."

"We're working together. I get it. You won't judge me. You won't offer your opinion."

"Correct."

"So you won't react when I tell you I've had six months of magical chaos."

Laura cleared her throat. "I won't."

"Or that it was the realest, surest thing I've ever known."

The cough came again. "Nope."

"Or that I feel in the deepest, most honest part of me that I've found my soulmate."

"Soulmates don't tell each other to fuck off." Laura paused. "Sorry. Start at the beginning. I've got this. We've got this. Just tell me your story."

"This isn't a story, Laura. This is my life."

CHAPTER THREE

Sitting in the front row in the darkened room, Sophie adjusted herself on the plastic chair. It was hard and uncomfortable and this definitely wasn't the high-end comedy club her colleagues had claimed. It was the basement room of Montel's, the dodgy bar she and her friends had frequented when they were seventeen, their fake IDs never requested once. Why Tessa and John would think this an appropriate choice for a work night out was beyond her. They were both shy introverts. They'd usually choose a play recommended by a parent of a student, or a talk in the local library by a visiting author no one had heard of, or even a guided walk around a nearby monument of interest, but a comedy evening? In a bar? The three of them had never done anything like this before and they'd certainly not shared alcohol unless you counted the thimble-full of sherry Tessa always offered around at their Christmas do. A Christmas do that consisted of the three of them standing awkwardly in the reception area of their music studio complimenting the decorations that were hanging from each of their doors before John made his yearly suggestion of a communal Christmas carol, which meant they could scuttle back to the safety of their individual music rooms and play their pianos, their singing echoing out of the open doors, festively filling the reception area; quite nice if anyone had actually been there to listen.

Sophie turned to her colleagues. John was sitting beside her clutching a pint of stout and Tessa was twisting an empty sherry glass around and around. "Would you like another?" asked Sophie, leaning in front of John's rather large bulk to get Tessa's attention.

"Don't leave us, it's about to start. I don't like being in the front row. John, you shouldn't have let that young man put us here."

"You know I don't like to cause a fuss, Tessa. We were early. You like to be early. They've given us the best seats in the house."

Tessa glanced around. "We're awfully close to the stage."

"Enough space for me to squeeze out and nip to the bar though," said Sophie, making the decision and taking Tessa's empty glass with her. It was the same dynamic between them at work: Tessa and John dithering from decision to decision until she decided for them. But one thing she never got involved with were the discussions about work nights out. Yes, she'd always attend the monthly activities because it was important to maintain good personal relations with colleagues, but she didn't want to spend time debating which way they'd socialise together because every way was awful, not because of who they were, but because of the limited activities they were open to: All of them dreadfully dull, with this evening just dreadful in an entirely different fashion. This was more inappropriate than awful. She and her friends would never have dared venture down to Montel's basement room to watch the 'entertainment', especially if the entertainment was called *Whooping Wednesdays*.

When she'd first joined Tessa and John's music school following the death of old Pamela from room three, she'd been excited about the idea of a fully-funded monthly night out, but she'd quickly learnt they would be evenings she'd have to endure rather than enjoy. She had tried early on to sway the decisions towards slightly more exciting activities like wine tasting or ballroom dancing – appropriate, she thought, for the likes of Tessa and John, and not completely inappropriate for her, but she'd been dismissed on the spot. It was something that never happened at work so she'd assumed that their introverted natures were rising up in self-protection… so what they were doing in a place like this was beyond her comprehension.

Collecting the drinks from the bar, Sophie edged back through the rows of people. She noticed most were young but they weren't the usual town-going type: women easily characterised by their pronounced eyebrows and men by their acutely sculptured facial hair. These people were eclectic. Funky eclectic. Funky weird. Sophie glanced down at herself. She was probably the most conservative-looking person in the room, bar Tessa and John of course, having opted, as she always did, for a plain t-shirt and jeans. Yes, she'd accessorised with a cute brown belt and stylish slip-on shoes so her outfit looked chic upon closer inspection, but she never wanted to draw attention to herself. It was the same with her hair: naturally curly brown locks tied back. It was a look that could be called unobtrusive, but when you got closer you'd see the carefully woven French braid was certainly not ordinary. Her make-up was the same too, nice but discreet, and she'd never adopt attention-seeking eyebrows for instance, because she liked to think of herself as muted. Unnoticeable, until you noticed.

"Hello, hello, hello! And who have we got here!" came the shockingly amplified voice from the stage that silenced the room after the initial mass whooping died down.

Almost back in her seat, Sophie froze, like a daft pheasant spotting the headlights and choosing to get run over instead of making a run for it to the safety of the grass verge. She stared at the woman on stage who was laughing into her microphone.

"Let me ask you a question," said the same voice. "When did you last have sex?"

Sophie felt her knees bend without any orders from her brain as her body tried to crouch-walk the final distance to the front. Hopefully the comedian was addressing everyone. She ducked her head and held the drinks forwards so as not to spill anything and draw more attention.

"You. Look. You're still in position!"

The laughter around Sophie got louder.

"You're either wide-gated or you've just done the dirty."

Sophie lunged onto the plastic chair, thrusting the drinks straight at John.

"Oh no! She's with her grandparents! Sorry, Gramps, I'm sure she's an angel. But what have we got here? You're not an angel though are you, Grandma? Just look at that twinkle in your eye."

Sophie watched as Tessa grabbed the sherry glass from John, swallowing the contents in one gulp.

"But why am I asking, I hear you cry?" The woman started to pace across the small stage. "Well it's been that long since I had sex that I bought a turtle-neck sweater two sizes too small." She shrugged. "I miss being choked."

Sophie spluttered into her glass as Tessa began slugging back John's stout while John was nervously rocking in his seat.

The woman continued. "I stood in the rain this morning. Just stood there. Drip. Drip. Drip." The comedian smiled. "It was nice to feel wet again." She paused until the groans of laughter died down. "And I like to drive over potholes. I do it deliberately. Bump. Bump. Buuuuuump. I see a pothole and I swerve towards it. Honestly I do." She smiled. "And I'm actually thinking about having children, just so someone will scream out my name." The comedian laughed at herself. "But everything came to a head at church last Sunday. Do you know what I did?" She nodded. "I licked the vicar's finger when he put the communion bread in my mouth."

Sophie laughed loudly.

"But that wasn't the worst of it. Last week, on holiday, I moaned. Publicly. A really loud sex moan. *Ahhh*. And why did I moan? Well, a mosquito bit me on the neck and I fucking loved it."

Tessa's gasp was audible.

"So, how is this happening, I hear you ask? Look at me. I've got naturally blonde hair which I style into this funky haircut. I wear bright, fashionable clothes." She paused. "I'm somewhat good looking, if I say so myself."

"Great body too!" offered a voice from the crowd.

The reply was quick. "I'll pay you later! But let me tell you how it's happening. I like girls. I'm a lesbian, and I'm in a relationship. And lesbians in relationships don't have sex. It's a fact. By the third date they're wrapped up under a blanket watching *The Great British Bake Off*. Now, a couple of days ago my girlfriend and I were tucked under a blanket watching *The Great British Bake Off* and she asked if she could try something new. I immediately sat up straighter because the last bit of action I'd had was on the way back from holiday when I deliberately kept my Swiss Army Knife in my pocket so I'd get felt up by the airport security lady."

Sophie laughed again.

"So, we're sitting there, my girlfriend and I, and she asks to try something new. She leans towards me, fluttering her eyelashes. It's a butterfly kiss, she says, as she flaps her eyelashes up and down my cheek. Now I don't mean to be crude, but I came. It had been that long since we'd done anything physical that I actually orgasmed."

"Oh dear, I think we should go," whispered John.

"Agreed," said Tessa, lunging out of her seat.

Sophie turned in shock as her two colleagues clumsily hot-footed it up the aisle. She glanced at the stage; the comedian was mid-flow but she had no option, she had to follow them. Crouching low, Sophie made a dash for it.

"Not you too," came the shout. "I can understand Granny and Gramps heading out, but you? Wait, I get it, I've hit a nerve. I see you with your long plait, twisted one too many times so your hair will get pulled."

Sophie ignored the laughter and continued her dash to the bar at the back.

"I'm sorry," came the shout, "I'm just being rude so someone will slap me. Right, I'm Jazz, you know who I am. As always, I'll be your compère for the evening, so without further ado let me welcome Mickey Murphy back to Montel's."

Distracted by the applause and whistles and trying to work out where Tessa and John had got to, Sophie didn't see Jazz jumping off the stage and jogging up the aisle behind her.

"Thanks for being such a good sport," said the now unamplified voice. "I'm Jazz. Can I get you a drink to say sorry? I always choose someone from the crowd to torment and you just happened to be right there when I started."

"Pardon?" said Sophie distractedly, as she spotted her colleagues now clambering up the stairs.

"Climbing their way to safety, I see. You stay though. Did I see you holding a sherry glass? Who drinks sherry? I could have gone after you for that instead."

"Pardon?" said Sophie again, flummoxed and embarrassed with no clue what to say.

"Drinks. You and me."

"Pardon?"

"Are you hard of hearing? I'm asking if you want a drink."

Sophie could feel her cheeks reddening. She turned back to the stairs. "Next time," she said, before pausing so she could look at the woman once more. "Next time."

"I really hope so," replied Jazz.

CHAPTER FOUR

"Why did you say: next time?!" Laura thrust herself forward, forcing a squeak from her expensively upholstered armchair. "Twice!"

Sophie folded her hands in her lap. "It was just one of those panicked things that you say when you're all flustered. Like when someone says 'happy to help', and you say 'me too', instead of 'thank you', or they say 'I like your outfit', and you say 'you too'. But when Jazz said 'I really hope so', we both just stared at each other before smiling, and that was our first moment."

Laura gasped. "You *never* used to be like this. Working with those old piano playing weirdos has done this to you! Why did they even take you there in the first place?"

"They said they'd been worried I might leave the studio and set up on my own. They thought I'd been looking a bit bored on some of our other nights out so they hatched a plan to surprise me with a comedy night."

"That comedically backfired."

"We ended up having ham and cheese toasties in Costa; it was nice."

"Listen to yourself, would you? Ham and cheese toasties in Costa with Tessa and John isn't nice."

"It is and it was."

"You're twenty-three!"

"And I'm happy."

"No, you're not! Two minutes ago you were crying your eyes out."

"Because of Jazz, not because of my lifestyle."

"I think they're interlinked. For whatever reason, the most outgoing and popular girl at school with the wildest and most bouncy brown hair is living the quietest and most unassuming life ever with her plait and plain clothing. And it's not even a sexy Lara Croft plait, it's a boring piano teacher plait."

"I am a boring piano teacher."

"You're not! You had the world at your feet, Sophie. Fame with the London Symphony orchestra. Fame with—"

"Youth orchestra."

"Whatever, you were about to go into the main one. You'd have travelled the world. You'd have been on TV. You had a scholarship to—"

"I love being a piano teacher."

"In Tessa and John's crappy studio?"

"It's a brand new building and I own an equal share of the business."

"Sophie, there's a *Vets For Pets* downstairs and the offices of *We Buy Any Car Dot Com* upstairs; it's hardly the Symphony Hall."

"It's modern and it's the way piano lessons are done now. Students come to me. I have my own room." She nodded. "Room three. And there's a reception area where parents can sit down and wait."

"I have been there." Laura shifted in her seat and it squeaked again. "Once was enough. My point is, I don't get you. You're so talented. Do you even play the cello anymore? You made the cello look so sexy, like that Vanessa woman did with the violin."

"Vanessa-Mae."

"Exactly, but your hair flicks were better. Plus, you worked that instrument between your legs. That's why they wanted you. They knew you'd be a hit on stage. I just don't get why you gave it all up to stay here in our crappy town and teach piano."

"More people want to learn the piano than the cello."

"You know what I mean. I just don't get you."

Sophie took a deep breath. "I don't think I get myself anymore because I Googled her. Jazz. That night when I got home. I opened up my laptop and Googled Jazz. Why would I Google her?"

"You tell me. She sounds crude and bolshy. One of those women always up in your face."

"She intrigued me."

Laura's look of disbelief intensified. "But why?"

"At first I thought it was because she was funny, but then as I was getting lost in page after page of jazz musicians I realised I was thinking about her presence." Sophie smiled. "She had an aura."

"Auras are a load of old bollocks."

"Life coaches are meant to embrace stuff like that. Jazz is into stuff like that. Auras. Orbs. The laws of attraction."

"Oh, is she now?"

Sophie noted the tone. "Just stop. You're judging. You've judged me, you've judged her, you've judged Tessa and John, you've judged my studio, you've offered opinions and you've hijacked that JCB and gone on a rampage all over my plot of land."

"I bet Jazz rampaged your plot of land."

Sophie smiled in remembrance. "She did a lot more than that to my plot of land, I can tell you right now."

"That's gross. I thought you were heartbroken?"

"I am, but I can still remember the good times."

"I'm not sure I want to hear about any times."

"Laura, you're a life coach, you have to hear it. You've got me talking now and it's actually nice to remember because everything was so good at the start."

"Fine. You searched for her online."

Sophie nodded. "She's a comedian. Really quite famous in the community."

"What community? There's a community of comedians? I've never heard of her. I need to see a picture of her right now please."

Sophie reached for her phone. "The LGBT community. You just search for Jazz lesbian comedian and she's everywhere."

"That's her?" Laura took hold of the phone and gushed. "But she's beautiful!"

"What were you expecting?"

"I don't know, just not that. She's absolutely stunning, Sophie."

"I know."

"She looks like a sharp-cheeked Scandinavian model."

"She often wears a different streak of colour in her hair."

"And she's broken your heart?"

Sophie nodded into the silence.

"I genuinely am sorry." Laura cleared her throat. "But a life coach must always be honest." She pointed at the picture. "You were punching. Above your weight, I mean. Jazz looks like she's Premier League and unfortunately you got relegated five years ago when you went from the person you were at school with your big hair and look-at-me attitude to this quiet piano-teaching church mouse, and if I'm honest I'd have to put you with the likes of Derby County or Cheltenham Town."

"Who?"

"Exactly. Jazz looks like Man United."

"She is." Sophie inhaled long and deep, remembering how it felt to have Jazz by her side. It happened that first evening at the bar: an overwhelming sense of safety, as if Jazz would protect her, no matter what. She spoke up. "Jazz felt like home. She made me feel like I belonged. Like I fit somehow. Like we were one from that very first moment."

"I thought she had a girlfriend?"

"Just part of her act."

"I thought you were desperate to get away?"

"I was, until I looked at her." Sophie smiled. "Have you heard the saying: Your soulmate's the stranger you recognise? Well it's true. In that moment her soul awoke my soul and I haven't been able to sleep since. Honestly, Laura, she's got the most authentic eyes I've ever seen."

Laura threw her hands in the air. "Why are you chatting such bollocks?! Eyes can't be authentic."

"Just look at them." Sophie held up her phone again. "And she always wears that blue feather earring in her right ear. Look how it matches the blue of her eyes. They're smiling eyes. Eyes that showcase her soul. Her good soul. And when you stand by her side you can feel she's a good person. She has a magical aura and nothing I say can describe it in the way it deserves. I can't do it justice. She's just special. That's what I need you to understand, and I felt it from that very first moment. I felt it when I was searching for her online." Sophie sighed. "I'm feeling it right now."

"Are you a lesbian, Sophie?"

"That's what you got from my speech?"

"I think it needs to be established."

"I don't know. I fell in love with a woman but I think it was more to do with her than her gender."

"Well according to that picture she's got a big pair of knockers and I'm assuming she's got a plot of land too, so you can't try and claim this was just some meeting of auras."

"It was."

"But you had sex?"

"We did."

"And she had lady bits?"

"Last time I looked."

"Oh, Sophie, this is going too fast. I don't think I'm qualified for this."

"You're telling me."

"Snarky. Fine, refocus. What happened when you found her online? I know you didn't friend request her as you're the only person left in the twenty-first century who doesn't do social media."

"See, you can't just *not comment*, can you?"

"It's a fact. You used to love the internet. You ran the school's website and newspaper, plus you couldn't get enough of myspace back in the day."

Sophie sighed. "You know what we should do? We should help each other out. I help you become a better life coach and you help me sort out my issues?"

"Fine. Step one: get back on social media."

"Never. But I did watch all her videos online and I read all her blogs and I think I fell in love that first evening."

"You did not! You became infatuated maybe as you stalked her, but you didn't love her."

"Step one for you: stop telling me what I did and didn't feel." Sophie looked out at the garden and paused at the memory. "The next time I met Jazz it was as if I'd known her forever."

"Maybe because you'd stalked her so much?"

"No. It was much more than that. It still is so much more than that." Sophie re-illuminated the photo of Jazz on her phone. "I see her and I'm right back to those memories, no matter how much I try and forget."

"We need to exorcise her. Let it all out. I promise I'll just sit here and listen. It'll be cathartic." Laura relaxed into her armchair. "Sometimes you need to say it out loud to realise just how silly you sound."

"It's not silly."

"Say it, and we'll see."

CHAPTER FIVE

Glancing at her watch as she turned another page of the paper, Sophie strayed from the routine she'd slipped into, her eyes drawn instead to a headline on the right-hand side of the page. She hadn't been reading the news, not that the tabloid she'd grabbed from the stand next to the milk and sugars was very informative, she just wanted a prop so it wouldn't be obvious she was staring out of the coffee shop's window. Usually she'd have no problem people watching, but tonight, whether Sophie liked to admit it or not, she was person watching. It was similar to the times she'd go food shopping and pick a nice cake for her parents, knowing perfectly well her mother and father were watching their weight and she'd end up eating it. Ultimately she was buying that cake for herself but she wouldn't let her conscious mind admit what her subconscious mind already knew. Tonight was the same: she wasn't ready to direct her attention to the facts. One: this wasn't her usual coffee shop. Two: she never usually went for coffee at seven o'clock on a Wednesday evening. Three: she wasn't really reading the newspaper, until now.

Lost in the story, Sophie jumped as a painted nail tapped on the headline.

"It's true you know," said the familiar voice.

Looking up and feeling shock hit the hairs on the nape of her neck, Sophie morphed back into the daft pheasant, eyes wide and nothing else moving. It was Jazz, standing right there.

"Science says no women are straight." The comedian's funky blonde hair with new additional pink streak moved beguilingly as she nodded. "True."

"I'm straight," managed Sophie.

"That's impossible." Jazz reached out and curled back the front page of the paper. "*The Sun* says so. Why are you reading *The Sun*? I thought you'd be more of a *Guardian*-type girl?"

"I am."

"Says the straight girl reading about lesbians in a tabloid. Do you remember me?"

"No." Sophie cursed herself the second the word fell out of her mouth. Of course she remembered Jazz. She was here in the coffee shop opposite Montel's in case she caught sight of Jazz. "Sorry, yes, I do," she said, cross that her subconscious mind had betrayed her. And, yes, while she always did something to wind down following her final student on a Wednesday evening – Billy Baxter, seven years old and only ever wanting to play *Eye of the Tiger* as he thrust his crotch forwards and backwards on the piano stool – a surveillance stint in a coffee shop wasn't it. Usually she'd take a bottle of wine around to her friend Laura's house, but for the past three weeks Laura had demanded she expel Billy Baxter as a solution to the *Eye of the Tiger* crotch-thrusting issue; hence why she'd told herself she needed to go somewhere alone to figure it out for herself. But if she was honest, Billy Baxter hadn't crossed her mind once.

What had crossed her mind as she'd flicked through each page of the paper she wasn't reading, was what time Jazz might arrive at Montel's on the other side of the road. Well here she was, at just gone seven, standing right beside her. "Sorry," said Sophie, composing herself, "of course I remember you. You're Jazz, the lesbian comedian."

"Just comedian's fine."

"Yes, sorry." Sophie knew she had to be careful. 'Lesbian comedian' was definitely an online tagline but she didn't want to appear too knowledgeable even though she'd watched every video this woman had ever appeared in and read every blog she'd ever written. "Are you compèring again tonight?" she asked, hoping her questioning eyebrows suggested she didn't know.

"Yes, are you coming? What was your name again? Actually I don't think you gave it to me. You rushed off after your grandparents didn't you? Was that a week ago? I really am sorry about that. Can I sit down? I've got a few minutes."

Sophie stared as Jazz turned a chair to face her, and that's when it happened again: the calmness she'd experienced momentarily at the back of the bar, an aura that descended around them in the chaos. Jazz definitely talked a lot, and she definitely talked quickly, but when their eyes connected there was a tangible sense of peace and it was the most comforting thing Sophie had felt in a long time.

"You don't talk much do you?" said Jazz, smiling.

"I haven't had the chance."

The laugh was loud. "Touché. I like that."

"I'm Sophie."

A hand was thrust out. "Hi Sophie, I'm Jasmine, stage name Jazz; everyone calls me Jazz though. You can call me Jasmine or Jazz, I don't mind."

Sophie connected with the fingers, so soft and welcoming. "Hi Jazz," she said, squeezing slightly.

Jazz shook her hand with force. "Did you like the show? What little you saw of it. You must come back tonight. Let me grab myself a coffee and I'll take you over. Do you want anything? Are you meeting friends?"

"I'm just relaxing after work."

"Sorry, do you want me to leave you to it? What do you do? What's your job?"

Sophie smiled. "I'm a piano teacher."

"No way! I thought you had to be at least fifty to do that!"

"Twenty-three."

"I'm twenty-five."

Sophie smiled again, the momentary silences seemingly freezing time, creating a bubble of tranquillity she hoped Jazz could feel as much as she did. It was clear that Jazz was a ball of energy, a spirited go-getter whose softer side was only exposed on the odd occasion her guard was dropped. Well that was the conclusion she'd arrived at after watching Jazz online, Jazz's tenderness and fragility only visible during the odd glance away from camera or solo written sentence where her self-deprecating words spoke louder than most. Sophie continued to stare. This woman was someone whose personality propelled her through life like a brilliant firework, someone who'd be totally different underneath all the bravado, even though the bluster and swagger were oddly endearing in their own right.

"Drink then?" asked Jazz again.

Sophie picked up her cup. "I've still got half a coffee."

"You'll need a top-up; we'll take it over. You can watch the rest of my set." Jazz swivelled off her chair and tapped the headline once more. "Straight women like to see my set."

****

Sitting on the stubby stool in the small broom cupboard, Sophie knew she had to ask herself some questions, the most important being what the hell was she was doing backstage at *Whooping Wednesdays*. In fact, it was more offstage than backstage, the little space that had a stool, a mirror and an assortment of brooms – hence her decision to call it a broom cupboard – giving her a side view of the stage. Sophie glanced down at Jazz's backpack that was propping open the door. In it had been a brightly coloured shirt that Jazz had changed into. She'd simply stripped off in front of Sophie, and while she hadn't meant to stare, she hadn't been able to stop. The space was so tiny that Jazz's breasts were simply present, plumped up in her bra, her smooth stomach right there too.

Sophie remembered the sight. It was beautiful. Jazz was beautiful. Of course she was going to look. It was that or stare at her own reflection in the cracked mirror and no one in their right mind would choose pulled back hair and plain clothing over a sexy silhouette, regardless of their sexuality. Sophie coughed, avoiding the temptation to question whether her sexuality could be similar to the cakes she bought for her parents and the coffee shop she'd chosen that evening: something her subconscious mind wouldn't let her conscious mind address. She peeked back at the stage. And why even address it? No one cared anymore. Montel's wasn't a gay bar but here was Jazz, an out lesbian, being enjoyed by all. Sophie smiled at the wails of laughter. Jazz was mid-monologue.

Getting up from the stool, she took a step closer to get a better look.

Jazz's voice was loud. "So whoever's controlling my voodoo doll I beg you, please give the pussy part a bit of a rub." The audience was laughing. "Okay, I need to level with you. I'm all about the laws of attraction. The ability to attract into our lives whatever we're focusing on."

Sophie took in a sharp breath as the comedian turned and stared directly at her, their eyes connecting in a moment that felt so much longer than it actually was. Sophie smiled but felt silly when she realised that Jazz was already focused back on the crowd.

"So tell me why I'm attracted to such crap sounding shampoos and conditioners? Honestly the worse it sounds, the more likely I am to buy it." Jazz's lips were pressed against the microphone, the voice suddenly deep. "Shampoo, for dry and damaged hair." The normal pitch returned. "Yep, I'll take that." The lips pressed harder. "Shampoo for brittle and dry damaged hair." The nod was happy. "Oooh, that sounds a bit better." The voice descended. "Shampoo for stressed out hair that's fragile, brittle, dry and damaged." Jazz laughed. "Sold! It's the same with face cream. I'm only twenty-five but I'm using a de-wrinkler for tired and dull skin. Skin that's lost its shine because of deep-set, stubborn lines. Honestly, I wake up every morning just to be abused by my make-up bag." The deep voice returned. "Foundation to hide your scary dark eye bags. Mascara for short stubby lashes. Lipstick for thin cracked lips." Jazz nodded. "Lube for old dry vaginas." She laughed. "And on that note let me welcome your second act of the evening, Mrs Deidre Dee!"

Sophie watched as Jazz applauded the old woman who was making her way up the steps. She'd been sitting on a table to the side of the stage with the other visiting comics, meaning Jazz was the only person with a dressing room and, small though it was, it spoke volumes about her standing in the show. Jazz was the real star and if Deidre's first joke was anything to go by it was rather obvious why. Sophie winced.

"How about this one then?" continued the old woman. "What do you call a prostitute with no arms and legs?" The pause was too long. "Cash and carry."

"Can she say that?" whispered Sophie to Jazz who was back in the broom cupboard now holding two glasses of sherry.

"Didn't you notice these next to the door? I asked Ben at the bar to keep them coming. They're doubles. And Deidre can say what she likes, the crowd love her."

"They love you more," said Sophie, taking the offering. "I don't actually drink sherry."

"Really? I've been drinking it since I saw you last week. It's good. I've decided Tio Pepe's my favourite. It makes a nice change from the gin and tonics."

Sophie watched as Jazz closed the door.

"I've got ten minutes," said Jazz.

"Right."

"So what are we doing?"

Sophie took a large sip of sherry. "What do you mean?"

"Well, are we kissing or what?"

Staring into the bright blue eyes, Sophie paused before nodding. "Okay then."

CHAPTER SIX

"Stop stop stop stop stop!" Laura was out of her armchair. "That's not how it happened!"

Sophie shrugged. "It was. She just asked if we were going to kiss."

"Why?"

"I don't know. Chemistry I guess."

"You'd only just met her! And who does that? How presumptuous!"

"I chose to go to the club with her. Plus I instigated the whole thing by being at the coffee shop in the first place."

"But she didn't know that."

"She probably did."

"She's manipulative. She got you drunk on sherry and forced you into it."

"She didn't. By the second half of the show I was down on my knees in front of her. She was on the stool. It escalated."

"Sophie! It must have been because of the sherry!"

"Maybe a bit, but I knew what I was doing. I knew from that very first night. Yes, Jazz is confident and forward, but I make my own decisions."

"And you decided to have a one night stand in a broom cupboard in the basement of Montel's?"

"It didn't get that far. We shared a taxi back to mine and sat outside and talked for a bit, but you know what it's like; it's hard with Mum and Dad. I couldn't invite her in. Not because she's a woman though."

"Would you have done?"

"If I had my own place? Of course."

"You've never had a one night stand!"

"I could tell from our first kiss that it was so much more than that."

"How?!"

"Well, she shut the broom cupboard door, I put my sherry down and we just stepped into each other's spaces." Sophie smiled. "It was so natural and so soft. At first anyway, and then she pushed me against the wall and really started to go for it."

"And what the bloody hell did you do?!"

"I switched places and gave as good as I got."

"Sophie!"

"What?"

"Who are you? Wait, was that rumour about you kissing Rebecca Lynch when we were in Year Twelve true? You always said it was a lie and I believed you because you were such a hussy with the boys."

"I don't want to talk about the past."

"If this happened five years ago I don't think I'd be batting an eyelid. Yes, I might be slightly shocked that she's a woman, but this behaviour wouldn't be out of character. You were a right goer back then. But now? You don't even like having your photograph taken and if it has to be taken you're always there with your hair tied back and your turtle-neck jumper on."

"I don't own any turtle-neck jumpers."

"What's that then?"

"It's a roll neck." Sophie sighed. "You're meant to ask about the kiss, Laura. You're meant to find out how I knew in that moment that she was the one."

"You're in a dingy broom cupboard in a crappy club. It's hardly a mountainside in Sardinia."

Sophie closed her eyes. "When our lips touched I tasted the rest of my life."

"Bollocks!"

"It's true."

"It can't be because you're here crying that it's over after she told you to fuck off."

"I tasted her soul that first evening."

"When you were down on your knees?"

"When we kissed."

Laura slapped her forehead. "That was a joke! Tasting her soul. Ha, even better: Dover sole!"

"Not funny. None of this is funny. I'm heartbroken."

"What did you do? How did it end?"

"I've only told you about the first night. Don't you want to hear the rest of it? The good times? The sex? The six months of pure magic?"

"Do I have to?"

"Yes, you're my life coach, and this is helping. It's making me focus on the facts." Sophie glanced towards the garden and inhaled deeply. "I think it's too easy sometimes to make monsters out of loves that you've lost."

"So this showgirl did something wrong? I knew it."

"No, it was me." Sophie shrugged. "Maybe Jazz did a few questionable things early on that I ignored but—"

"Stop. Tell me right now. I want to hear every single sketchy thing about her."

"A life coach has to be impartial."

"She made you cry. I don't like her."

"Well I liked her. I still like her. I'm just so confused. It's as if…" Sophie leaned forward in her seat, placing two fingers on the coffee table. "Okay, imagine two magnets. When they're facing the right way they slam together. The connection's unstoppable because of a force that's defined by the laws of nature. The magnets are joined and they're strong and that connection's real and palpable. You can see it and you can feel it and there's an energy that means they'll always slam together."

"I'm imagining your body slamming against Jazz's."

"Trust me it slammed, but my point is, when one magnet turns to face the other way, when one decides to take a different view point, there's no way the magnets will ever come together. They'll no longer connect with each other. In fact they'll repel each other."

"Nope. You've lost me."

"Oh, Laura, I'm just trying to explain how the smallest difference of opinion between us seemed to send us spiralling away from each other, and that shouldn't happen. But then I sort of concluded that if you're going to have the huge highs of the energetic unstoppable connection you're inevitably going to have the huge lows too. I guess you can't play with fire and not get burnt." Sophie's eyes darted to the floor the second she'd said it. "Let's move on."

"No. You tell me right now what this bitch did."

CHAPTER SEVEN

Taking her seat at the small table, Sophie marvelled once again at just how thoughtful Jazz was. Jazz knew she loved tapas and had gone out of her way to find this unique floating restaurant on a converted barge moored to a jetty outside town. It was home to no more than ten tables and a cosy humming atmosphere with beautiful views out across the river. The plan was to enjoy dinner before Jazz dashed off to her comedy performance, a performance that had included a plus one for Sophie, but the fact it also included accommodation in a rather plush hotel meant Sophie had other plans for the evening.

Picking up the menu, she sighed happily. All of her favourite things were listed: roasted sharing camembert, pork belly with cider poached apples and caramelised onions, Moroccan spiced lamb, halloumi with honey and mustard salad. "Oh, Jazz, this is perfect."

"You definitely want to head back to the hotel on your own?"

"Definitely," said Sophie, wickedly eyeing Jazz over the top of the menu. They'd had to dump their stuff and head straight to the restaurant after Sophie had had to cover a lesson for Tessa, even though she'd rearranged all of her own afternoon lessons the second she found out she and Jazz would finally be spending a proper night together – their only sexual encounters so far happening in the broom cupboard, the back of her car and in the toilets of bars. Tessa had begged and Sophie knew it was important to cover for each other when needed. Plus Jazz had understood; in fact Jazz had been brilliant about it. She knew that work commitments sometimes got in the way of plans. Sophie smiled. Jazz was understanding, thoughtful and romantic.

"What are you smiling at?"

"You, greeting me today with a red rose. You, finding this place. You, understanding that our planned afternoon sex session had to be postponed."

"Only for three hours. I'll be back by ten, I'm the opening act."

"And I'm going to be the closing act."

"What have you got planned for us?"

"Just you wait and see." Sophie recalled the innocuous bag now sitting in their hotel room, full of all the sex toys they'd spoken about in their heated text messages. "You do delete our chats, don't you?"

"What's made you say that?"

"I'm a respectable member of the community."

Jazz laughed. "I've Googled you, you're not there. You should let me set the studio up with a website. Pictures of the three of you. You'd get loads more students."

"We're at capacity. Piano teaching's something that's spread by word of mouth."

"I hope you'll spread your mouth later on."

Sophie tutted.

"What? I'd say crap like that in a text. You on the other hand are way more reserved in person."

"We had sex in my car!"

"I mean in the things you say."

"You think I'm all talk and no action?" Sophie's smile across the top of the menu was naughty. "Just you wait."

"You're not going to be one of those women who tease in the bedroom, are you?"

"What do you mean, one of those women? How many teasers have there been?"

"Enough to know what I like, and all that 'tickle me with a feather' nonsense doesn't do it for me. I like proper rough and ready, take me now, shit."

Sophie laughed. "I know you do, but what if I were to," she slipped her foot out of her shoe and slid her toes up the inside of Jazz's leg, "warm you up gently?"

Jazz reached under the table and grabbed the foot. "I'd just thrust it right in there."

"Stop it!" giggled Sophie. "You just wobbled the table! We're meant to be having a sophisticated dinner on this sophisticated barge." She pulled her foot away. "Now get back to ordering your saveloy sausage."

Jazz looked at the menu. "It's actually sautéed chorizo with red wine."

"So you can do posh?"

"I can, but let's be honest, this croquetas de jamón they've got listed half-way down is just a ham croquette, isn't it? I buy them in the freezer section at Tesco. Twenty-odd in a pack and only a couple of quid. And what's this? Gambas al ajillo?"

"Garlic shrimp."

"They're prawns then. Garlic prawns." Jazz nodded. "They're also down the freezer aisle in Tesco." She put her hand up and politely got the attention of one of the waitresses. "Hello, excuse me, can you tell me what the spicy lamb albondigas is please?"

"Meatballs," said the waitress.

Jazz nodded, smiling across the table at Sophie. "Thank you." She waited until the waitress had almost walked away. "Sorry," she said again, "and what's the jamón Iberico de bellota?"

"It's like ham on toast."

"Great."

The waitress paused before turning.

"And the patatas bravas?"

The waitress swivelled back around. "Spicy potato wedges."

"Right, thank you."

"Is that all?"

"Yes."

"You're sure?"

"Yes." Jazz waited before raising her voice once more. "Sorry, no, last one. The puntillas?"

"Tiny fried baby squid. Are you ordering it?"

"No, I'm having the saveloy sausage."

Sophie interrupted. "Can we have another five minutes please?" She tried to smile politely until the waitress had walked away. "You're not on stage, Jazz!"

"I thought you liked my little shows? And anyway I'm just making the point that things shouldn't pretend to be what they're not. Just like people shouldn't pretend to be what they're not."

"Puntillas will just be the Spanish word for squid."

Jazz shook her head. "It's not. Puntillas in Spanish means lace. Like the lace edging you get on a napkin. That waitress is winging it."

"You know Spanish?"

Jazz smiled. "I do."

"So why are you asking so many questions?"

"Just putting on a show."

Sophie tapped the table. "Well stop. I want to be the one putting on a show this evening."

"You don't have forty-five feathers in that bag at the hotel, do you?"

Sophie nodded. "Yes, the feathers of forty-five different birds."

Jazz shrugged. "Fine, as long as you just bind them all together and shove them right in there."

☁

Laura gasped. "I see what you mean! She was sexually inappropriate! No one likes penetration, not even us straight girls! I see why it raised a red flag!"

"I haven't even told you the story yet."

"There's more? I don't want to hear it!"

"You do."

"I don't!"

"Can I try you?" Sophie looked around at the simply designed space. Laura and her feng shui expert were right, the room was calming and open enough to make you feel as if you had the space to talk without the distraction of the typical clutter you might find in a normal living area. "You've done a really good job in here and the light green theme is definitely calming me."

"Thank you." Laura narrowed her eyes. "Wait, you're buttering me up, aren't you? Fine, I want to get good at this. Tell me what happened in the hotel."

Sophie smiled. "You might want to hold on to those expensively upholstered arms of that chair of yours."

Racing back to the hotel room, Sophie knew she didn't have long. She'd walked with Jazz to the theatre, arriving at the stage door fifteen minutes before Jazz was due on. That was one of Jazz's weaknesses. Time management. Or maybe she was at fault? Always obsessing about getting everywhere early. Jazz wasn't late after all, but surely one needed preparation time? Time to compose oneself before a big show? Sophie pushed open the door to the room and momentarily enjoyed the quiet and order. That's what she felt like she needed right now. Time to compose herself before *her* big show. It had all seemed like such a great idea at the time, realising Jazz's deepest and darkest sexual fantasies. Sophie dropped to her knees and unzipped the bag. Okay, so they weren't that deep or that dark but they would require some assembly and the fact that Jazz had no clue what was about to happen meant everything had to be arranged to a tee.

Pulling the pile of black strapping from the bottom of the bag, Sophie forced herself to focus. She'd already had a practice run on her parents' lounge floor two nights ago when they'd taken themselves off to choral practice – a weekly rehearsal that lasted at least an hour, giving her time to lay out the under-bed restraint system. It was pretty simple really, a long black strap running vertically from top to bottom with four horizontal black straps coming from the sides with cuffs for the wrists and ankles. The horizontal straps could be lengthened or shortened depending on the width of the bed, but in essence it would strap Jazz down in a spread eagle position.

Turning to the large bed, Sophie nodded at herself. This was it. The moment she'd been dreading. It was all well and good laying it out on the floor but for it to work it had to be slid under the mattress. She continued to stare; the mattress was huge, not to mention all the posh throws and pillows that were placed just so, meaning she'd have to get it looking exactly the same so Jazz wouldn't suspect a thing until she whipped down the wrist cuffs and started the show. Taking hold of the strapping, Sophie moved to the bottom of the bed and crouched down to lift up the mattress. She froze. It was too heavy. Dropping the restraints she lifted with two hands; the mattress only rose a matter of centimetres. "Dammit," she gasped. She'd got everything mapped out in her mind, all based on the ultimate fantasy that Jazz had described in texts. She had to make it work. Maybe she could lift the mattress onto her back and crawl underneath with the harness?

Looping the top strap around her waist, Sophie tied the two wrist restraints together, tight enough to survive the commando crawl, but loose enough to undo when in position at the headboard. This was it; Indiana Jones was going in. Getting into a squat position, Sophie yanked the duvet back as she tried to remember what her personal trainer had said that one New Year she'd decided to get fit: knees bent, back straight, lift through the arms and legs. "And lift," she instructed herself, pulling the mattress up momentarily before it slipped out of her fingers. "No!" she gasped, trying once more. It was no good, the whole thing was too big and heavy, she'd have to edge herself in shoulder first.

Checking the loop around her waist, Sophie used her right hand to create a tiny opening between the mattress and the base of the bed before slamming herself shoulder first into the space and wriggling frantically to try and get some leverage. It reminded her of a caving trip she'd gone on at school; the only thing missing was a head torch. She smiled. It was working. Her left shoulder and the top of her left arm were under the mattress. She pushed up with her legs, the mattress was lifting. There was enough space for her head. Bending her neck, Sophie twisted, shoving herself face first into the gap before mounting the mattress higher onto her back. And just like that, both shoulders were in. Now for both arms so she could begin her commando crawl. Pushing harder with her legs, Sophie dared to reach out with both hands in front. And that's when it happened; her foot slipped and she shot forward into the inner-sprung abyss, the mattress immediately slamming down on top of her.

Sophie wasn't sure what she heard first: the panic of her own heartbeat squashed in the musty darkness, or the knock on the door and a chirpy voice calling "Room service." "No!" she shouted, unsure whether it was at herself, or her situation, or the man at the door. Either way it was muffled and hadn't worked as the knock came again.

"Ice, madam!"

Sophie cursed inwardly. Why hadn't she just waited for the ice bucket at reception instead of asking for it to be delivered? She knew why, she was short of time, and her current predicament wasn't helping. "Leave it outside," she shouted, instantly conscious that her temperature had started to rise along with her heart rate. She needed to get out, she couldn't breathe.

"Ice, madam. I'll bring it in."

Dammit, the man hadn't heard her and as she wriggled she realised she couldn't move. She was stuck: pinned to the bed base by the world's heaviest mattress.

"Not now!" screamed Sophie once more, after inflating her lungs with difficulty. Frantically she tried to drag herself back out. It wasn't working because she couldn't reach the floor and there was nothing to push against. She tried another frenzied wriggle but all she could feel was her hair, now loose from its plait, getting incredibly static. She jumped as the space was lit up by a spark. She was about to combust. This was how she was going to die.

"Madam, are you okay?"

Sophie gasped at the incredibly close voice. She stayed still, unsure of quite what to do. It was instantly mortifying, like those times you played hide and seek as a child and you didn't know your feet were visible from under the curtain until later when the adults laughed at your cuteness. Maybe if she didn't move the staff member would go away. Who was she kidding? She couldn't move anyway, she needed his help. "I've slipped," she muttered.

"Peekaboo!" said the voice as the mattress was lifted off her.

Sophie rolled over, dropping onto the floor in a spider's web of black leather strapping. She knew she looked like a kinky parachute jump gone wrong.

"Would you like a hand?" asked the smiling man. "Or shall I pop your bottle in the ice bucket first?"

Sophie shook her head, making her static hair fizz around her head. She hadn't got a bottle, the ice was for agenda point three. That's how she'd organised the evening in her head. Agenda point one: strap Jazz down. Agenda point two: tease her with a sexy dance. Agenda point three: put ice in her pussy.

"Just put the bucket over there." Sophie could barely speak as lack of oxygen and embarrassment collided in her chest and burst around her blood stream. She focused on her breathing. She could hide the bucket later on. The priority was getting rid of the guest and getting this harness in position.

The waiter frowned. "Are you going to make a porno?"

"No!" gasped Sophie, hauling herself to her feet as she yanked the straps from around her waist.

The waiter was peering at the open bag. "Solo fun?"

Sophie also looked at the black leather flogger, now visible on top of the lacy red underwear and patent stiletto heels. "Could you help me with this please?"

She handed over one of the straps with a nonchalance that astonished her. Usually she'd be mortified in any situation that was even slightly out of the ordinary. Not that there had ever been such an occasion before, in fact asking another woman in a pub loo for a tampon was out of her comfort zone, but the desire to pleasure Jazz was over-riding any embarrassment she was currently feeling. Plus she'd read somewhere that hotel workers saw all sorts, so a woman trapped under a mattress wrapped in a maze of black strapping probably wasn't anything much.

"Of course, madam, but I've never seen anything like this before," said the waiter.

Sophie decided to ignore that and be matter-of-fact.

"You hold the right arm cuff and I'll hold the left. If we stand either side of the bed we should be able to pull it under the mattress and get it to the top."

The waiter did as instructed and it worked.

"Thank you," said Sophie calmly when the contraption was finally in place and the bed neatly remade. As she smiled confidently, handed him a bank note and ushered him from the room she could feel the adrenaline start to flow. This was working, this had worked, this was actually going to happen.

CHAPTER EIGHT

"No! I do not want to hear the details of agenda points one to eight!" Laura hadn't returned to her armchair for the best part of ten minutes, having been wildly pacing the room instead. "But again, I see what you're saying; the warning signs were there."

"What do you mean?"

"All that kinky shit! I can't believe you actually did it! Did she strap you up too? Wait, I don't want to know. It's just weird. You were right to get out."

"It wasn't that. I loved the sex. It's so empowering being able to fulfil someone else's fantasy."

"Who are you?!"

Sophie rubbed her temples. "I'm not sure anymore."

"Does this happen a lot? This fulfilling of fantasies? Because as far as I'm aware you've only had two boyfriends and they were the shyest, geekiest men ever born." Laura paused. "Apart from Dom in school. He was a hunk. You two were the cool power couple, but then you went all *give me a man who looks like Harry Potter* as soon as you stepped away from your fame and fortune and became this piano playing geek."

"Maybe Jazz sparked my sexual awakening? Maybe she showed me who I truly am. I'm wild and carefree and I love pushing the limits sexually."

Laura nodded. "I give Bobby a blow job on his birthday."

"And Christmas?"

"Once a year is enough."

"Well I'm a sexual being."

"You look like Johnny English! You're sitting there in your plait and black turtle neck!"

"Roll neck."

"Who cares! I just can't marry up the Sophie I know to the Sophie you're describing."

"Everyone has fetishes behind closed doors."

"I don't!"

"You would if you met Jazz. She oozes sex appeal. She makes you want to do terrible things."

"I knew it! She made you wear a strap-on didn't she?"

Sophie ignored the comment. "She always made me want more. I could never get enough of her. I was completely satisfied but then immediately hungry for what was coming next."

"You, by the sound of it."

"I did. Lots."

Laura slowed her pace around the room, pausing at the painting of the paddy fields and then again at the topiary framing the French windows. She lifted her hands into a zen pose before sitting back down. "Fine. So what was the problem?"

"Okay, so she came back from the club. I had all the lights dimmed and I was sitting on the edge of the bed waiting for her."

"The bed that had the harness on?"

"Yes, but you couldn't see the straps. I'd hidden them under the pillows at the top and the duvet at the foot of the bed so when she finally lay down I figured I'd be able to pull them out and surprise her. Anyway, she lets herself into the room. I've got some romantic music playing and she sees me in my red underwear and heels. I stand up from the bed and take the black flogger from the sideboard. I'd placed it just within my reach so I didn't have to move. I cracked it through the air and said, *"You've been a naughty girl."*

"This is gross, fast-forward."

"I told her to stand still or I'd flog her."

"Poor woman, she's just got in from her comedy set. Welcome home, honey, I'm going to whip you fully clothed at the front door."

"Stop it. It was sexy. I stripped her there and then and she didn't move a muscle, but I could see her pulse beating in her throat. She was mesmerised."

"Probably scared of being hit."

"Do you want to hear this or not?"

"Not really. Just tell me what the problem was. Where was the warning sign? Did she get cross because the ice you'd hidden down the side of the bed for her pussy had melted? Or were your stilettos not pointy enough? Or did the restraints come undone?"

"None of that. It was all amazing. I had her naked and spread eagle on the bed while I stood on the mattress in my heels and red underwear, with my legs spread either side of her, cracking my flogger."

"I'm surprised you didn't fall."

"I didn't."

"So what was the problem?"

Sophie coughed. "Okay, so we had sex for ages. I mean all sorts of scenarios, all sorts of positions. It was truly amazing and it was everything we'd talked about in our texts. But after we'd done all the fun stuff I asked if we could make love."

"Right."

"Well, I asked her if I could make love to her."

"Okay."

"So we moved under the covers. We're both naked. All the toys are away and it's just us and it's perfect. The music was still playing so I just held her in a spoon position, you know? Anyway I was behind her and my lips were resting on her neck and I started to stroke her, really slowly. I stroked her stomach and her thighs and I played with her nipples, gently."

"Move on."

"I was behind her and I was holding her. I was gently kissing her neck and I was in such a happy place. It was as if in that moment I'd found complete peace. She was my one. I just knew it. So there I am, feeling all the feels, in one of the most romantic moments of my life to date and I move my hand gently between her legs so that I can start touching her softly."

"And?"

"And she starts snoring."

Laura slammed her hands on the chair arms as she wailed with laughter. "She fell asleep?!"

Sophie nodded.

"That's hilarious!"

"It's not. I was heartbroken. I was making love to her for the first time. Yes, we'd had sex, but this was different; this was my way of showing her how much I cared. I hadn't said the words yet but I wanted to show her the feelings." Sophie shrugged. "But it obviously wasn't enough. I obviously wasn't enough."

"Wait a minute, what do you mean?"

"Out of all the fun stuff it was the making love that mattered the most, but she clearly didn't feel the same way."

"She fell asleep! You said she'd just done a late night comedy performance. You said you'd been having sex all evening. It's hardly her fault. She was probably just knackered!"

"Are you defending her?"

"Of course! Remember last year when I wanted to be a masseuse? They said the greatest compliment is when a client falls asleep."

"But you're not fucking the client, Laura!"

"And nor were you. You were making love. You were relaxing her."

"Yes, with a view to making her come slowly and softly and deeply."

"I bet she appreciated the sleep more than another orgasm because it sounds like you'd already given her a right seeing to."

"I can't believe you're saying this."

"She hardly did it deliberately, did she?"

"It doesn't matter. It spoke volumes about everything."

"No, it didn't." Laura shook her head. "Oh god, Sophie, what did you do?"

"I left. I wrote her a note saying 'You fell asleep', and I left."

"That's so childish!"

"I was hurt!"

"Irrationally!"

Sophie shook her head. "You know what, Laura, I'm not doing this. You're not helping."

"You've never liked to hear the truth, have you? All those times people sat you down and told you to go with the orchestra. All those times people questioned why you'd changed your mind. It didn't make sense. In fact you haven't made sense for the past five years, Sophie. Something changed in you and I think Jazz was bringing the real you back. You got scared, so you made up a silly excuse to walk out."

"It wasn't a silly excuse, I was hurt, and anyway that wasn't the end of it. That was early on in our relationship. We made up. We got things back on track. Until the next time."

"The next time you behaved irrationally?"

"Enough. I'm leaving."

"Okay, I'm sorry," said Laura, following Sophie to the door. "Please just give me another example of one of these 'warning signs', as you called them."

"Why?"

"Because this is helping me too. I'm having to be analytical and focused and, if I'm honest, I feel like I'm getting to know you all over again. Maybe not the old you, just a part of you that I didn't know existed."

"This was a bad idea."

"Sophie, you say you've had no one to talk to. Talking helps."

"Talking just reopens the wounds."

"What wounds?" Laura reached out for her friend. "She hurt you? How did she hurt you? Give me another example."

"You'll only take her side again."

"This isn't about sides," said Laura, rubbing Sophie's shoulder. "It's about taking a fresh look at things. About being objective. And if anything I'll always have your back."

Sophie let go of the door handle and sighed. "Fine. Four months in and she couldn't remember my surname."

Laura pulled away and gawped at her. "Maugham? For god's sake, Sophie, I only learnt to spell it last year!"

CHAPTER NINE

Closing her eyes, Sophie smiled at the low buzz of her surroundings as a feeling of complete relaxation descended over her. It reminded her of lying on a beach in some exotic location where the overriding sound might be the gentle lapping of waves once you'd zoned out the noise of children playing and beach vendors calling their wares. This was the same, she thought, as she lay on the grass, totally zen. Okay, so the local park wasn't anywhere near the sea, but her ability to focus meant it didn't really matter. People were talking and playing as they shared their picnics in the sun, but this, and the low hum of nearby traffic, wasn't the centre of her attention. All Sophie could hear as she closed her eyes were the chirps and singing of birds, and the myriad sounds of summer while a warm breeze tickled the wisps of hair on her cheeks.

"Close your eyes," she instructed Jazz, lying beside her. "I'll tell you which bird is making which call."

"It's that brunette over there with the big tits. She's got a right holler on her."

Sophie rested her hand on Jazz's forearm and squeezed. "Close your eyes."

"They've been closed for ages. I'm enjoying the sun."

"And you can't hear the birds?"

"Only that big-titted brunette hollering at her fourteen kids."

"There," hushed Sophie, stroking her arm. "That chirrup. That constant chirruping note. That's the male sparrow. He'll sing the same song incessantly to announce that he has a nest."

"I hear it."

"The female sparrow only uses that song on the odd occasion they want to attract a new mate after losing one."

Jazz laughed. "I like the female sparrow's style. Only talk to the men when you're trading them in."

"And that one," continued Sophie. "That loud trilling. That's a starling. Maybe a couple of starlings."

"Sounds like they're screaming."

"That's it. And listen." Sophie squeezed again. "You know this one. *Oh-oo-oor.*"

"Is it an owl?"

"No," said Sophie, laughing. "Listen. *Oh-oo-oor.* There. Or maybe it's more like *coo roo-c'too-coo.*"

"You have a good bird call. Now move your hand lower; I want to hold it."

"It's a wood pigeon," said Sophie.

"Give me your hand."

"We're in the park."

"You've held my hand before." Jazz rolled onto her side, pushing her sunglasses on top of her head. "No one's paying us any attention. In fact, let's upgrade that hand hold to a kiss."

Letting her head loll, Sophie squinted as her eyes adjusted to the sunlight. She smiled. Jazz was in her space, making her feel all the things she felt when in the presence of such a phenomenon, this magic being who'd come into her life and turned it upside down. It was a mixture of sweet calm and total frantic attraction. Jazz completed her but at the same time made her realise what she was missing. She wanted this freedom, this carefree live-life attitude, this 'If I want to kiss you in the park, I'll kiss you in the park' attitude. "You're a really special woman, Jasmine."

"I love it when you call me Jasmine."

"Seriously, you are. You're stunningly beautiful. Your personality's so lively and infectious. You're good at your job. You—"

"So you do find me funny then?"

"Ish."

"I interrupted, carry on."

"See. It's that cheeky smile. You're a happy soul, Jazz." Sophie paused. "I sometimes wonder what I can give you."

"You give me wood pigeon bird calls and great sex." Jazz moaned. "*Really* great sex and I *really* want to kiss you right now."

"And I want to kiss you too. I want to kiss you all the time. It's becoming an issue."

"Not if we come out as a couple."

"Wouldn't that devastate your comedy fans?"

Jazz coughed. "And your parents and friends, maybe? Whoa! Icy stare! I'm joking! You know I'm joking."

"I'm sure they'd be fine."

"So how come..."

"How come what?"

"How come... no, it doesn't matter. I've never pressured you and I never want to pressure you." Jazz reached out for Sophie's face, gently rubbing her thumb across the cheekbone. "I understand how hard it can be, coming to terms with your sexuality."

"I don't think I'm struggling with it, am I?"

"We're four months in and I haven't met any of your friends."

"I'll arrange it."

"I don't want to feel like I've pushed you into anything. Honestly, I'm happy with the pace of things and you've met my friends and that was cool, wasn't it?"

"Everything's been cool. You've been cool. You're the definition of cool." Sophie smiled. "Everything about you is good, Jazz. I've never met anyone like you before. You make me want to live life. You honestly are the most thought-provoking person I've ever met."

"Thought-provoking?"

"Yes."

"And ever?"

"Yes, ever." Sophie smiled. "Well I did meet Howard Donald from Take That once and he was interesting, but he didn't turn me on like you do."

"And how do I turn you on?" asked Jazz, moving her hand to Sophie's bare legs and parting them slightly as she ran a nail up her thigh.

"I need you to kiss me."

"You want me to kiss you here?"

"Yes here," said Sophie before screaming with laughter as Jazz lunged forwards with her face, planting a huge kiss on the inside of her thigh. "Not there, you dingbat!"

"Come here then," said Jazz, pulling Sophie almost on top of her.

Sophie didn't resist, returning the kiss with as much passion as was given. She paused before whispering into Jazz's ear. "I'm sorry to inform you but there's a weird-looking man watching us."

Jazz jerked her head around once more. "Where?"

"There. By the hedge. With the sunglasses on."

"He looks asleep."

"He's not, he's watching us."

"Good job I like to put on a show then," said Jazz, returning her lips to Sophie's.

"There," mumbled Sophie in between kisses. "I see his eyebrows moving."

Jazz jerked her head to the side once more. "He's just lying still."

"He's not, he's watching us."

"Do you feel uncomfortable? Do you want to move?"

Sophie groaned. "I want you. I always want you."

"Well you're not allowed to have me here regardless of whether that weird man is watching or not, so why don't we nip to the toilets over there?"

Sophie looked to the direction of where Jazz's eyebrows pointed. "Are they nice?"

Jazz smiled. "You have to pay."

"And what may I ask will we be doing in these toilets of yours?"

Jazz's fingers were back on Sophie's thigh. "A bit of this maybe?" She moved her lips to Sophie's neck. "And some more of this?"

Sophie reached for her bag and stood up. "Worth every penny."

****

Pushing her twenty pence piece into the slot, Sophie nodded at Jazz who was doing the same thing at the turnstile beside her. It was as if they were horses geeing themselves up for the gate release, or skiers about to start a downhill slalom. "Oww!" gasped Sophie as her metal bar didn't turn. Reaching down for the returned coin she tried again.

"Lick it," said an old woman who was leaning on a mop on the other side of the barrier.

Sophie looked at the dirty coin before trying again.

"Lick it," repeated the woman.

"Do you have another coin, Jazz?" Sophie tried to ignore the tuts from the people behind her, aware that the girl next to her was also having difficulties.

"Lick it," said Jazz with a smile.

"I'm not licking it," said Sophie.

"Just lick it," said a voice from the queue.

Jazz spoke with a lilt in her voice. "Let's sneak in unnoticed, they said. We'll be in and out before anyone suspects, they said."

"Give it here," said the old woman, resting her mop beside the barrier.

"And she's licking it," continued Jazz, whose running commentary no one was actually listening to, Sophie noticed with relief.

"Try now, love," said the old woman.

Sophie used her thumb and forefinger to grasp the slathered-up coin by its edges.

"And now she's dropped it," said Jazz.

"She's dropped it," came a moan from the queue.

"It was slippery!" snapped Sophie, fumbling on the floor for the wet coin. "And I'm in," she said, finally pushing through the barrier to a solo clap from the queue.

"And will the little old mop lady be joining us?" asked Jazz, taking hold of Sophie's arm as she pulled her around the corner towards the cubicles. "I mean you've already been intimate with her juices."

"Why are you yanking me so fast?"

"Because there's going to be a surge of people and we need to get into that cubicle at the end."

Sophie quickly crammed herself into the space behind Jazz, unsure whether the mop woman who'd suddenly re-appeared at the hand driers with a rag and some spray had looked their way. "You think she saw us?"

"It's fine. I might be wearing a catheter bag. You might be changing it."

"So I'm your carer now?"

"You're my lover," said Jazz.

"I like being your lover," whispered Sophie, pushing Jazz against the cubicle wall.

"Careful! The wall just wobbled!"

"Try here," urged Sophie, moving Jazz backwards against the cubicle door.

"Now the lock's rattling!"

"Just kiss me," moaned Sophie, pulling them both into the centre of the cubicle.

"You really want it, don't you?"

"Almost as much as you do."

Jazz grabbed the back of Sophie's neck, kissing her deeply.

Sophie groaned, responding with as much fervour as was possible without knocking them both off balance. "Do you think the floor's clean?" she asked between kisses.

"Why?" managed Jazz.

"I want to get down on my knees. My tongue between your legs." Sophie forced their bodies closer. "I want you so much."

"She'll see your knees."

"Who?"

"Mop woman."

"She's not standing outside, is she?"

"This is nice, keep doing this. Touch me with your fingers."

Sophie smiled, her thumb riding underneath Jazz's t-shirt, her mouth on Jazz's neck. "I want to push you against the wall and make you come really hard."

"You can't, it'll collapse."

Sophie laughed. "Come here then. Sit on top of me. I want to feel you close to me." Drawing them both back, Sophie closed the lid of the toilet, sat down first and pulled Jazz onto her knee, both facing the cubicle door. "See, this is nice. I can spread your legs with mine. I can unzip your jeans."

Jazz turned her head. "But you can't kiss me."

"No, but I can bite your neck." Sophie pulled across Jazz's hair with one hand and plunged her other hand straight into Jazz's trousers.

Jazz groaned. "I'm so wet."

"Lean back onto me. I'm going to bite you as I pull on your nipples and fuck you with my fingers."

"I love it when you talk like that."

"I know, you told me. You also told me you like it really fast and really hard."

"Mmm hmm."

"Right above your clit."

"Mmm hmm, oh Sophie."

"Yeah?" Sophie pulled Jazz further on to her knee, leaning them backwards as she worked her right hand quickly... and that's when it happened. The motion sensor flush, sensing the motion and flushing the toilet with a huge roaring gush of water. "Dammit," gasped Sophie, shocked at the ferocity of the noise.

"Keep going," urged Jazz, leaning her head back onto Sophie's shoulder.

Sophie moved to the other nipple, rolling it roughly between her finger and thumb.

"Harder on my clit."

Sophie adjusted herself on the seat to get a better angle; the flush immediately roared once more. "Sorry," said Sophie, trying not to lose focus.

"Harder."

"On it," said Sophie, biting on the neck as she squeezed the nipple.

Jazz groaned, pushing back onto Sophie, the movement again triggering the flush. It roared loudly.

Sophie tried not to laugh, instead burying her face in Jazz's shoulder as she tried to move her right hand faster.

Jazz groaned. "I'm close."

Sophie could feel the sweat building on the back of her neck.

"That's it," whispered Jazz, starting to rock in Sophie's lap. "That's it!"

"Stay still."

"I can't! I'm close, keep going."

Sophie couldn't stop Jazz's movement transferring to her. The flush roared loudly. Sophie let out a giggle, aware that she was about to lose all ability to control her arm. "Sorry," she managed.

"That's it! Harder, harder, harder."

Sophie stifled her laughter as the flush roared once, twice, three times.

"Yes!" gasped Jazz, throwing her hand to her mouth as she curled her body in on herself.

The flush boomed once more.

"And there's one for luck," said Sophie, pulling her hand back out of the trousers as she squeezed her fingers to get the circulation flowing once more.

"You think anyone noticed?" whispered Jazz.

"The roaring flush that went off twenty-six times? Quite possibly."

"My noise."

"You couldn't hear it over the flush. Let me out first."

"Wait, I want to pleasure you."

"You can owe me. I think we've risked enough."

"Go now while we can?"

Sophie nodded. "Better to get away with one bit of fun than get caught for two. Stay in here. Follow me in a minute." Opening the door slightly, Sophie squeezed herself out and was immediately greeted by the little old lady leaning against her mop.

"You licked it," said the woman.

Sophie gasped. "I did not lick it."

"She wanted to lick it," said Jazz, emerging from the cubicle behind her. "Young love, what can I say?"

Sophie felt her cheeks flare as she dashed to the basins, rinsing her hands quickly before shaking them dry-ish. "You came out too quickly!"

"She's cool," said Jazz, still behind her. "Don't worry about it. She'll see all sorts in here."

"We're so naughty!"

"You're so naughty. You're incorrigible."

"You encourage me."

"Different words, but let me encourage you to hold my hand." Jazz smiled. "Hold my hand as we walk back to the park."

Taking the lead, Sophie guided them into the warm sun. "It looks like I'll be adding good at homonyms to the never-ending list of things I'm learning about you. You speak Spanish, you—"

"What's a homonym? Is it because I'm gay?"

"You know exactly what a homonym is. Words that sound alike but have different meanings." Sophie smiled. "It's cool to be clever, you know. You don't have to hide it."

"The only thing I'm not hiding are my feelings for you." Jazz spun Sophie by the hand and shouted. "I'm in heaven!"

"Are you?"

"Total heaven! You said I was perfect earlier, but you're the perfect one. You've just given me an amazing orgasm after an amazing few hours lying in the sun. You're becoming braver in public; you've said we'll meet your friends and family. I'm just really happy, Sophie. I know I joke around a lot, but you're everything I've been looking for."

Sophie smiled as they walked across the grass towards their spot near the hedge. "Really? That makes me so happy." She smiled again. Jazz was everything she didn't know she'd been looking for, breathing a fresh excitement into her life that she hadn't felt for the past five years; opening her up to so many new thoughts, feelings and experiences. This park for instance, in the next town along. She'd never been here before, always choosing the local one that was more convenient than nice. In fact there was nothing really that nice about where she'd grown up and chosen – to the confusion and shock of so many – to stay. A high street awash with charity shops, new-build estates constantly cropping up on any spare bit of land, supermarkets seemingly around every corner. The only redeeming feature was The Grand Theatre. Sophie tried to shut off her train of thought. *Had been* The Grand Theatre.

"And I'd definitely take your name," continued Jazz, oblivious to Sophie's suddenly ashen face.

"Pardon?"

"When we get married. Jasmine Morgan. It has a nice ring to it."

Sophie stopped walking and pulled her hand free. "What did you say?"

"Jasmine Morgan. Morgan's much better than my surname. Chill! I'm only joking. You'd have to ask me first."

"Who's Morgan?"

"You."

"How do you spell Morgan?"

"Morgan, like Morgan Freeman."

Sophie wrapped her arms around herself. "What's my surname, Jazz?"

"Morgan! Sophie Morgan. It's Morgan isn't it? I'm sure you've told me it's Morgan."

"We've been together four months."

"And?"

"And you're talking about marriage but you don't even know my surname."

"I was joking, but what is it?"

Sophie shook her head. "Forget it."

Jazz gasped. "No! What have I done? What is it?"

"If you don't know my surname then I don't think it matters."

"What are you doing, Sophie? Where are you going?"

"I said forget it."

"Forget what? Wait!"

Sophie spun back around and hushed her voice. "I just fucked you in the toilets."

"And?"

"And you don't even know my surname!"

53

"I've fucked a lot of people in toilets whose surnames I don't know."

"Oh, that's very clever of you, Jazz. Fine, whatever."

"What's going on? What are you doing, Sophie?"

"I'm going."

"Where? Why?"

"Because you don't know my surname!"

"What is your surname?"

Sophie shook her head. "Jazz, just listen to me for one second. I know your mum's called Vanessa, your dad's called Tony. You have an older sister called Sonia and a younger brother called James. Sonia's married to John and James is a playboy. Your middle name's Margo. You grew up by the sea side. Your gran used to live with you; she's called Betty. Your first car was a Rover. You had two cats growing up: Jimmy and Jam. You—"

"What are you doing?"

Sophie stared straight at Jazz. "And you don't even know what my name is."

CHAPTER TEN

"Don't you dare walk away from me too!" said Laura, keeping her hand on the door. "Morgan and Maugham are so similar!"
"Oww! Mm-oww-gham! Totally different sounds and totally different letters!"
"She was close."
"She didn't know it!"
"You don't have any social media accounts!"
"So?"
"So your surname's not flashing up every five seconds."
"It hurt me!"
"Just like her falling asleep hurt you?"
"Yes! And that's not irrational of me. I'm honest with my feelings."
"So be honest about why these things hurt you so much."
"Because it was crap of her! I'd told her my surname on numerous occasions."
"No, you loved her and you wanted her to love you just as much back! But, Sophie, you've got to understand that we don't all have photographic memories like you, and we're not all as on the ball with everything as you are. You're so intelligent, a cello and piano playing genius. Most normal people struggle to keep up with the pace of your brain. I struggle all the time."
Sophie gasped. "It was my name!"
"So you reacted like a loon and she told you to fuck off?"
"No, this was only four months in. We made up."
"Oh for fucks sake, Sophie."
"What?"

"You're confusing me. It's no wonder she was confused! One second you're telling her she's the most thought-provoking person you've ever met, then you're flouncing off over something stupid, but it obviously wasn't that big a deal if you made up again."

"I forgave her because I loved her."

"And maybe she forgave you because she loved you too."

Sophie laughed. "You're saying she had to forgive me when she was the one who forgot my surname? That's laughable."

"Forgive your behaviour."

"Seriously? Are you being serious right now because if you are then I'm done."

"I'm being serious, Sophie."

"Right. Let me out please."

Laura kept her hand on the door handle. "We haven't spoken about Billy Baxter yet. You always speak about Billy Baxter on a Wednesday."

"I'll speak about Billy Baxter next Wednesday because I'm not speaking about this anymore." Sophie nodded. "I think you should get yourself another case study."

Laura paused before removing her hand from the door and stepping back. "That's the most sensible thing you've said the whole session."

****

Watching from the doorway as her friend marched down the hall past her parents' lounge and dining room, Laura smiled. Sophie would be back; she always came back. Silly arguments between them had been a staple in their relationship for the past twelve years, having met on the first day of secondary school and fallen out over who had the best collection of highlighter pens. The bond they'd made over their shared love of fluorescents, however, drew them back together after a few hours of cooling off, and while neither were real hot-heads they were both only children, another thing they'd bonded over, with neither accepting their other friends' assessment that their sibling-less status made them overly sensitive.

Laura listened to the silence after the front door slammed. She listened a bit more; Sophie's car hadn't moved yet. She waited. Usually the fact that someone was an only child was a fantastic talking point in life coaching, or so session three of the night course had suggested, as only children didn't have siblings to take jabs at them and thicken their skin during childhood, making them more reactive as adults. They also had to learn independence at an early age with no older siblings to help them out, making them less likely to ask for help when they got older. And sure enough, a car engine cranked into life and there was Sophie driving away because she didn't want to ask for help. Driving away or walking away being another trait of the person who hadn't learnt to resolve sibling squabbles in a confined space.

Laura grabbed her bag. Well, another trait of the only child was the ability to keep oneself amused, and while what she'd spontaneously decided to do wasn't necessarily about amusing herself, it was a way to fly solo and get the job done. She marched to the front door and stepped out into the cool evening. Clearly there was much more to Sophie's story than she was letting on and it didn't take a life coach, albeit one who was still learning, to figure that out. It was much more than Sophie being silly and sensitive. Sophie was pushing Jazz away; but why, when she clearly loved her? Laura checked her watch and began to walk quickly. She was about to find out.

****

Heading down the stairs into the basement room of Montel's, Laura smiled to herself. The place hadn't been decorated in five years; even the smell was the same. She remembered the first time she and Sophie had sneaked in with their fake IDs, hiding in a corner booth upstairs, just happy to be grown up, or at least pretend they were grown up. In fact Sophie, with her bouncing brown hair, face-full of makeup and revealing outfit had probably looked older then than she did now with her prim clothes and plait.

Laura descended the final step and fingered her own short hair. If this Jazz woman was attracted to a dowdy-looking Sophie then it shouldn't be a problem getting her attention. Laura didn't mind admitting that Sophie was naturally better looking than she was, but Sophie had stopped making an effort and there was a lot to be said for sharp hair, clothes and makeup. She fingered her do once more, expecting everyone to be looking her way. They weren't. They were staring at the stage. Laura turned. And there she was, Jazz, standing behind the microphone, lit up in the spotlight.

"And on that point," laughed Jazz, "just before I hand over to Kellie Kracker, can I ask one final question: does anyone else pack underwear like they're going to shit themselves every single day of a trip?"

Laura spluttered from her position at the foot of the stairs. Jazz was crass. Sophie didn't usually like crass. Or maybe she did? She'd suddenly started liking women after all, not to mention all of that BDSM stuff she'd talked about. Laura focused. Jazz had jumped off the stage and was hurrying up the aisle towards the bar. This was her chance. Stepping forward, Laura walked directly into Jazz's path, but Jazz managed to dodge her and continue on to the bar. Laura turned around, shocked. They weren't going to collide but the least she'd expected was some sort of recognition in the woman's eyes – not recognition that she was connected to Sophie, of course. Sophie's lack of social media accounts was the reason she'd had the confidence to turn up here and hopefully stay incognito – it was more the fact that Jazz hadn't noticed a good-looking woman. "That was close," said Laura, moving to the bar and fake laughing.

"What was?"

"We almost collided."

"Did we?"

Laura stared. Why wasn't Jazz flirting? Why wasn't she rabbiting on like Sophie said she did. "I crossed your path, sorry."

"Oh, I didn't notice."

Laura frowned. This woman didn't notice? This lesbian woman didn't notice another woman standing right in front of her? "On the aisle."

"Oh right, sorry."

Laura watched as the comedian signalled the barman; she'd lost her, their brief interaction was over. She stared at Jazz's side profile.

She had such brilliant bone structure with cheeks that looked like they were smiling even though her lips weren't. Laura froze, Jazz had turned to look at her.

"Can I help you?"

"Sorry, I thought... I just... I just wanted to say you have a wonderful aura."

"Do I?"

"Yes, and I'm sure I saw an orb hovering over your shoulder. It stole my attention. I didn't mean to stare."

"You believe in orbs? What colour was it?"

"Orange."

"Really? An orange orb? Orange orbs symbolise comfort and healing. That's reassuring, thank you."

Laura was about to speak when she realised she'd lost Jazz's attention once more. This was going to be so much harder than she'd originally thought: Sashay in, smile at the lesbian, strike up a flirty conversation, invite her for free life coaching.

"Was it definitely orange?"

Laura nodded, relieved that the attention was back. "Definitely, and from your tone I sense you've been through something that's requiring a lot of comfort and healing." She threw out her hand while she had the chance. "I'm Laura. I'm a life coach." She watched the eyes carefully, still no recognition.

"Jazz. Jasmine. Jazz. Are you here for the show?"

Laura waited until a laugh from the crowd died down. "I was upstairs. I was meant to be meeting friends but something drew me down here. I think you might have drawn me down here."

"Really?"

Laura nodded. "This is going to sound bizarre but I'm a big believer in fate, in signs, and I'm looking for another case study. Free life coaching if you want it?"

"What's the catch?"

"There is no catch. Oh look, there's another orb. It's green."

Jazz turned. "Green means communication and psychic development."

"Utter nonsense," said the barman, handing over a drink to Jazz. "I've been listening. It's just the shimmer off the stage lights reflecting in the mirror behind me."

"Ben, you're a non-believer."

"It was just a thought," said Laura, turning as if she were about to leave. "I'll find someone else."

"Why me?"

Laura shrugged. "Why not?"

CHAPTER ELEVEN

Watching the little girl, whose legs were dancing in mid-air as they dangled from the piano stool in room three, Sophie couldn't help but smile. Her name was Darcy and she was sporting the same plait and black polo neck she'd proudly showcased five lessons ago. 'I want to be just like you, Sophie,' she'd whistled through the gap in her front teeth. The sweet but utterly ridiculous sentiment had almost made Sophie cry. No one would want to be like her if they knew the truth, but it was heart-warming to think some good might have come from her decision to reject the fame and focus of the orchestra and stay put. She smiled again at the little girl's outfit; she'd even got the simple but chic brown belt and slip-on shoes correct.

"Is that the right note?" questioned Sophie, trying not to grimace at the mis-placed fingers, the unintentional flats turning the jovial *Maypole Dance* into something more sinister. "Shall we try that line again?" she said, pulling her chair close so she could lean over and help with the finger placement.

The little girl immediately reached up and stroked Sophie's plait. "I wish my hair was brown."

"No, all the best people have blonde hair like you." Sophie couldn't stop the image of Jazz flashing into her mind.

"Do you have a boyfriend with blonde hair?" The stroking continued. "Or a girlfriend?"

Sophie laughed.

"My mum says you should always ask both. You shouldn't assume."

"And did your mum ask you to ask me?"

The little girl pulled a naughty face. "She says I talk about you too much already. But that's only because you're beautiful, and good at the piano, and kind to me when I don't practise."

"Have you practised this line?"

The little girl giggled. "No."

"Okay, well put your thumb on the middle C and do a huge reach up with finger four to the A."

"My hands aren't big enough."

"They are; stretch, stretch, stretch, stretch, streeeetch. That's it!" Sophie smiled as the correct note sounded out. "If you practise with your hands up it's easier. Remember I told you the trick with the two pence piece? Put it on top of your hand and try and play without it falling off."

"It always falls off."

"Because your hands are sagging below the keys. Bring them up like tap-dancing spiders and imagine the spiders are like puppets on a string." Sophie reached out, playing the *Maypole Dance* in the sprightly style it was intended.

"I'll never be as good as you."

"Just try your best. That's all you can ever do." Sophie realised how hypocritical she sounded the second she'd said it. She hadn't tried her best with Jazz, or Laura for that matter. Half-stories that never told the absolute truth. She glanced at the clock on the wall. She needed to make amends, with Laura at least. "Uh-oh," she said, "we've gone over our time again."

"We always go over our time," giggled the little girl.

Sophie nodded to signal the start of the sing-song. *"Time flies when you're having fun,"* sang both of them in unison, ending the lesson in the same way as usual.

"My mum's got a Mars bar in her bag. Do you want it?"

"That's very kind of you, but you have it."

"I'm not allowed it. I was naughty at school. Mrs Walsh came into the playground to talk to my mum. She said I'd deliberately spoilt Jessica's painting."

"Did you?"

Darcy focused on her own swinging feet. "We were doing portraits of each other but she made me look like a pig with a snout."

"So you spoilt it?"

"It was an accident."

Sophie nodded. "Always say sorry, no matter what."

"Do you always say sorry?"

Sophie couldn't shy away from the suddenly present, expectant eyes. "It's something I'm working on."

"I bet you never do anything wrong. You're so kind and caring." The little girl jumped off the stool, throwing her arms around her teacher. "And you make me want to be better and better and better."

Sophie smiled into the small shoulders. "And you make me want to be better too."

****

Placing the new buffalo-hide leather cushion that had finally arrived from South East Asia onto her armchair, Laura nodded to herself. She hadn't been deceptive, she'd just played into what she knew of Jazz's character. Sophie had said Jazz was carefree and spontaneous, so suddenly deciding to take on life coaching with a stranger wouldn't be anything out of the ordinary, especially if Jazz had felt like fate had guided her there. Laura glanced around at the rest of the room. A quick Googling of orbs and their meanings on the way over to Montel's had done the trick. But this whole thing wasn't a trick, and it wasn't deceptive, it was simply life coaching. The fact it was with her best friend's secret lesbian lover was by the by. Laura nodded again. This was fine. This was all above board.

"That's the front door," came the shout from the lounge. "Oooh, she's a pretty one, Laura. I doubt there's much wrong with her life."

"My job's not about fixing people, Mother!"

"Sorry, you did tell me what this latest venture was about, didn't you? I still don't understand it though. Shall I let her in?"

"No! We spoke about that too!" Laura dashed along the hallway, closing her mother into the lounge.

"Tea and biscuits?" came the muffled call.

"Stay in there, Mother!" Laura stood at the front door, straightening her summer dress before greeting her client with a smile. "Hello again, welcome, welcome, do come through."

"Girls, can I get you some malt loaf? Homemade."

Laura spun around. "Mother! I told you to stay in the lounge. Sorry, Jazz, that's not a very professional start. My mother, Maureen, will not be joining us."

Jazz smiled. "But I hope her homemade malt loaf will."

"Oh what a delightful young lady! I had to come out to see if you're as beautiful in the flesh as you looked through the window, and you are. Truly stunning. You'll have an easy job with this one, Laura, not like that woman I heard you talking to yesterday who—"

"Mother!" Laura turned to Jazz. "I'm so sorry. It's just through here. I'm having a few teething problems hosting my office at my parents' house."

Jazz moved along the corridor between hangings of posh artwork. "Do you live here as well?"

"Of course she does. Steven and I have been trying to ship her off for years, but she's having none of it." The woman stopped. "I'm teasing, my darling; it shows Jazz here that you're likeable."

Laura ushered Jazz past the expensively framed pieces towards the door at the end. "I can only apologise once more."

"It's fine. I live with my parents too."

"See!" Came the triumphant shout. "Common ground already! I'll be in with the malt loaf shortly."

"Please don't, Mother."

"Please do," returned Jazz.

Laura shut the door. "And let's breathe."

"It's fine, honestly," Jazz was laughing. "Oh wow, this room's lovely and airy."

"My space. My office. My life coaching." Laura signalled towards the sofa. "Our life coaching. Please take a seat and let me run through a few things."

****

Placing the laminated sheet of reminder points back on the coffee table, Laura smiled. "So that's it really. Where shall we start?"

Jazz shrugged. "You tell me."

Laura made a professional looking steeple with her fingers under her chin and nodded. "Well, is there anything in your life you'd like help with? Any barrier you need to overcome? Any professional or personal problems you'd like to discuss?"

"I thought you said you weren't an agony aunt?"

"I'm not, but to achieve our goals we sometimes need to dig deeper. Do our personal lives affect our professional achievement? Has anything happened that needs to be 'put-to-bed', so to speak, before we can move on?" She stopped. She had to be careful. It was always going to be a gamble whether or not Jazz would mention Sophie and it would be better getting there organically rather than forcing it. "I mean, are you happy?" There. Blunt, direct, but not obvious.

Jazz tugged on her blue feather earring. "I'm always happy."

"Take a moment. Look out of the French windows to the garden, if you like?"

"Why?"

"It'll calm you."

"I'm always calm."

"You said that quite sharply."

"I didn't, and I think the fact I'm here already says a lot about me. I tend to go with the flow really."

Laura inclined her head towards the painting that her father had commissioned. "And are you achieving your goals?"

Jazz followed the stare. "Is that India?"

Laura ignored the question. "Does that painting make you contemplate the goals you've achieved in your personal life? Your professional life?"

Jazz returned her attention. "In an ideal world I guess I'd like to be further along in my career than I am now."

"You're only twenty-five, aren't you?"

"How do you know that?"

Laura broke the eye contact and reached behind her back for the expensive cushion. "I Googled you after I met you." She pulled it onto her lap and looked back at Jazz. "Like I said at the bar, you're a case study and I'm relatively new to all this. I've just tried to get a step ahead of the game. It's all free, remember."

Jazz continued to stare. "Even I know you shouldn't Google a client. Googling people gives you a preconceived idea of who they are. It's like people always expecting me to be funny."

Laura maintained the eye connection; she'd not seen the smallest spark of personality so far. "Is it because you're sad about something?"

"Is what?"

"Nothing. Sorry, I think I'm still a bit thrown by my mother, thinking she's going to come crashing in with her malt loaf."

"I do like malt loaf; I wasn't trying to ingratiate myself with her."

Laura forced a smile; this Jazz character was actually quite fancy and articulate, making the idea of Sophie falling for a lesbian comedian more feasible, if the lesbian comedian was actually just another boring intelligent person like Sophie. "Let's start with your career then. You said you hoped you'd be further along by now. What do you mean? What do you think's held you back?"

Jazz turned to the windows. "I'm not sure you can help me."

Laura clapped her hands together. "Great! You've just admitted you need help!"

"I meant in a qualified capacity."

"Just talk. You're nervous, you're anxious, you may be a little bit shy."

"Perplexed is more the word."

"We're both new to this. Let's help each other."

"How do you know I haven't had life coaching before? Counselling even?"

"Have you?"

"No."

"Exactly. This is what it's like. You're doing fine. Just talk. How often do we get to open up to people who actually want to listen?"

Jazz laughed. "I think that says more about your life than mine."

Laura waited.

"Fine. I left school at sixteen. I knew I wanted to act. I knew I could act. I'd been acting since I was twelve. I had main roles in all the school productions and local theatre productions. I even did the odd television advert when I was a kid. But then I started to enjoy playing the funnier parts and was told I had good comedic timing. I had the full Equity card and everything."

Laura waited again.

"I got lead roles in *Steaming* and *Born Yesterday* – can you remember when The Grand Theatre started their own production company so it wouldn't just be touring shows coming to town? Do you remember that?"

Laura didn't reply. Session three of the night course had focused on waiting every time the client was on a roll so the client could let everything out without unnecessary interruptions.

Jazz continued. "Well, they did and it was fantastic and our shows really started to take off to the extent that a group of investors wanted us to tour. So anyway, we're getting ready for a production of *Chicago—*"

"Oh, I know that one!" Laura couldn't help herself.

"You know Roxy?"

"The funny murderer?"

"Yes, well I was set to be Roxy and then some chavvy teenagers burnt down the theatre. Remember? Five years ago. Huge news. Well, that was the end of it for me. Everything stopped right there and now I'm introducing other comedians in the basement of Montel's."

"You do so much more than that! You have loads of stand-up gigs and I read online you might be performing at the Apollo."

Jazz tugged on her earring. "See, that's why you shouldn't Google people, and you shouldn't believe everything you read on the internet."

"*Live at the Apollo*, I watch it sometimes."

"I'm not sure about it."

"Why not?"

"I've been asked to re-join the theatre. *The Sound of Music*. Me as Maria. Lead role. The Grand's almost re-built and they want to start up where they left off with a resident production company who'll hopefully also tour. It's what I've always wanted."

"There's no mention of your acting career online." Laura paused. "If it meant so much to you, why aren't you doing it now?"

"That sounds judgmental."

"Sorry, no, this is all just… *news*."

Jazz shrugged. "Acting's my passion. I tried to get work after the fire but the profession's completely oversubscribed and suddenly I'm twenty-five."

"You're hardly past it."

"I need to decide what to do. My comedy career could take off with an appearance at The Apollo but this could be a great chance to get back into acting."

"Do both."

"I can't. It's a full-time residency at The Grand with the possibility of—"

"Touring, yes, you said. Right, let's backtrack, we're getting lost in this unnecessary detail. You said you felt past it in the acting world. Do you feel past it with the women?"

"Excuse me?"

"Well I'm straight as a telegraph pole, but I can appreciate that some women might like you."

"What?"

"Sorry, that came out wrong, but this is good, we're getting somewhere." Laura nodded thoughtfully. "Can you give me an example, with someone possibly, where things were good but then they went wrong? Like, I don't know, a girlfriend maybe? A time when you were happy, but then something bad happened that you felt was out of your control?"

"Why?"

"I want to find out how you deal with difficult situations. It says a lot about a person." Laura paused. "Everyone has a story about an ex. It's the easiest avenue to explore."

"And then?"

"And then I'll be able to guide you more appropriately with your decision."

"I'd rather just discuss my career options without bringing in that crazy lady."

Laura clapped her hands together. "Brilliant! We've got progress! Tell me a story about her and you'll see how it shapes our discussions."

"No."

"It'll help." Laura waited.

"Why?"

"I know what I'm doing."

"I'm not sure you do." Jazz paused. "Sorry, I just… this is all just so…"

Laura stayed silent.

Jazz didn't speak.

Laura nodded gently.

"Fine, but can I be frank? Because if you're as straight as a telegraph pole then it won't affect you, will it?"

"By all means," said Laura, grasping the buffalo-hide cushion that little bit tighter.

"So, I've been seeing this woman called Sophie."

CHAPTER TWELVE

"Don't hold my hand," said Sophie.

Jazz smiled, admiring the pretty profile of the woman she'd fallen unashamedly in love with. She hadn't had the nerve to say it yet even though she knew she felt it with every spark of her being. Releasing her grip, she nodded. They were approaching Sophie's music studio so it was understandable Sophie would be nervous. "Of course, I'm sorry, I wasn't thinking." Jazz reached out and cuddled her girlfriend instead. "I'm just excited." This was progress and it had been a long time coming.

"Don't do that either."

Jazz laughed. "Am I allowed to talk to you in there?"

"No."

"Right."

"Oh Jazz, are you sure you want to do this?"

Jazz stopped their walk. "Me? Of course I do. Don't you?"

Sophie was staring at the modern building over the road. "They're just a bit peculiar."

"Well you're a bit peculiar and I like you more than I should." Jazz smiled. It was true. Sophie was one of the most complicated women she'd ever met. Simple on the surface – a piano teacher who kept herself to herself, but with so many layers it was like you were getting to know her afresh every day.

"What do you mean, more than you should?"

Jazz paused. This was a layer she'd become aware of early on – Sophie's inability to handle any sort of criticism, or perceived criticism. "I was only joking."

"Not one of your funnier ones."

"No," said Jazz, shaking her head and slapping the back of her own hand. It wasn't a big deal. Everyone had their own little idiosyncrasies and it was actually quite entertaining to see where Sophie's line was before trying to figure out why it was there and when she'd crossed it. The fact she knew she'd never fully figure her out was part of the appeal. Sophie was different to anyone she'd ever met: so beguiling and so goddamn wild in bed it was criminal. If she were honest she'd fallen crazily in love with her that very first evening. Just seeing this naturally beautiful woman down on her knees in the Montel's broom cupboard was all it had taken. Such outrageous behaviour from someone so seemingly un-outrageous. A delicious puzzle that needed piecing together, made so much harder because of the many missing parts: Friends. Family. Life story. Jazz smiled. But this was a piece: meeting her work colleagues. Yes, they were over four months into their relationship and, yes, she'd rather they were meeting Sophie's friends and family, but a step was a step. "Have you thought about what you're going to say to them?" she asked.

Sophie continued to stare at the building. "It's all I've been thinking about. Hi Tessa and John, remember that rude comedian who called you Granny and Gramps? Well guess what? We've been fucking, and here she is. She wants to say hello."

"Can we call it making love?"

Sophie's eyes were back. "Have we made love?"

Jazz laughed. "Oooh, touché!"

"Why are we doing this?"

"Arguing about that one time I accidentally fell asleep? Because you keep bringing it up. You always bring it up. It's on your list of: what shall I bring up today."

"I mean this. Here."

"I know! I was joking!"

"So?"

"We're here, Sophie, because it's what normal couples do. They meet people from the other person's life, but if you're not ready I understand. I've not pushed you into anything and I'm happy where we are."

"Are you?"

"Well, no, but I don't want to tell you that."

"That's just it. You never tell me anything. I just never know where I am with you."

"With me?" Jazz laughed. This was another of Sophie's idiosyncrasies. Her ability to project all of her issues onto others and honestly believe she wasn't talking about herself. She was also very good at starting silly arguments when she got anxious. "Shall we just go for dinner instead?"

"You said you wanted to meet them."

"I'm happy to do whatever you want."

"Are you?"

"Well I'd obviously rather meet them than not."

"So why don't you just say that?"

"You don't make things particularly easy for me, Sophie."

"Me? You're the one who keeps changing your mind. First you want to meet them, then you don't."

Jazz took a deep breath. As fascinating as Sophie was there was only a certain amount of figuring out she had the patience to do at any one time, and unfortunately she'd concluded a couple of times by now that Sophie possibly wasn't intriguing, just childish. Taking another deep breath, Jazz reached out and rubbed Sophie's arm. She didn't want this to be one of those times. "I understand how this is all new to you. It's hard coming out."

"Who said I was coming out?"

"Coming out as having a girlfriend, as seeing a girl... a woman... me."

"I'm not afraid."

"I didn't say you were."

"So what are you saying?"

"Nothing."

"Yes, you are. Just say it, Jazz."

"There's nothing I want to say. Perhaps it might have been easier to meet your friends first because they're younger and it wouldn't seem like such a big deal to them, but I'm letting you lead this thing."

"See! Why didn't you say that at the start? Why do you keep things bottled up? Why do I have to pry it out of you?"

"Me?"

"I have no clue what's going on with you."

Jazz reached again for Sophie's arms, but this time she didn't let go. "I'm fine. I'm happy and I want you." She smiled as she rubbed the rigid limbs. "I want all of you, Sophie, and I'll wait as long as it takes. Am I really that fussed about officially meeting Tessa and John? No. Would it be nice to see your studio so I can picture you when you're at work? Yes. Am I intrigued about the banter you have between you and your colleagues? Yes. Is that just so I can get more material for my stand up? Quite possibly."

"It better not be."

"We're almost five months in. You need to know when I'm joking."

Sophie sighed. "Am I being silly?"

"I think you're understandably nervous."

"I'm sorry, I'm being a pain, but you're right; I'm incredibly nervous. Will you forgive me and link my arm?"

"I, Sophie, my dearest, would put you on my shoulders and bounce you over there like a kangaroo if you asked me to."

Sophie restarted their walk. "An arm-link will do."

☁

"I get it," said Laura, shifting uncomfortably in her armchair. "You met someone you thought you liked but she turned out to be a gaslighting maniac."

Jazz shook her head. "I didn't say that."

"Have you ever questioned whether it was because she was an only child? Was she an only child, I mean? Because people have called me a gaslighter before and I'm an only child and it's not nice."

"Who said anything about gaslighting?"

"See, you're doing it to me. You've told me a story that paints Sophie, this Sophie girl, in a very negative light and now you're acting like you haven't."

"I haven't even told you the story yet."

"That wasn't it?"

Jazz laughed. "No. Like I said, her strange and totally over the top reactions are one of her quirks. Mostly I don't mind them. They fascinate me."

"Why?"

"Because when you meet someone so different you have to expect a few idiosyncrasies."

"I still don't know what that means." Laura paused, remembering how Sophie had described Jazz. "You mean if you play with fire you're going to get burnt?"

"Anyone who plays with fire deserves to get burnt in my book."

Laura nodded. "Bad analogy, sorry. You have fire issues. I should have thought."

"I don't have fire issues, I just wish the perpetrators had been caught. You know the police had CCTV. It wasn't publicly circulated because of the estimated age of the kids involved, but we all got to see it."

"You just bit back."

"What do you mean?"

"Maybe it wasn't all her. I justifiably suggested you might have issues with fire and you immediately disagreed."

"You're allowed to disagree with people."

"Maybe the two of you just had a clash of personalities?"

"We didn't. We were the perfect match. We had a few teething problems but she was everything I could dream of in a soulmate."

"It doesn't sound like you two were soulmates."

"We were. We are. I guess we just fell for each other's kind of crazy and it's so sad because I don't think she ever fully understood just how much of me belonged to her. How much of me still belongs to her. She's broken my heart and I won't be able to love anyone else because she'll always have it."

"I read a meme on Instagram the other day that said: *I'm worried that I've already met my soulmate but probably told them to fuck off.*"

Jazz pulled at her feather earring. "Well..."

"Oh you didn't tell her to fuck off, did you?"

"Everyone has a limit and I think I'm a lot more laid back than most people."

Laura studied the woman sitting on the sofa. She wasn't leaning forwards like Sophie had been, or wringing her hands, or scuffing her shoes. She was just there: cool, calm and collected. "Do you think people deliberately try and rile you to get a reaction?"

"I hope not and it's not like I hold back with my thoughts or emotions."

"It seems like you've got a bit of a wall up to me."

"I've just told you some really personal things and I've only just met you. That's the opposite of a wall. Is this part of the coaching? Are you meant to give me a hard time?"

"A-ha! You like to play the victim."

Jazz instantly sat forward. "I don't."

"You reacted again. Maybe it was your reactions, not Sophie's, that were the problem."

"It wasn't me."

"What wasn't you?"

Jazz looked away. "What happened. How it went down."

Laura nodded. "Tell me. I'm listening."

CHAPTER THIRTEEN

Tightening her link around Sophie's arm, Jazz held open the glass door beside the brightly coloured vets' franchise. There was an open staircase ahead of them with a large sign directing people up to the offices of *We Buy Any Car Dot Com* and a smaller sign quietly announcing the *JTP Music Studio* on floor one. "JTP?" queried Jazz.

"John, Tessa and Pamela."

"You've not mentioned a Pamela before."

"She's dead."

"Oh, sorry."

"It's fine. It's why I'm here."

"Oh, yay to Pamela's death then," said Jazz, tapping the metal engraving. "But why's your name not on the sign?"

"I can't jump in her grave. I've already jumped into her room and onto her piano."

"I thought you've been with the studio for years? Let me guess, it's that not-drawing-attention issue again?"

"I'm just not precious about stuff like that. It's been the *JTP Music Studio* for decades."

"This looks like a new building."

"Four years old-ish, I think. Apparently, it was the move out of the village hall that did it for Pamela."

"Did she die on this staircase? Faux-marble's nice and all that but it looks pretty slippery."

"It's not, come on, and she probably took the lift anyway." Sophie pointed at the small glass box.

Jazz laughed. "Oh gosh, I hate those things. You have to keep your finger on the button for it to go up or down, don't you? There's one in the library. I made the mistake of getting in it once and everyone was staring at me when I couldn't get it to work. It was like I was on the frog hopper ride. Up and down, up and down, up and down."

"Oh, you exaggerate everything!"

"I don't. Honestly, I felt really bad because a queue of wheelchair users appeared out of nowhere and everyone in the library could see me bouncing around like I didn't have a care in the world."

"Come on, this is it." Sophie pointed to the first-floor landing and waved her hands at the open-plan reception area.

"Oh, this looks like a library too." Jazz moved towards the bucket chairs in front of the floor-to-ceiling windows and sat down. "You just need a book case. I'd quite happily sit here and stare at the view."

"Of the car park?"

Looking around, Jazz smiled. "It's open and light. I like it."

"Stop being so sweet."

"I'm not. I genuinely like it. It's a simple and functional area. And I like your water dispenser too." She stood up and tapped the huge plastic bottle. "Who changes it? Tessa or John?"

Sophie laughed. "You're being silly. Come back here; you can see my house over there. Look past the car park and that other industrial estate and then over the roof tops and it's just to the right-hand side of that brownish area."

Jazz put her arm around Sophie's shoulder and lifted her hand to her eyes. "I feel like we're in that bit of the Lion King movie where Simba says: 'What's that shadowy place over there?' And the dad says: 'That's Sophie's house; we don't go there.'"

Sophie batted away the contact. "You're not funny."

"Right, are you ready? Shall we go and say hello or shall we continue to stare at the roof tops and the memory of that one time we sat outside your house after our evening in the broom cupboard?"

"They'll be in John's room. They practise their duet pieces together on a Monday evening."

"Don't you join in? Make it a trio?"

"I don't need to."

"Why not? Are you much more talented than they are?"

Sophie shrugged. "I think it's more about Tessa and John wanting to spend time together."

"Do they like each other?"

"How should I know?"

"It's your job to know! It's your job to encourage. Remember Ben from the bar in Montel's? He's got a crush on Kellie Kracker."

"That old woman?!"

"No, that's Deidre Dee. Kellie Kracker's the one with the big tits. Bigger than old Tessa's if I remember correctly. I can still picture your Tessa bouncing up that aisle. It's no wonder bad boy John wants a duet."

"Sophie?" The timid voice was right behind them.

Sophie and Jazz spun away from the window. Sophie spoke first. "Tessa! John! I didn't see you both! Sorry, we were just…"

Jazz couldn't help but stare at the woman's breast area. It was like a breast ledge, a whole other independent section of her body. There were her feet, ankles, legs and wide bottom, her waist roll and then her breast ledge. Jazz dared to look past the neck that wasn't quite there, to the head. The woman's plump face was red with embarrassment. Dashing over she took the woman's hand, shaking it forcefully. "I'm a comedian. A bad one. I'm not funny, but you already know that because you walked out, didn't you? You were right to walk out." Jazz stopped shaking and took a step back, nodding her head in appraisal. "I'm also a lesbian and I notice breasts. I noticed your breasts. They're robust and that's good."

John threw out his hand as if to protect the assessed area. "Sophie?" he repeated.

"Sorry, I didn't mean to tread on your toes, John," continued Jazz. "And I was being supportive. Good on you to go for it. I mean, I would if I wasn't with Sophie."

Both Tessa and John spoke in unison. "With Sophie?"

Sophie cleared her throat. "I… Jazz and I… We… We went for drinks."

"Is that what it's called?" said Jazz with a smile.

"We..."

Jazz positioned herself between the elderly pair, gently guiding them towards the bucket seats in front of the window. "Please sit down, we've got an announcement."

"We haven't got an announcement," said Sophie.

"We have. We'd like to thank you for bringing us together. I believe you organised that comedy night for Sophie. Well, it was perfect. Yes, the initial performance was cut short, but she came back for more and the rest is history."

John coughed. "Sophie?"

"Sophie's happy," said Jazz with a smile. "We're happy. You two made us happy."

John coughed again. "You're an item, as they might say?" He turned to Tessa and clapped his hands together. "I told you, Tessa."

Tessa nodded. "You did tell me, John."

Sophie frowned. "What are you talking about?"

"They're talking about you," said Jazz.

"Oh, this is wonderful," said Tessa. "We've only ever met your friend Laura the masseuse and that was brief. But now you've brought your partner to see us, a partner that we were instrumental in supplying. I told you she'd like the comedy club, John."

"You did tell me that, Tessa."

Tessa rubbed her hands together. "Oh, this is wonderful; it feels like we've progressed more in these few minutes than we have over the years. Thank you for being so open with us, Sophie."

"She's just a bit shy, is our Sophie," said Jazz, throwing her arm around Sophie's shoulder and squeezing.

"Is that why she doesn't want to duet?" asked John.

"I am here," said Sophie, waving her hand. "And, no, I just think it's nice to give you two some alone time so your love can blossom as well."

"Oh, how ridiculous!" said Tessa, pulling herself out of her seat. "Isn't that ridiculous, John?"

"Utterly ridiculous, Tessa!" said John, making a hearty attempt to un-wedge himself from the chair.

"Ridiculous, Sophie," said Tessa, picking up her bag and pressing the button for the glass lift. "John, on that note I think we should go."

"Yes, Tessa, I think we should."

Dumbfounded, Sophie watched as her colleagues squashed themselves into the small box and descended the short distance to the ground floor. They were both red-cheeked. She whispered through her teeth. "Why is it okay for you to tease them and not me? You've only just met them but I've known them for years! You talk about Tessa's tits and she's putty in your hands; I mention a possible attraction between the pair of them and that's it, they're done."

"Some of us just have the gift of the gab."

"They hate me, don't they?"

"Shush, they've come out at the bottom." Jazz peeked over the bannister. "I actually think they're very fond of you and it seems like they know you better than you know yourself."

"In what way?"

"They had your sexuality pegged."

"They did not!"

"That's what they were getting at."

"Were they?"

"Yes! You should let them in. In fact you should let more people in."

"Maybe I like being an island?"

"Do you?"

"Life's just easier that way. Now they're going to be asking questions and prying into our lives."

"That's what normal people do."

"Stop saying I'm not normal."

Jazz engulfed Sophie in a huge hug. "You're far from normal. You're absolutely unique. One of a kind."

"Annoyingly so?"

"Endearingly so."

"You must be a glutton for punishment because I know when I'm being a pain and I can feel myself being a pain, but I can't seem to stop it."

Jazz wrapped her arms tighter around Sophie and whispered in her ear. "My conclusion thus far is that you're on edge about something. Whether that be your sexuality or what I'm not sure, but you're definitely a bit anxious and that's what causes the snaps."

Sophie pushed Jazz away. "I haven't got mental issues!"

"I know! I'm just…" Jazz shook her head. "I'm not as articulate as you. What I'm trying to say is that… well… I love you." She paused. "I love you *because* of your flaws, not despite them."

"What?"

Jazz took Sophie's hands in her own. "I'm being serious, Sophie. I love you. I've felt it for a long time now. Maybe from the start." She smiled. "You're my once in a lifetime and I've fallen head over heels in wild passionate love with you."

"No, you haven't!"

"I have. I love you."

Sophie shook the hands away. "Stop it."

"I won't. I love you."

"You don't love me."

"Sophie, I do. I know what I feel. I feel love, true love, and it's overwhelming and all-encompassing. It's a once in a lifetime explosion of emotion and I have no clue where it's come from, I just know that it's here. I honestly love you with every inch of my being."

"If that were true you'd tell me somewhere better than the reception area of my piano studio and you wouldn't mention it in the same breath as my issues. *Hi Sophie, nice studio, you're a weirdo but I love you.*"

"I've been so close to saying it so many times."

"That I'm a weirdo?"

"That I love you."

"I don't believe you."

"Wait, wait, wait!" snapped Laura, out of her armchair and pacing around. "How did you react so calmly! You've laid your heart on the line and she's thrown it back in your face."

"What do you mean?"

"You told her you loved her and she told you that you didn't."

Jazz shrugged. "I knew her, and when you truly know someone you understand their reactions."

"She reacted like a tool!"

"Everyone can be a tool at times but if you feel real love for someone you can see through all of the nonsense and on this occasion she panicked."

"It was rude!"

"But she's not rude. Well, she doesn't mean to be rude. Like I said, I know her… or I knew her."

"Well her friends and family didn't know her, especially if she was choosing to introduce you to her crappy colleagues instead of them."

Jazz frowned. "Are you meant to get as invested as this in a client's story?"

"What do you mean?"

"You. You're pacing around. You seem quite frantic."

Laura abruptly sat back down. "I'm just not sure if I'm following. You loved her like she loved you?"

"Well, she hadn't actually told me she loved me at that point, but I knew she did."

"How?"

"Lots of reasons, but what happened next confirmed it for me."

"Tell me. I need to hear the whole story."

CHAPTER FOURTEEN

Taking hold of Sophie's hand, Jazz pulled them away from the window. "Room three you say?"

Sophie suddenly smiled. "Wait. You love me?"

"Of course I love you. You're incredible."

"But you don't know me."

"I know enough, Sophie. I see you. You have a good soul and, yes, you might have a little bit of surface shit going on, but it's your soul that matters."

"Surface shit?"

"Shit that won't matter in the long run."

"Well you have surface shit going on too."

"I know I do. We all do. But I feel this, Sophie, and I know you feel it as well. There's a real magic between us. You're different."

"Different bad or different good?"

Jazz squeezed Sophie's hand. "This might sound rehearsed but only because I've been thinking about how I can explain it to you." She smiled. "Imagine a field full of beautiful flowers. They're all so pretty and they're shining in the sun. You pick one for its beauty, but what happens? It dies. I see all those beautiful flowers. I appreciate all those beautiful flowers and I've picked some of those beautiful flowers before." She shrugged. "But the moment of enjoyment's temporary. It goes away. You, however, you're that wild flower in the corner of the field, blowing in the wind. The one that's not intentional. You weren't seeded like the others, Sophie. Your beauty doesn't conform. Yet there you are, rare and exquisite."

"So you're saying you've had enough of the pretty fangirls at the bar and now you're trying a piano teacher?"

"No, I'm saying—"

"Four months in and you need to know when I'm joking too." Sophie laughed. "Come on, come into my room. I understand what you're saying and I think what I wrote last week says something similar too. Let me play it for you."

Jazz followed Sophie's lead. "I'm excited," she said.

"About me playing?"

"About all of this. Seeing your room. Hearing you play. Just being here. It's amazing."

Pulling a key from her pocket, Sophie unlocked the door to her music room. "Ta-dah," she said, half laughing, half sighing.

Jazz popped her head around the door frame. The space was small. Tiny in fact. An upright piano with a stool filled most of it. A poster with music notes on it was Blu-tacked to the wall above the piano and there was a chair in the corner. A plain plastic chair. "Wow," she said. "It's…"

"It's crap but it does the job."

"I was expecting a grand piano and fine art on the wall. Maybe a sofa and some cushions."

"I teach *Old MacDonald* to six-year-olds; I'm not sure they'd appreciate it."

"Don't you want a nice plump chair?"

"They're not here to entertain me. I have to sit up and help with their fingering."

Jazz stepped into the room and lifted the lid of the piano. She ran her fingers over the keys and purred. "Miss, will you help me with my fingering, please?" She placed the tip of her finger between her lips and bit gently.

"Wrong. Just wrong."

"Come on then, Stevie Wonder, play me something." Jazz moved to the plastic chair.

"Am I okay to sing too?"

"You sing?" laughed Jazz, rolling her eyes and clamping her hands. "Every day I learn something new. It's like you're a Kinder Egg crossed with a Russian doll: endless layers of surprises."

"Shush, I need to concentrate."

Jazz looked around the room. There was no natural light and no real space for any plants or decorations; it really was just a room with a piano. And that's when it happened. The most beautiful melody paired with the softest singing voice. It was as if someone had thrown fairy dust into the air, lighting it up with a feeling of enchantment. Jazz raised her hand to her mouth. She couldn't breathe, but she didn't want to react either; not that she could if she tried; she was frozen, awestruck. The notes were perfect and the words were heartfelt. She bit hard on her lip as she listened, lost in the power of the song.

"*In her eyes I found magic, in her smile I found heart. I found courage that my life could once again start. I found beauty and pleasure and everything true. I found knowledge that my life has meaning with you.*"

Jazz closed her eyes.

"*You're the one I was made for, the one I hold true. But I must take a breath and be honest with you.*"

"Oh, Sophie," she whispered, unable to stop herself.

"*I push you away to save you from me. I need to make peace and find clarity.*"

Jazz wiped away a tear.

"*I'm not who you think and I'm not worth your love. A bittersweet punishment sent from above.*"

Jazz jumped from her chair and sank onto her knees beside the piano. "Talk to me, Sophie. You have nothing to be scared of."

Sophie lifted her fingers from the keys and spoke softly. "It's just a song."

"So why are your eyes watering?"

"Why are yours?"

Jazz caressed Sophie's leg. "Because I'm moved."

"A song writer makes things up. They dramatize."

"But why are you sad? What are you holding back from me?"

"I'm not sad." Sophie turned on the stool and smiled. "I'm happy. You make me so happy, Jazz. I just…"

"Just what? Talk to me."

"I can't"

"Why not?"

"I just know it's going to end."

"Why?"

"Because…"

Jazz shuffled closer. "Because you love me back and it scares you?"

Sophie's breath quickened. "I do love you, Jazz. I'm crazily in love with you. I'm writing songs about you nearly every day and I can't think of anything other than you. Of us. Of our future. You consume me, every second of every minute. And I'm a different person since I've met you. I feel alive again. I feel like I want to be here."

"So what happened? Tell me why you've been hiding?"

"I…"

Jazz shook her head. "Actually don't. It doesn't matter. I love you and I'm here for you and I don't care who you were or what you did."

"You would care."

"Have you killed someone?"

"No."

"Well then."

Sophie rubbed her forehead. "I'm just so scared of getting close to you and it all going wrong."

"I know that. Don't you think I've known that from the start? When you love someone you don't have to understand what they're going through, you just have go through it with them, by their side."

"Oh, Jazz, you're so amazing."

"Kiss me then."

Sophie smiled as she stroked her thumbs across Jazz's cheeks. "You're a really special person."

"Says you," whispered Jazz, kissing her softly. "That voice and that melody. Your talent's overwhelming, mind blowing."

"You're the mind blowing one," said Sophie, kissing deeper.

"I can sing too," murmured Jazz.

"Duet?" managed Sophie.

Jazz pulled out of the embrace. "Let's join together in another way first," she said as she lifted Sophie from the stool. "Get on the top of the piano."

"I can't. It's too thin."

"You're thin. Trust me." Jazz continued to kiss as she perched Sophie on the piano top. "Now lie back so I can part your legs."

"I'll roll off."

"You won't." Jazz appraised the scene. "It's like you're Julia Roberts in *Pretty Woman* where Richard Gere tells the old men to leave the room so he can play Julia on the piano."

"She was on a grand piano."

"And he had his head between her legs, like this."

Sophie groaned. "Pull my jeans down."

"I am, take your plait out."

Sophie looked startled. "What?"

"Take your hair out. Julia Roberts had her hair down. Let it cascade over the other side of the piano."

"No."

"For me?"

"No."

"I've never seen you with your hair down."

"I don't like it down."

"Just once? This is a real fantasy for me. Look at you, sitting up there, legs ready for me to part. I want to grab hold of your hair as I push deep inside you with my tongue."

"Take my jeans off."

"I am. Take your hair down."

"Maybe as you're making me come."

"Yeah?" said Jazz, moving her mouth between Sophie's thighs.

"Yeah," moaned Sophie, back in position, her hand dangling down and hitting a key.

Jazz groaned. "That happened in the film; that's turning me on." She moved deeper between the legs, groaning every time Sophie's fingers plinked the keys, somehow tunefully. "That's totally turning me on."

"You're turning me on," said Sophie, arching her back as she moaned. "Keep going."

Jazz moved her hand from Sophie's side up to her hair, finding the bobble at the end of the plait and pulling it out.

"What are you doing?"

"Fucking you."

"Leave my hair."

"No."

"I said leave my hair."

Jazz stopped. Sophie was sitting up, frantically trying to find the bobble.

"Where is it?" snapped Sophie.

"Let me finish. Forget about the hair. It doesn't matter. Lie back down. Let me finish."

"I don't want you to finish. I want you to go."

"What?"

"I want you to go."

"I'm not going."

"Just go!"

🌧

Laura screeched. "So what did you do?"

"I just went," said Jazz, folding her fingers in her lap.

"You didn't tell her to fuck off?"

"No, I was too confused. I didn't know what I'd done wrong."

"Did you ask her?"

"Of course I did, later on, over text."

"And?"

"And she said you should never change for anyone. She had this big long rant about how people should want you for who you are not who they can make you."

"You were only trying to replicate Julia Robert's hair!"

"I know, and the second she said stop I stopped. But I didn't understand it. I still don't understand it. As we were texting I tried to use the example of whether or not she'd let me dress her one day. I asked her to imagine we were going to someone's wedding and I wanted our outfits to complement each other and the only thing that would complement my outfit would be for her to wear a yellow dress."

"What the hell are you wearing then?"

"It's just an example. But my point was: would she wear something that wasn't so great for the simple reason I'd asked her? I'd begged her?"

"Oooh be careful, that's sounding a bit like control."

"It's not. It's like telling someone you like their hair longer. Why wouldn't that person even think about the possibility of growing it if they knew you liked it that way?"

"Because you're telling that person there's something wrong with them, that they can be better."

"Everyone can be better. She was just so bloody sensitive all the time. She felt like everything was a personal attack."

"So you told her to fuck off?"

"No, we made up."

Laura laughed.

"What?"

"Nothing, I've just heard... nothing. Carry on."

"That's it. You asked for an example in my life of a time where I felt things were going well before it all went wrong. Well in that moment, in that room, with her singing and playing to me, it was pure perfection."

Laura shook her head. "But if that perfection's always going hand in hand with crap nonsense, then surely it's not worth it?"

"But what if that crap nonsense is temporary? What if it's caused by something that'll go away? That's what I thought anyway. I thought we could get past those teething problems and live the dream."

"Did you?"

"Well no." Jazz rolled her shoulders. "I don't know what was going on with that woman and, frankly, I don't care anymore."

"You do!"

"Maybe I did, but it all got too much."

"What happened?"

"It doesn't matter. I'd rather talk about my job."

Laura sat up straighter and tried to refocus. "Right, okay. But one last question; did she know about your acting?"

"She didn't, but then…"

Laura waited.

"Look," said Jazz, sighing. "Jazz the comedian is just Jazz the comedian. Very few people actually know I'm Jasmine Jones, the once aspiring actress."

"So you kept secrets from her?"

"Why are we still talking about my ex? I don't talk to anyone about my acting past until it comes up."

"Is that because you view it as a failure?"

"Well, I've been unable to get any more parts so, yep, I guess that's about right."

"Isn't it the fire's fault?"

Jazz shifted in her seat. "There are other places to act."

"Right." Laura performed a solemn nod. "I think that should be the focus of our next session. For now, I'd like to remain on the subject of Sophie."

"Why?"

"Because I need closure. You need closure." Making the thoughtful steeple once more with her fingers, Laura tapped them gently against her chin. "I'm just not understanding this so-called magical connection. It seems to me that she was a real pain in the arse."

"You've lost me. Why are we talking about this again? I've just outlined a genuine career conundrum."

"Do both. The acting and the comedy."

"I've already told you, I can't. If I commit to the theatre that's it, it'll be non-stop: rehearsals, press events, two performances a day, a tour. Then it'll start all over again with the next production."

"Which is exactly the reason we need to make it the focus of our next session. But now we need closure on today's topic: Sophie. Why put up with the bullshit?"

Jazz didn't reply.

Laura stayed quiet.

The voice that eventually came from the sofa was tired. "Even the most perfect thing has its flaws."

Laura nodded encouragingly. "But how was she perfect?"

"You said we didn't have time."

"Just one example. Please? I desperately want to see the good side of this woman."

CHAPTER FIFTEEN

Yawning under the duvet in the room she'd slept in for almost twenty-five years, Jazz stretched. Her job made regular sleep patterns difficult to maintain. Often she'd get in from a gig at gone two in the morning, especially if she was headlining. She stretched again and let out a little moan. Laughing to herself, she flung her hand towards the pad of paper sitting on her bedside table. This latest pad was backed in black vinyl with the PwC logo in the corner of each sheet of paper, some freebie she'd picked up at a conference event somewhere. Never precious about what she wrote her jokes on, she was just conscious that she always had something close by. This was her black bedroom pad, she had a pink Hello Kitty pad ready to slot into whatever bag she was carrying and a Moleskine notebook – a present from her parents at Christmas – that stayed in her car; not to mention the Word app on her phone, full of all the funny things she'd thought of while in the bathroom or out at dinner where it was easier to apologise and pretend you were replying to a text instead of grabbing a notepad and saying: 'You were just utterly ridiculous; I'm going to write that down.'

She scribbled quickly. *Who loves it in the morning when they stretch and their inner porn star moan accidentally escapes? *do action and sound* It's like you hear it escape and it excites you, so you yawn and stretch again, only this time you stick your boobs out as well. *do boob action* Come on, ladies, we all do it, don't we? *do action and sound again* In fact, let's do it now. All of us. Yawn, stretch, moan. *audience action and laughter* And gentlemen, there you go, that's what real pleasure sounds like.*

Jazz circled the whole thing, drawing three big question marks in the margin. It should work and she could probably camp up the audience involvement, picking on the really loud women and the really quiet ones. She could picture it now: The collective noise of moans escaping from the crowd. She drew another question mark. Could she try it tonight? Usually she'd test new material at one of her compèring slots. Some jokes just didn't work and it was much easier to just move on by introducing the next, and much funnier, comedian than having your whole set, based around that one gag, die on stage. She put the pad down. She'd wait. Tonight was important. It was being televised and she needed to get everything spot on.

Stretching once more, she found her phone. Five missed calls and five voicemails. She groaned. All from Sophie. It had been two days since the plait pulling confusion and she wasn't sure how much more discussion and de-briefing she could take. This was one of their differences; she could easily let things lie after a blow-up whereas Sophie couldn't. Like the constant little digs about that time she fell asleep and that time she confused a few letters of her surname. Yes, some might say she'd fucked up, but she'd apologised and life was too short to continually pull people up on their mistakes. Everyone made mistakes. Everyone. Taking a deep breath, she clicked to listen to the first message. She could feel herself frowning, assuming it was going to be another rant about hairstyles and the importance of not changing people, but as she heard Sophie's voice Jazz burst into a joyously loud laugh. Sophie was singing. Heartily.

"*I just called, to say, I love you. I just called, to say how much I care. I just called, to say, I love you and I wish you the very best of luck tonight.*"

Jazz clicked through to the next one.

"*Because you're once, twice, three times a lady, and I love you. Yes you're once, twice, three times a lady, and I'm thinking of you.*"

Jazz laughed again.

"*She's a lady, woah woah woah, she's a lady. I'm talking about that little lady, and that lady's a star.*"

Jazz played the next message on loud speaker as she sunk her head into her pillow, smiling from ear to ear.

"You're simply the best, better than all the rest. Better than anyone, and you'll rock it tonight."

"I do love you," she whispered as she clicked through to the next message.

"I'll make love to you, if you want me to, and I'll hold you tight, baby all through the night, but not tonight as you're up north and I'll miss you."

Jazz listened to the pause.

"Seriously, Jazz, ignore my silly singing. I just want you to know how much I care and how proud I am of you. Tonight's a big deal and I'm so sorry I can't come with you; damn my eighty-year-old grandma's birthday party, how dare she? Seriously though, you'll be amazing. I love you and I might have accidentally, perhaps, most probably, sent you a little care package that should be arriving in the post this morning. It has to be signed for and I didn't want you to miss it, that's why I called, but then I started to sing, so now I'm going, but just to leave you with one final thought: *Baby love, my baby love, I need you oh how I need you. But all you do is treat me bad.* Oh wait, wrong song. You didn't break my heart and leave me sad; I was silly and irrational again and I'm sorry. I love you. You're too good for me. Enjoy your care package and I'll see you when you're back. Take care. Have fun. Byeeeeee."

Jazz dropped her phone onto her pillow and laughed. That's all it ever took. One simple sorry and everything was forgotten and forgiven. Who knew why Sophie didn't want her plait pulled out? But quite frankly who cared? When Sophie was the sweetest, most thoughtful person like this, none of that nonsense mattered. This was the real her. The funny, sweet, endearing and thoughtful woman she'd seen from the very first moment they'd met. Jazz smiled again. She was happy, so happy.

"Knockity-knock-knock," said her mother as a head popped round the bedroom door.

Jazz pulled the duvet higher around her chest and sat up against the headboard. "It's fine, Mum, I'm up."

"You told me to wake you for your train."

"I told you to check I was awake for my train."

"I'm checking, and," the woman, who looked remarkably similar to Jazz except for a more sensible haircut and slightly less height, came into the room, "this came for you."

Jazz looked at the large box. "Thanks, just pop it down there."

"Don't you want to open it? I had to sign for it."

"No, it's fine thanks, Mum; just pop it down there."

"It's handwritten."

"Down there."

"With a heart next to your name."

"Mum." Jazz laid her palms flat on the duvet.

"What? I'm interested, and who was that on the phone? Beautiful voice. I heard you laughing."

"Mum!"

The parcel was placed in an exaggeratedly apologetic fashion on the end of the bed. "Fine, but I'll have to come up on the train with you and watch your set. Watching your set's the only time I ever find anything out about your love life."

"It'll be on Freeview Comedy."

"Live?"

"Yes, live! You know this."

"Tuesday night, salsa night. I'll watch it on catch-up." Jazz's mum tapped the top of the box. "She knows tonight's important, right? That's why she's sending you a good luck package."

"Were you listening, Mother?"

"Me? Of course not."

"Out."

"She sounds like a nice one."

Jazz couldn't stop the smile from forming on her lips. "She is. A really nice one."

"Well for goodness sake, why don't you invite her over?!"

"I have."

"And she hasn't come?"

"Obviously not, Mum, and she's not in that bloody box either so stop messing with it."

"The good ones are worth waiting for."

"I know."

"Look at me. I didn't meet your father's parents for over two years."

"He didn't realise he was going out with you for over two years."

"You're not funny, Jazz."

Jazz nudged the box with her foot under the duvet. "She thinks I am."

"Tell me about her."

"No."

"Please? All of my other little chicks have flown the nest and you're the only one I've got left. Look at me, sitting here, all alone."

Jazz watched as her mother perched on the end of the bed next to the box.

"Cheep cheep, feed me."

"I thought you were the mother?"

"Cheep cheep, feed me with love and information." Jazz's mum smiled. "With some sort of sign you're okay."

"Oh, Mum, you know I'm okay."

"You're twenty-five, sleeping in until eleven, in the childhood bedroom you've never left without a whiff of a serious relationship to behold."

"You want to come in here and smell sex?"

"Jazz!"

"You can't have it both ways. I'm trying to be respectful not bringing women home and I'm staying home so you don't die alone in your nest and get eaten by some cat."

"Is Dad the cat? To be fair he'll eat anything, won't he?" Jazz's mum squeezed Jazz's legs through the duvet and smiled. "Shall we open it?"

"Oh bloody hell, just open the thing."

Jazz's mum wailed. "This is so exciting! Pass me that pen!"

Jazz watched as her mum stabbed at the tape sealing the top of the box. "Careful, there might be something delicate in there."

"There's not. It's lots of little things, all wrapped up. I poked a hole in the side earlier and peeped through. Right, here you go: card."

Jazz took the white envelope. It felt a bit like Christmas morning, her mum watching on with eager eyes, desperate to see happiness brought through the unwrapping and elation at whatever gift had been given. Jazz laughed. "She says: *Sorry it looks like a death card; it's all the corner shop had.*"

Jazz's mum frowned. "Hold it up. Oh gosh, it *is* a death card. *Thinking of You.* That's a cross and a weeping eye!"

"She says: *Just to let you know that I'm thinking of you. You'll be an absolute super star tonight. Shine bright and go wow them. Love, me.*"

"Who's me? Who is this giver of death cards?"

"She's called Sophie and she's much funnier than she lets on."

"You find that card funny?"

"It's hilarious. Oh bless, look, all the gifts are numbered. Right, number one. It says: *Every couple has a song but we have a drink. Our drink is sherry.*"

"Sherry?"

Jazz ripped open the heart-design wrapping paper. "It's a miniature bottle of Croft Original."

"Your grandma used to drink that. Does this Sophie girl look like your grandma?"

"Gift two says: *Because you always wear them.* Oh my goodness, look!" Jazz pulled the silky shirt from its wrapping. "How cool is that! Oh, I love it! It's so bright and so me! I love the blue and gold Versace-style pattern."

"Not Versace though. Where's it from?"

"You know I'm not precious about designers." Jazz fumbled with the label. "John Rocha."

"Your grandma wears John Rocha. Seriously, she does. From Debenhams."

"Why are you laughing?"

"I'm not. This is just so sweet and you're so happy. Keep going."

"Okay, gift three says: *Your burgundy nail polish is always chipped. You need to keep on top of it with this.*"

"What is it?"

"Burgundy nail polish."

"Oh, I love her! I've told you about that before!"

"Gift four." Jazz swiped the pile of ripped wrapping paper to the floor. "This says: *To eat on the train, they're your favourite.* Ha! Crisps! Three packets."

"Is she a feeder? Your grandmother's a feeder."

"Gift five says: *Just in case.* Oh, I love it," laughed Jazz. "Look: *The Big Fat and Very Silly Joke Book.*"

"Hit me with one."

Jazz flicked through the pages. "Okay: What did the finger say to the thumb?" She paused. "I'm in glove with you."

Jazz's mother threw her hand to her mouth. "That was the first one you found?!"

"Top of the page."

"It's a sign! Your grandmother believes in signs. I believe in signs. You believe in signs. It's a sign, Jazz!"

"That I need to take gloves with me tonight in case it's cold up north?"

"That she loves you, because this is an effort, Jazz. Anyone can click on Interflora and get flowers delivered, not your father mind, but this takes effort and thought, not to mention how totally lovely it is. And all of these little personalised messages too. What's that big one? Open that next."

Pulling the oblong shaped gift out of the box, Jazz read loudly. "Gift six: *To keep you company.*" She unwrapped the package in the same manner as she had the others. One tear and one huge yank, the paper instantly discarded. She gasped, but it was too late; her mother had snatched the gift first.

"What the bloody hell is this?! She clearly doesn't know about the secret suitcase of sex toys you keep stashed in that wardrobe over there, because this little thing's far too vanilla for you!"

"Mother!"

"It is! It hasn't even got ridges or anything, and it's only half the size of the ones you usually use."

"Mother! Give it back."

"This would suit your grandma more."

Jazz laughed. "You're not funny, Mum."

"I am. That's where you get it from." She nodded. "But you won't be getting any pleasure from this little purple thing, will you?"

"Hand it over." Jazz studied the dildo. "It's old-school. She likes old-school."

"Like your grandma."

"Don't talk about Grandma when I'm holding a dildo." Jazz picked up another package. "Last one. Gift seven: *To play with on the train*. Actually I'm not sure I should open this."

"They don't make love eggs that big."

Jazz fingered the squashy round package. "How would you know?"

"You get that from me too. Just open it. It's not like I haven't seen that suitcase. In fact, I accidentally offered it to Deidre Chambers. She was off on another city break and couldn't find her case. Asked if we had one. I brought her up here and everything."

"You did not!" Jazz ripped open the paper. "It's a squashy brown American football."

"It looks like a dog toy. Why would she get you a dog toy?"

"Because she's funny and random and there'll be some strange explanation that will make no sense whatsoever but it'll be endearing all the same."

"Is it a stress ball?"

"I don't know. But I'm taking it on the train with me."

"Don't forget to take that little purple dildo as well."

"Mum, that's enough. You've worn me out. I need to pack."

"That little purple dildo?"

"Yes."

Jazz's mum smiled. "Seriously, I'm happy for you, Jasmine. You're smiling your proper smile, not your on-stage false one, your proper one. It's heartening." She stood up from the bed and made her way towards the door. "I love her already."

Jazz squeezed the football tightly. "That makes two of us."

CHAPTER SIXTEEN

Reaching for the arm of the sofa, Jazz pushed up on it and shrugged. "Sophie was magic. But we all know that magic's not real. It's an illusion."

Laura gasped. "Wait! Where are you going? I need closure. Why did she freak out about her hair? What was the soft ball for? How did your TV performance go?"

"No clue, no clue, and you can watch it online if you really want to? I think it was that show that got me the Apollo gig."

"We need to talk about the Apollo gig." Laura spoke quickly. "Sit down. I need to build up your confidence. I need to get you in the right frame of mind so you say yes and give it all that you've got."

"Have you even been listening? I haven't said yes because it'll clash with the re-opening of the theatre." Jazz stayed by the door. "And, no offence, but all of this talk has made me feel worse than I did before."

"Sometimes you have to re-open a wound. Like when there's grit in it. You have to scrape that grit out before it'll heal."

"You're likening my ex to a piece of grit?"

"A foreign body. Something that shouldn't be there."

"Why shouldn't she be there?"

"Sophie's bad for you, just like that grit, and you're bad for her."

"How do you know?"

"It's obvious."

"How?"

"You're both broken."

"Both?"

"You and Sophie. You'll never heal unless you both properly de-grit once and for all. And then you can't ever ride that bike again because you'll just fall off and get another graze, which means more grit."

"Do you know her?"

"Who?"

"Sophie."

"Of course not."

"So why are you talking like you—"

"Coo-ee! Only me. Oh excuse me, can I squeeze in? I have your malt loaf and two cups of tea."

"Mother!"

"Sugar on the side if anyone wants it. I bet your client doesn't eat sugar though, does she? I can tell from her build." Laura's mother placed the tray on the coffee table. "Sorry for noticing, but I notice these things. I noticed when you walked in. You're not only beautiful but you're buff as well. That's what you youngsters say nowadays, isn't it? *Buff.* It's funny when you say it aloud. The way it just pops out of your mouth. *Buff.* It's more like a noise than a word. So, how's it going, ladies? Have I interrupted? It feels a little bit frosty in here. Is everything okay? Shall I turn up the heating?"

"Mother!"

Jazz rubbed her earring-free lobe. "It's fine, I was on my way out." She smiled. "I'll take the malt loaf to go though, if I may?"

"Sure, how wonderful, let me just nip and get you a sandwich bag."

Laura watched as her mother exited the room before fixing her stare right on Jazz. "You're definitely trying to ingratiate yourself with my mother. Why?"

"Excuse me?"

"That smile. That gushing over her shop-bought *shhh, Doreen's having her Soreen* malt loaf."

"What are you talking about?"

"That advert. *Shhh, Doreen's having—*"

"No, the accusation of ingratiation."

Laura nodded. "You *are* secretly posh."

"Because I like malt loaf?"

"And you're charming on the surface."

"Only on the surface?"

"The way you use your words. Who are you, Jazz? I think you're being deceptive."

"Me?!"

"Wanting everyone to like you."

"What?"

"Then painting them in a bad light when they don't."

"What are you talking about?"

"Suggesting I know Sophie because I correctly called out the solution to your problems: to never see her again. To never get on that bike. To never ride her. I'm assuming you rode her? My point is you got prickly when I tried to tell you what to do."

"So you're telling me you don't know Sophie?"

"Of course I don't and if you—"

"Coo-ee, me again! Malt loaf in a sandwich bag and I've popped in a couple of jam tarts too. Laura doesn't like the apricot ones, do you, my darling. Oh hang on, is that the door?" Maureen stepped into the hallway and crouched, directing her gaze through the glass panels at the end. "Looks like it's Sophie. Oh darn it, she likes the apricot ones, doesn't she? I might need to steal one back."

"Sophie?" asked Jazz.

Laura tried to pull Jazz back into the room. "My grandma!"

Jazz frowned. "Your grandma's called Sophie?"

"Your grandmother's dead, Laura. Why are you talking about your dead grandmother? Is this part of the therapy? Should I leave you girls to it?"

"I think you should answer the door," said Jazz.

"Don't answer the door, Mother."

"Well, I just can't leave poor Sophie standing there."

"Leave her standing there," gasped Laura.

Jazz stepped into the hallway. "You'd leave your grandmother standing on the doorstep?"

"Please, Jazz, come back in here. Mother! Tell Sophie to go."

"To go? The least we can do is give her one of her favourite apricot jam tarts. Sorry, do you mind? I can't send her away empty handed. Could I just get at that clasp? Tough little buggers these sandwich bags, aren't they?"

"I'll do it," said Jazz, keeping hold of the goodies and walking past the framed artwork straight to the door. "I'll give it to her."

"Jazz, don't!" shouted Laura, but it was too late; Sophie was there, in full view, standing on the front step.

"Sophie, hi," gushed Maureen, popping her head around Jazz's shoulder. "We have to send you away, sorry. I think they're in the middle of a séance with someone's grandma or something like that. I won't pretend to know the ins and outs of this therapy malarkey but it's rather highly charged. Would you like an apricot jam tart?"

"Jazz?" said Sophie, motionless.

Jazz didn't speak.

"Or would you rather have a bit of malt loaf? I can nip back into the kitchen and grab you a slice?"

"Jazz?" whispered Sophie once more.

"Is that a yes? Or I have a couple of Viennese Whirls?"

"Mother, please just go back into the lounge for a minute."

"Are you going to sort out the malt loaf, Laura?"

"No one cares about the bloody malt loaf!"

"Highly charged," whispered Maureen, edging backwards and heading in the lounge's direction.

"Jazz?" said Sophie again.

"Yes, it's bloody Jazz," snapped Laura. "Stop staring at her like a lunatic."

"Jazz?"

"Oh for god's sake, will you both just come into my room? We can switch this up to a couples counselling session if you like?"

Sophie spoke again. "Say something, Jazz."

Jazz handed over the sandwich bag before barging her way past Sophie. "You like apricot jam tarts. Something else I didn't know about you."

"Where are you going?" asked Sophie, perilously spinning around on the doorstep.

"What bit of *fuck off* didn't you understand?" Jazz was shaking her head. "Engineering this ridiculous situation as if I wouldn't find out. What did you think would happen? I'd chat to guru Laura for half an hour then fall into your arms on this very doorstep?"

"What?"

"Just leave me alone, Sophie."

"I haven't done anything!"

"Isn't that what you always say?"

"Jazz, wait! I haven't got a clue what's going on."

"And I've heard that one before," shouted Jazz, turning the corner onto the street. "I don't want to see you again, Sophie."

"Jazz!"

"Just leave her," said Laura from her position in the doorway. "She's got issues."

"What's going on?!" demanded Sophie, looking from her pseudo-guru friend to her rapidly disappearing ex-lover. "Why was she here? Did she come looking for me? I should go after her."

"Why would she look for you here?"

"You wouldn't be that hard to find."

"What?"

"Is she using you to get to me?"

"She knows who I am?"

"She's the one in your house, Laura!"

"But that's because... wait, hang on, you spoke to Jazz about me?"

"Of course I did. You're my friend. I was coming around to say sorry."

"Oh god," gasped Laura, throwing her hand to her mouth. "This makes it so much worse. She *is* deceptive! And she *is* scheming. She'll have censored everything she told me. She'll have tainted the story her way. She's an unreliable narrator! Tell me, did you freak out when she tried to pull out your plait?"

"No!" Sophie looked aghast before shrugging. "Well, yes... but it wasn't a freak out, I just... how do you know? What the hell's going on?"

"Oh dear, I think you need to come in."

CHAPTER SEVENTEEN

Squashed into a corner table at the back of the working men's club, Sophie turned to her friend. "This was such a bad idea." One quick search on Laura's smartphone and they'd discovered where Jazz was performing that evening. It was dark and dingy but thankfully full, making their entrance and slinking shuffle to the seats at the side that much easier than they'd expected. Both had been fully prepared to have it out in stage-lit public – Laura admittedly more prepared than Sophie because she felt like the butt of her own joke – with Sophie just wanting answers about what had gone on. "So," said Sophie, whispering across the scratched table. "Let me line this up. If Jazz knew who you were, why did she come to your house? Why did she agree to the life coaching? Did she think I was involved? If she did, then she still has a flame."

"She doesn't have a flame."

"Maybe she was hoping I was trying to get to her through you."

Laura shifted her chair further into the shadows. "I was so sure she didn't recognise me."

"She's not going to recognise you, is she? But maybe after you introduced yourself as Laura she remembered I had a friend called Laura and put two and two together?"

"What exactly did you tell her about me? Did you tell her I was a life coach?"

"You were a masseuse when we first got together, then you started the dog walking service."

"I was never a dog walker! I had a pedigree pooch pampering business."

Sophie shrugged. "Either way, this life coaching's recent. I don't think I mentioned it."

"Still, even a low-level stalker would be able to find out what I looked like if they really wanted to. I assume you told her things like your age, where you went to school, any parties and events you were going to? Half an hour on Facebook and she'd find me, and then you."

"I'm not on Facebook."

"But pictures of you are." Laura tapped one of the deeper scratches on the table. "Bobby's birthday last week. You're in the background of loads of shots. You're not tagged, but you're there. Imagine Jazz meeting you and wanting to know more about you. She knows all the details I just mentioned. She knows you have a friend called Laura. Half an hour in and, boom, she finds me, and there you are too in one of the pictures, so she knows I'm the Laura you're talking about."

"Jazz is too cool to do all that."

"You Googled her."

"So?"

"So people do it."

"Which means you're saying she *did* know who you were, which means she chose to play along and come to the life coaching. But why? The only answer is that she still has some hope for us."

"Or she's a game-playing bitch?"

"Her? You're the one I should be angry with!"

"But you're not though, because this whole thing's opened up a new dialogue between you two."

"It hasn't! I'm hiding at the back of a working men's club with no plan of action."

"I'd hoped we'd see her at the start and it would all just happen, but we might as well watch her set first, then confront her."

"And say what?"

"We'll ask her why a game-playing bitch would pretend not to know her new life-coach."

"I think you've been fired."

"Good. She's got far too many issues."

Sophie sighed. "Oh, Laura, what if she didn't know?"

"She did! She acted like the big I am on the doorstep."

"Maybe she didn't want to lose face? Maybe she responded how you responded."

"What do you mean?"

"You said you went on the attack when she asked if you knew me. Did you really call her deceptive?"

"I panicked. I started waffling on about Mum's malt loaf as well."

"Maybe she panicked?"

"But she painted you as the baddie, Sophie. She knew who I was and she used it to slag off my friend to my face."

"Or she didn't and I am the one who got things wrong between us?"

Laura shrugged. "We'll see. Look, here she comes. Let's see what she's like when she thinks we're not here."

"We're never usually here."

"Still, she might use what's gone on."

"She'd never do that."

Laura gasped. "Wouldn't she? That's my mum's joke! She's up there talking about words that sound funny when you say them! My mum said that today! *Buff!* She's stolen her idea!"

"Shush! Let me listen." Sophie slid even lower in her seat even though there was no possible way Jazz could see them from the brightly-lit stage.

Jazz was pacing in the spotlight. "*Plop*. When did you last say the word *plop*? You all just said it, didn't you? I saw your lips move. There was a silent plopping across the room. What about *belch*. Say *belch*. Say it now. Yeah, that's it, really belch it out." Jazz laughed. "Words are funny, aren't they? There's one in particular that I like. It means ASAP, as soon as possible. Who knows it? It's my favourite word; well it's two words actually." She nodded. "*Lickety-split.*"

Sophie laughed.

"That's not funny," hushed Laura.

Jazz nodded again. "It's the straight women not laughing, isn't it? Men, you like the word *lickety-split*, don't you? Well, I'd like a bit of the old *lickety-split*, but I'm single again. Owwwwww. I hear you, but it's okay. Don't be sad for me; I've learnt lots of new things. For example: did you know that narcissist spelt backwards is arsehole?" Jazz smiled. "Hey, if they can make shit up so can we."

Sophie inhaled a sharp breath through suddenly wide nostrils.

"I would tell her to go fuck herself but I'm pretty sure she'd be disappointed."

Laura grabbed her friend's hand and squeezed as they both gasped together.

"I think I'm just going to box the whole thing off as part of my self-hate phase."

"I can't listen to this," said Sophie, beginning to shake.

The laughter was loud. "She had more issues than the National Geographic." Jazz nodded. "And what should you do if you miss your ex?" The pause was thoughtful. "You re-load and try again."

"HOW COULD YOU?!" screamed Sophie, standing up, unsure of when she'd done so or why her tears were now flowing.

Laura grabbed at Sophie's jumper, trying to pull her back down, but Sophie stayed standing, now-silent rage fixing her stare to the stage. "How could you?" she said again, this time with less volume.

"Ladies and gents," said Jazz, "I'll be back in a lickety-split. Go and take a plop if you need to."

"Run!" gasped Laura.

Sophie felt the tugging but was completely bewildered. "What?"

"Run! She's coming!"

Looking back, Sophie could see that Jazz was making her way through the tightly packed tables. "Let's run!" squeaked Sophie, suddenly feeling panicky and alert. She let her friend's hand grab hers and lead her out towards the exit.

"Sophie, wait!" shouted Jazz.

Sophie glanced back again. It was like a scene from a movie where every possible person that could get in the way got in the way.

"Never!" she yelled, feeling like a child running away from another child. She gasped at her own vision of herself. She might as well stick her thumbs on her temples, put her tongue out and wiggle her fingers while shouting: *Naa na na naa nar.*

"What are you doing?" yelled Laura, as they crashed out of the venue and onto the street. "Why have you stopped running?"

"This is silly."

"Let's go! Quickly!"

"No," said Sophie, shaking off her friend's grip as she wiped away her tears. "I don't want to run away from this. I need closure."

"That was bloody closure! She said you had more issues than the National Geographic! She said you were shit in bed!"

"I didn't mean her!" said Jazz, suddenly out of the club and on the pavement beside them. "My other ex."

"Oh, as if!" Laura was hands in the air and scoffing. "Just look at her! Look at what you've done to my friend!"

Sophie sniffed. "It's fine. I'm fine. I guess your 'fuck-off' really does mean fuck off, doesn't it?"

Jazz reached for Sophie's arms. "I wasn't talking about you."

Laura continued her wild ranting. "As if! What are you going to do? Say it's like that song?" She started to sing. "*You're so vain, you probably think this song is about you.*"

"Why are you singing, Laura?" Sophie was shaking her head. "Now's not the time for singing."

"*I bet you think this song is about you. You're so vain.*"

"Laura!"

"What? That bloody song *was* about him after all."

Jazz shook her head. "Those jokes weren't about you. I'd never do that to you."

Sophie frowned. "But you'd go to a life coaching session knowing the life-coach was my friend?"

"I didn't know."

Laura squealed. "You did! You said so!"

"I think I figured it out during the session."

"You're lying!"

"Laura please. I want to hear what Jazz has to say. We came here to hear what Jazz had to say."

Jazz folded her arms. "I should be asking you the same question."

"What?! I haven't gone on stage and slagged you off!"

"That wasn't about you. But *you* got your mate to set up some warped life coaching session so you could see me squirm."

"I didn't! I had no clue what she was up to!"

"And you expect me to believe that?"

"And you expect me to believe you weren't just being mean to me in front of a live audience?"

"I'd never do that! I love you!" Jazz paused. "I loved you."

Laura grabbed Sophie's wrist. "She's lying. We should leave."

"I've watched all of your sets online," said Sophie. "I've never seen that routine before."

"Of course you haven't," snapped Laura, "because it's new and about you!"

Jazz pulled her phone from her pocket. "I don't post these crappy gigs. There's a chance I'll be performing at The Apollo soon. I don't want people to know I still do working men's clubs." She scrolled quickly. "Here! On my Dropbox. Two years ago at the Hare and Hounds pub."

Sophie took the phone and clicked the video that was saved in Jazz's online storage account. She watched in silence. The same jokes. The same delivery.

"That wasn't about you, Sophie," said Jazz, quietly.

Laura interrupted. "Yeah, but you resurrected it tonight, didn't you? Coincidence or venomous timing?"

"Neither, just..." Jazz sighed. "Look, I'm sorry you had to hear that but I didn't write it about you."

"Was it directed at me, though?"

"I didn't know you were here!"

"You know what I mean."

Jazz smiled. "You're amazing in bed."

"Gross!" said Laura.

"You are, and you don't have issues, you're just layered."

Laura interrupted again. "She does have issues. You both do. I think you should start couples counselling. I'm happy to host. Plus I still haven't heard what your big falling out was about, your final fuck off."

Jazz shrugged. "There wasn't a final fuck off."

Sophie gasped. "There was!"

"No, it was more a case of not wanting to keep doing this. It's like reading the same book over and over again. Why do it when you already know how it ends?"

"Because it's enjoyable?" said Sophie.

"But it always ends the same way," Jazz wagged her finger between them, "with this."

Laura interrupted. "This just looks like a lot of miscommunication and misplaced emotion to me. I can sort that out. It's my job."

Both Sophie and Jazz laughed at the same time and in that moment their eyes reconnected.

"Oh gross. Look at you both. I see it now. That weird energy." Laura waved. "Hellooooo! Anyone home?"

"I've missed you," whispered Sophie.

"And I've missed you too," said Jazz.

Laura huffed. "How long has it been?"

Jazz was still gazing. "It feels like a lifetime."

"How long?" demanded Laura.

Sophie didn't shift her gaze from Jazz. "About a week."

"You've been split up a week? A bloody week! You've been crying like she died, Sophie! And you, Jazz, you've been... well you've been... you know what? I don't know what you've been doing. I'm still not sure if I trust you."

"Do *you* trust me, Sophie?" asked Jazz, their eyes still connected.

Sophie nodded. "With my life."

CHAPTER EIGHTEEN

"Okay," said Jazz, squeezing Sophie's hand that little bit tighter, "instead of our story always having the same old ending let's switch things up and turn our novel into one of those *choose your own ending* ones."

"What do you mean?"

"Earlier on I said we shouldn't do this again because it's like reading the same book when we already know how it ends."

"With you telling me to fuck off?"

Jazz ignored the dig. "With frustrating miscommunications. So why don't we actively choose a different ending? Why don't we actively outline the options? For example, right now we're standing under the glowing street lamps outside my house." Jazz smiled. "My parents' house. We've been here before and you've always gone home."

"I've been inside."

"Not when they've been in."

"I'm not coming in when your parents are at home."

"And that's what you've always said and it's that choice that perplexes me and frustrates me and, if I'm honest, hurts me."

Sophie reached out, pulling Jazz into a cuddle. "I don't mean to hurt you." She peeped over Jazz's shoulder towards the slivers of warm light escaping from the downstairs curtains. "But it looks like they're still up."

"And?"

"And I'd have to meet them."

"And?"

"And it makes things more real."

"Don't you want things to be real?"

"I..." Sophie paused. "It's just a big step."

"It's a choice, I guess. Are we doing things properly this time, or not? Do you head home, leaving me to question your long-term motives, or do you come in, say hello to my parents and cuddle up to me all night?"

"You want me to stay the night?"

"Of course I do. Don't you want to?"

"I do, I just..."

"What?" Jazz stepped out of the embrace. "See, it's this sort of drama, where there needn't be any, that gets to me. It's boring, Sophie. You say it's not about coming to terms with your sexuality; so what is it? Why won't you make things real?"

Sophie tried to manoeuvre herself back into the warm arms. "I left Laura at the working men's club and chose to walk home with you. That's an actively good choice."

"She was heading into town to meet friends."

"And I chose to come here."

"You hate town."

"Not with you, I don't."

"But I'm not in town. I'm here, outside my house, asking you to come in."

"Okay."

"Okay what?"

"Okay, I'll come in."

"Really?"

"Yes." Sophie put on a funny voice. "*Choose to go home: turn to page two*, right back to the start of our story. *Choose to go in: turn to page two hundred*, uncharted territory."

"Good. Right. Wow."

"What?"

"My mother's inside. I can see her in the window."

"You've not been calling my bluff, have you?"

Jazz shook her head. "I just haven't had time to prepare myself for the reality of this moment because I never thought it would actually arrive."

"Well it's here. Let's get in there and just do this."

"Bring the old Sophie back!" joked Jazz.

"You don't mean that."

"I don't. This is just wonderfully terrifying." Jazz smiled. "And I'm so incredibly proud of you."

"I haven't done anything yet."

"You have. You've decided to change the ending. Look, your feet are actually moving." Jazz followed the walk across the driveway towards the front door. "Now, next choice. Sneak in or say hello?"

"*Hello*!" wailed the voice as a blast of hot air enveloped them from the flung open front door. "I'm Jazz's mum, Vanessa! Come in! I've been watching you from the window, your dad told me off for curtain twitching. You must be Sophie! Jazz has told me all about you. You have a beautiful singing voice and she loved that care package you sent a few weeks ago. What was the soft ball for?"

"Mum!" snapped Jazz, staring at the blustering.

"Is it a sex toy? Only I was talking to Deidre Chambers, our next door neighbour, and she said you could shove it in someone's mouth before taping—"

"Mother!"

Sophie smiled. "I see where Jazz gets her fast talking from."

"People say we look similar too," said the older woman proudly. "Come in, come in."

Jazz put her arm around Sophie's shoulder as they stepped into the hallway. "Mum, this is Jessica. Jessica, this is Mum."

Jazz's mum gasped. "You're not Sophie? Sophie who sent the sex ball?! I'm so sorry! I thought you were Sophie."

Sophie laughed. "I think Jazz is joking."

"You *are* Sophie who sent the sex ball?"

"What are you lot wailing about?" called the deep voice from the lounge.

"Sophie's here! Sophie who sent the—"

"Mum!" snapped Jazz, taking Sophie's hand and leading her through to the cosy lounge. "Dad, this is Sophie. Sophie, Dad. Right, we're heading upstairs."

"Nice to meet you," Sophie managed before being yanked back into the hallway.

"Food? Drink? Sustenance?" asked Jazz's mum.

Jazz ignored her, continuing their march up the stairs past the dazzlingly floral wallpaper.

"See you in the morning?" continued the hopeful tone. "I could make pancakes or muffins or—"

Jazz slammed the door to her bedroom.

"They seem nice," giggled Sophie with a smile.

"How are you so chilled?! That was horrific! We made the wrong choice! We should have turned to page two."

Sophie fondled Jazz's face. "But there's no kissing on page two."

"Wait, I need a moment."

"And there's no bed on page two," said Sophie, pulling Jazz backwards onto the covers.

"But they're so..." Jazz stopped talking as Sophie's lips met her own.

"Sorry ladies," said Jazz's mum, head peeping round the door, "just before you get started, I moved your suitcase to the top shelf of your cupboard, Jasmine."

"Mum!"

"I thought you might need it." She turned to Sophie, who was now bolt upright against the headboard. "We had Jazz's little cousins to play this morning and they do tend to snoop. I didn't want to explain some of my daughter's contraptions to my sister-in-law. She's somewhat of a prude and if little Rosie had come downstairs with—"

"Out!" snapped Jazz.

"We are, going out I mean," continued her mother. "Last orders at the pub so you're free to make as much noise as—"

"Out!"

Sophie couldn't contain her shocked laughter as the door was finally closed.

"Why are you laughing? This is just ridiculous. My parents are ridiculous. It's ridiculous that I'm still living at home. It's ridiculous that, wait, where are you going? What are you doing?"

"Top shelf didn't she say? Why haven't you shown me this before?"

"Sophie don't."

It was too late, Sophie yanked down the black suitcase and was un-fastening the zip. "So what do we have in here then?" she said with a smirk, before gasping. "Good god, Jazz, it looks like you're off to build the Clifton suspension bridge!"

"What?"

"All these chains! And nipple clamps too!" She rummaged through the suitcase. "No! Is that a spiked paddle?!"

"It's not spiked."

"These are metal spikes!"

"They're not sharp, feel them."

Sophie tapped the implement against her thigh. "Why would anyone want to be hit with that? I thought my session with the under-bed restraints was your ultimate fantasy? Where's all this stuff from?"

"Just bits I've collected over the years. You're not judging me, are you? Your leather flogger's in there too and that purple dildo you sent me."

"So who's the spiked paddle woman?"

Jazz sat up straighter. "Right, we're at a story choice. Choice A: have a chat about exes, get jealous and judgemental, or choice B: just not go there."

"Aren't you intrigued about my history?"

"Hearing about someone else's history only gets you jealous and judgemental so I'm choosing choice B: let's just not go there."

Sophie shrugged. "Okay, but FYI I don't have a suitcase full of metal shit."

"It's not metal shit, it's…" Jazz slid off the bed. "Here, feel these. They're metal love eggs."

"They're cold."

"Now move them gently in the palm of your hand. Can you feel the insides knocking against the outsides? They both contain another smaller, heavier metal ball." Jazz smiled. "Imagine them inside you. Imagine I'm taking you from behind, my hand wrapped around your stomach, my fingers working your clit. I'm moving you as I fuck you, these balls knocking into each other deep inside you."

Sophie grimaced. "I'm only imagining which other bitch has had her insides knocked about by these bad boys."

"You are not!"

"I am! I can't believe you've kept all this stuff from other relationships."

"A lot of this stuff is solo stuff. Stuff I bought for myself, to use on myself."

Sophie pulled out a metal chain. "So you tie yourself up, do you?"

"Okay, not that, but it's not been inside anyone."

"And this double-ender?" Sophie pulled out a large rubber dildo.

"What?"

"You've had this inside different women."

"Maybe."

"And you don't think that's gross?"

Jazz gasped. "Men don't chop off their knobs and grow new ones with each sexual partner!"

"I hadn't thought of it like that."

"Exactly, so why should I throw out perfectly good sex toys that I've washed and stored neatly?"

"Because they remind you of past lovers?"

"And the guy having sex looks at his erection and says: Hi old friend, I remember when you ploughed into Sheila last week, but now we're working on Maggie?"

"Maybe."

"No! He's focusing on who he's with and he's using his instrument accordingly." Jazz closed the lid of the suitcase. "There's no way I'd use half of this stuff on you anyway."

"Why not?"

"You're too vanilla."

"Excuse me?"

"Not vanilla, just not hardcore BDSM."

"And you are?"

"I have been with some people."

"Who?"

"See! We're back to that story choice. Look how angry you're getting because we're talking about exes."

"I'm not angry, Jazz, I'm just confused."

Jazz secured the suitcase and lifted it back onto the wardrobe. "I think we should cuddle up in bed."

"Wouldn't you rather chain me up and mark me with that paddle?"

"No."

"Why not?"

"Because you're not into that."

"I might be."

"Are you?"

"I don't know until I try."

"Really? With my mother and father downstairs?"

"They've gone out."

"Don't test me, Sophie, because I really will go there with you."

"Good. I want you to go there."

Jazz moved towards the bed, lifting Sophie in one movement. "Let's start with this then, shall we?" she said, throwing Sophie onto the bed and straddling her waist, while pinning her arms above her head. "Stay still."

Sophie watched as Jazz bent her head and carefully took the long necklace from around her own neck. It was the one Jazz often wore: a chunky looking chain that was made up of lots of little silver crosses. "What are you doing with that?"

"Tying your wrists together."

Sophie felt the necklace bite into her skin as Jazz knotted her wrists tightly. "You've done this before."

"Maybe."

"That was like a boy scout tying a fisherman's knot."

"Is it too tight?"

"Tie it how you usually tie it."

"I have."

"So that necklace *has* seen some action before." Sophie laughed. "It's like you're wearing your own on-the-go sex aid without anyone having any clue whatsoever."

"It's just a necklace."

"That you tie your bitches up with."

Jazz pushed her hand against Sophie's mouth and whispered into her ear. "Your smart mouth is making me want to fuck you harder."

"Good," said Sophie, shaking her head free of the hold. "I want you to lose yourself on me. I want to see who you really are."

Jazz flopped onto her bottom in between Sophie's legs. "You know this is just role-play, right?"

"Don't spoil it! Get back up here!"

Jazz stayed where she was. "If we're doing this you're going to need a safe word."

"Why?"

"That's how it works. We push each other to our limits but have faith that it's not real because at any given moment we can say our safe word and it'll all stop."

"What's your safe word?"

"Red."

"Fine, I'll be white. Keep going, I'm anticipating what implement you're going to use on me."

"What implement do you want me to use on you?"

"All of them."

Jazz laughed. "Oh, Sophie, I love you."

"This isn't meant to be romantic!"

"There are just so many sides to you."

"Lots of places to paddle me then."

Jazz jumped off the bed and yanked the suitcase back off the wardrobe. "I'm going to use the nipple clamps first."

"No, my nipples aren't sensitive so it won't do anything for me."

"This is for me," said Jazz, freeing the metal pincers that were caught up in a string of anal beads. "Keep your hands above your head."

"They're tied."

"But you can move them up and down if you want to."

"I'm happy like this."

"Good, because I'm going to pop each button on your shirt."

"Don't rip it though; it might not be all bright and jazzy like yours but it's from Monsoon."

"Be quiet."

"I'm just saying I don't want you to—"

Jazz re-straddled Sophie's waist and pulled the shirt apart with one fast yank, sending buttons flying off in all directions.

"Jazz! What are you doing?! I told you not to do that!"

"And I told you that your mouth would get you into trouble!" She pulled hard on the centre of the bra, spilling Sophie's breasts out of the cups.

"Ouch! That hurt!"

"It's meant to. Now lie back and let me fuck your nipples."

"Wait!"

Jazz paused. "White? You're saying your safe word?"

"No, I said wait!"

"I'm not waiting," whispered Jazz, untwisting the metal pin.

"You're not going to put my nipple in there!"

"I am."

"It looks like one of those clamps they used to have on the side of the tables in D&T at school!"

"I'll start wide," said Jazz, pushing the clamp over Sophie's left nipple.

"Wait!"

"White? You want me to stop?"

"I said wait!"

"Stop saying wait! It sounds like white."

"Jazz, don't!"

Jazz lined up the other nipple. "They've gone hard. You want this."

"I don't want this."

"So say your safe word."

"No."

Jazz turned the pins. "Look at them, trapped in there."

Sophie gasped. "How tight does it go?"

"Total clamping."

"And you like this? You like seeing me like this? Arms tied above my head, shirt ripped open, nipples being assaulted?"

"Keep talking, you're turning me on." Jazz unzipped her jeans "I'm going to fuck myself on you," she said, taking her jeans off completely and undressing Sophie from the waist down before grabbing the metal love eggs from the suitcase. "I'm going to push these deep inside you. They're going to be knocking around as I fuck myself on your face." Jazz straddled Sophie's shoulders. "You won't be able to see what I'm doing back here but you'll feel it."

"Wait, they're big."

"I'm not waiting any longer," said Jazz, pushing both balls straight into Sophie.

Sophie cried out. "Fuck me, Jazz!"

"That's what I'm doing," said Jazz, positioning herself right over Sophie's mouth as she held onto the headboard. "I'm going to fuck you hard," she said as she worked herself to and fro on Sophie's mouth. Sophie's body moved underneath her. "You feel them banging inside you?" moaned Jazz, using one hand to keep hold of the headboard and the other to reach back and twist the nipple clamp one more notch.

"Wait!" came the muffled shout.

"I'm not waiting any longer," said Jazz, twisting over the other shoulder to tighten the other clamp.

"Wait!" came the scream even louder.

"I'm not waiting, I'm coming. I'm coming in your mouth, with your hands chained up, your nipples in clamps and two metal love eggs buried inside you. That's it, try and lift yourself up," groaned Jazz, moving with more force. "I'm coming, I'm coming in your mouth." Jazz screamed out in pain. "You bit me!" she gasped, throwing herself back with such force that she fell off the side of the bed and into the open suitcase of sex toys.

"I said white!" cried Sophie, using her bound fists to bang on the bed. "White!"

Jazz rubbed her own shoulder. "Wait! You said wait!"

Sophie looked down at her clamped nipples and started to cry. "White!"

"Why are you crying?" gasped Jazz. "You're the one who just bit me!"

The whisper was barely audible. "I said white."

CHAPTER NINETEEN

Sitting side-by-side on Laura's life-coaching sofa, both Sophie and Jazz had reached the conclusion that this was the best option, or possibly the only option. They were too fresh in their relationship to seek real couples counselling, plus neither thought the £80 per session that a quick Google search had found would be money well spent. Yet both realised they needed help because the previous evening had been difficult to say the least, with neither knowing quite how to respond to the other. Sophie was angry that Jazz hadn't stopped at her safe word but was more ashamed at how she'd responded, and Jazz was angry at Sophie's response but even more upset that she'd misheard the safe word.

"You responded by biting her pussy?!" screeched Laura.

Jazz shook her head. "We want you to try your very best to be an independent, professional sounding board. To listen as we talk through our side of things and possibly mediate how we respond to each other so we can see things from each other's point of view."

Laura laughed. "You'd need a proper counsellor for that!"

"We're asking for your help," said Sophie.

"That's easy! You're bad for each other! You get back together at," Laura tilted her head from side to side, "what was it? About eight thirty last night? And by ten you're sexually assaulting each other!"

"It was a miscommunication," said Jazz.

"No! The bit before the *Silence of The Lambs* snacking."

Jazz frowned. "The sex?"

"Yes! That style of sex is just weird! You're taking Sophie on a path she doesn't want to go down."

Sophie spoke up. "I wanted to try it."

"You didn't enjoy it!"

"I did, until the nipple clamp went too tight and I said my safe word."

Jazz sighed. "It sounded like wait."

"It was white."

Laura lifted her hands to the pair of them. "I'm not sure which one of you used that magnet description about how you slam together when things are good and push apart when things are bad, but look at you now." She nodded. "Jazz, you're fixated by the grass in the garden, and Sophie you're mesmerised by my grade one piano certificate on the wall. It's like you're literally repelling each other."

"So help us," pleaded Jazz, her attention back on Laura.

"Why? You clearly don't work."

"We do," said Sophie, focusing on Jazz. "Everything's just so highly charged with us." She took hold of Jazz's hand and smiled as their eyes met. "That's our potion and our poison."

"Aren't potions and poisons the same thing?" asked Laura.

"No, a potion's something that helps you and a poison's something that, well," Sophie laughed lightly, "poisons you." She sighed. "I guess our passion and energy's just crazy. Last night was crazy. I felt lost in this charge of intensity."

"It's like we get sucked into this other world, isn't it?" continued Jazz. "Our connection's like a raging fire and it's nice to sit around a raging fire if you're camping in the great outdoors, but it's not nice when that raging fire gets out of control and burns down everything you care about."

Laura drew her fingers up into a steeple. "Are you talking about the theatre again, Jazz, and the fact your career went up in smoke?"

"That's not what we're here for," said Sophie.

"I think it might be linked."

"It's not," Sophie was firm.

"You're talking metaphorically, right?" asked Jazz. "Like I associate fire with something negative so I step away before it gets out of control?"

"Or you start the fire yourself and use it as an excuse to walk away?"

"No one started the fire," snapped Sophie.

"Simmer down," said Laura, before laughing. "Do you like what I did there?"

Sophie shook her head. "We're not getting anywhere. I think we should stop this."

"And what? Split up?" asked Laura.

"No, just... I don't know. Learn to control our emotions maybe?"

"I don't need to control my emotions," said Jazz. "I responded appropriately when you sank your teeth into my vagina."

"You were fuming!"

"I wasn't fuming! I was measured! Your choice to bite me was extreme."

"What was I supposed to do?"

Laura tapped her finger steeple against her chin. "Play dead. I'd have played dead. Jazz would have noticed and jumped off, then Jazz would have felt guilty for riding you too hard and you'd have stopped that ghastly sex session without being the bad guy."

Sophie gasped. "I'm not the bad guy and I don't play games! Every single one of my reactions in this whole relationship has been genuine."

Jazz nodded at Laura. "So you think she's the bad guy? You think Sophie responded inappropriately?"

"That's an interesting question. Why does it matter to you?"

"Oh for god's sake, Laura," snapped Sophie. "Stop trying to act like a therapist!"

"You can't have it both ways. You either want me to help you, or you don't."

"But this isn't helping. We're just going around in circles, we always just go around in circles with us both believing we're the one in the right."

"Okay, so let's focus." The finger steeple morphed into a two-fingered pointing gun. "Tell me about how it ended the first time. Tell me why Jazz said fuck off." Laura shot her pistol. "Jazz, I want to hear your side of the story and don't hold back just because she's here."

"I do have a name!"

"Hush, Sophie, this isn't your moment. Jazz, what was the final breaking point for you? Last time I mean, not this time, or the seemingly billion times before. I'm talking about the *last* last time, the one that had Sophie in here crying her eyes out because she thought she'd lost you."

Jazz turned to her girlfriend. "Can I?"

Sophie shrugged.

"Okay, well it seems a bit silly now and I do believe we're making progress because we got through last night and we're still talking."

"Barely," said Laura, "and maybe you only chose not to flounce off this time because you were seriously concerned about being called a sexual deviant?"

"Me flounce off? It's always Sophie who flounces off."

"You told her to fuck off."

"To make a stand!"

"Talk, you're fired up, this is good, tell me the story."

CHAPTER TWENTY

"We're here!" Jazz abruptly stopped the car in front of an overgrown hedge.

"Steady!" said Sophie. "Is this even a space?"

"It's fine, I know the owner."

"What owner? Where are we?" They'd travelled further into the countryside than on their previous jaunts and Sophie had no clue where they were.

Jazz pointed past a row of bushes at a small wooden building. "Cheryl's Cycle Hire."

"That shack in the undergrowth?!"

"It's the start of the Teddington Trail."

"You've brought me all this way to go on a bike ride? You said we had something to celebrate."

"We will once we complete the twenty-six-mile ride."

"You're joking!"

"No! This is going to be fun." Jazz reached into the back seat for her Ortovox backpack. "Watch your head. I've got snacks, drinks, cash for the pubs en-route. It's a gorgeous day and I've even brought you some sunglasses."

"I've got my own sunglasses."

"But these are cycling sunglasses," said Jazz, opening up the backpack.

Sophie looked at the offering. "I'm not wearing those. They look ridiculous."

"You'll need wrap-arounds. We'll be going at quite a speed."

"I won't."

"You will."

"I won't. I failed my cycling proficiency in year five."

"When you were ten?"

Sophie nodded. "I never actually got the official certification to say I could ride a bike."

"I've seen you riding a bike. You're fine."

"Recreationally, when we're pootling down to the park." She fingered the sports sunglasses. "But this looks far too high profile. And what's that pipe sticking out of your backpack?"

"Suck on it," said Jazz.

"No!"

Jazz narrowed her eyes. "Suck on my pipe, Sophie. Oh come on, have a bit of fun; there's a camelback in here. I've filled it with vitamin water."

"Professional, and like I say, I'm not certified."

"It just means we don't have to keep stopping." Jazz popped the plastic tube into her mouth. "You get thirsty, you grab the pipe and suck."

"When I'm biking next to you? As if! There's no way I'll be able to streamline my approach as we're hurtling down this trail at twenty-billion miles an hour with my wasp-eye shades on before aligning next to you and sucking your refuelling pipe into my mouth as we're still speeding along." She glanced back to the shack. "I can't even do a wheelie."

"It's fine, all you have to do is reach over my back and grab it."

"How?"

Jazz smiled. "We're spending the day on a tandem."

♣

Sophie's arms were folded firmly around her waist as she stared, tight-lipped, at the view of the garden. "I didn't moan that much," she muttered.

Jazz shrugged. "I'm just telling it how I remember it."

"With me being all moany and ungrateful?"

"You did take a little bit of encouragement at the start."

Laura spoke up from her side of the coffee table. "She doesn't like doing new things or going to new places."

Sophie swivelled back to the room. "I do!"

"You did when we were teenagers, but then you changed and became all insular."

"I went on a twenty-six-mile tandem ride with wasp glasses on! That's not insular!"

"Exactly. Jazz was bringing the real you back, she *is* bringing the real you back, and it scares you so you put up all these whiny, moany barriers that your subconscious *does* actually want Jazz to break down. If I was Jazz I'd have pulled my pipe back and pedalled off on my own."

"I think she's worth it." Jazz tapped the sofa seat. "Come and sit down."

"Will you two stop being so condescending? Honestly, Jazz, if I'm so horrific why do you even bother? And Laura why bother being my friend if the person I've chosen to become is such a let-down?"

"For exactly that reason," said Laura with a nod. "I know you've *chosen* to become this person which means you can choose to revert to the old you at any point." She smiled. "And when you do I'll be ready with the hairspray to zhoosh your big curls. Remember when that was my job on nights out?"

Sophie nodded at Jazz. "Go back to the story."

"Wait," said Laura, "remember when I chose to become a goth? You put up with me even though I looked like I'd been punched in both eyes and my hair was greasier than a chip pan."

"You were a goth for four days!"

"But you stood by me."

"But I'm not going through any sort of phase and I'm not asking anyone to stand by me."

"You asked me to stand by you when you were getting on the tandem," said Jazz, grinning.

Laura nodded. "See, we're making links. Continue with the story, Jazz."

Sophie gasped. "This is such psychobabble!"

"Fine, just tell us why you started plaiting your hair five years ago."

Turning very deliberately back to the French windows, Sophie stayed silent.

"Exactly, so we have to figure it out by dissecting Jazz's anecdotes about your bike ride."

Sophie's shoulders shrugged. "We got chased by a cat who gave us a puncture and then we found a human skull in a field."

"Fuck off!" laughed Laura.

"No, that bit came later."

"Tell me! Right now!" Laura was nodding at Jazz. "Give me the whole shebang right from the start."

"Just hoik your leg over," said Jazz, holding the front handlebars of the tandem as firmly as possible as she stood beside the bike.

"Why are my handlebars so low and why's your saddle so high? I'm going to be face-full of your ass all the way!"

"Not for the first time."

"This isn't funny, Jazz. I look ridiculous. I'm sure that woman gave me the most unfashionable helmet. Why's yours streamlined with a point at the back while mine looks like a mushroom? Is she an ex? She seemed very pally."

"Cheryl?"

"Yes, Cheryl from Cheryl's Cycles."

"Just get your leg over."

"That's what she tried to do when she tightened your helmet strap."

"She tightened your strap too."

"Yes, with a yank that pinched some of my neck skin, but she did yours really sexily."

Jazz laughed.

"You're not denying it then?"

"Just get your leg over!" said Jazz. "That's it, now put your feet on the pedals. I'm going to tilt the bike slightly as I get on."

"Woah!" screeched Sophie. "What are you doing?"

"Getting on!"

"Your backpack just hit me in the face!"

"Sorry, lean back."

"I can't! I have to hold on to the handlebars!"

"You don't. I'm the one in charge of the steering, your handlebars don't move."

"But you've tilted us! I can't just grip with my thighs!"

"Imagine the saddle's my face."

"Jazz!"

"What? And we're up." Jazz nodded. "Right, now to start. This is the trickiest bit. It's easiest if you just lift your legs so they're not on the pedals."

"And put them where?!"

"Just out to the sides."

"My vagina's not that powerful!"

"What?"

"No hands, no feet, just my vagina holding onto the saddle for dear life!"

"Don't make me laugh, I have to have a really strong push off."

"Do you two need a hand?" asked Cheryl, helpfully stepping out of the shack at that moment.

"No, thank you," said Sophie sharply.

"Yes please, thanks, Cheryl," said Jazz with a grin. "If you could give my back a bit of a push to get us started."

Sophie spoke up. "Jazz said her back, not her bottom."

The woman from the cycle shack spoke seriously. "I have to be careful not to press too hard on her backpack as it might pop her drinks reservoir. The saddle gives a much firmer push-off."

Sophie raised her voice again. "You're touching her bottom."

"And three!" shouted Jazz, lunging them forwards. "Now pedal!" And they were off, onto the path that led bikers along thirteen miles of countryside to the end point of High Peak before they had to turn around and return to the car park.

"Never!" said Sophie, lunging to Jazz's side of the sofa. "I did not have a spat with Cheryl from the cycle shack about her push-off position!"

Jazz nodded. "You did and it was the only time you pedalled hard the whole journey, when you were getting away from her."

"It was like she was birthing a cow, her hand literally disappeared! But I only told you that afterwards."

"We needed a big push-off and it got us started, didn't it?"

"Yes, but I didn't confront her!"

"You were mumbling. I heard you."

"But not that!"

"Oh, will you both stop squabbling!" snapped Laura. "Are you even aware that you're doing it?"

"I can't have her making stuff up!" said Sophie. "I might have been a bit moany but I didn't confront Cheryl about her attempted fisting of Jazz's arsehole!"

"This is Jazz's version of events."

"So?"

"So, at least she's talking."

"And making me out to be a real moaner!"

"I don't view it as moaning," said Jazz. "I've always found it quite funny."

"No, Sophie's definitely a moaner. It's the only child in her. I'm the same."

Sophie shook her head. "But I don't want to be a moaner, or perceived as a moaner, and I certainly don't want to be recounted as a moaner."

"So stop," said Laura. "Treat this session like one of those reality programmes where people go on TV and don't realise who they are until they watch it back. Of course it's edited, everything always is when someone's telling a story from their point of view."

Sophie turned to Jazz. "Why couldn't you just point out my moaning to me if it was such a big issue, instead of showcasing this whole shit show now in front of my friend?"

Jazz shrugged. "Like I said, I've always found your little quirks quite entertaining and I did try and calm you down when we got the puncture, remember? But you didn't take it very well."

"Oooh, tell me about the puncture," laughed Laura.

"You weren't calming me down, you were criticising me and no one likes criticism."

"I don't mind it," said Jazz mildly. "Maybe it's my line of work? I'm used to it, I guess? Or it could be because of my brother and sister, like you suggested, Laura, who've given me broad shoulders?"

Sophie threw her hands in the air. "So why are you even with me then, Jazz?"

Jazz laughed. "This spark! This fire! You're so deliciously complicated."

"She's not," said Laura. "She just thinks you're siding with me and that gets her goat. But let me address something more intricate with you, Jazz: the way you're now using fire in a positive manner."

Sophie shook her head. "Stop talking about fire."

"Oh gosh, you haven't got fire issues too have you, Sophie? I assume Jazz has told you all about her promising early career in the theatre?"

Jazz nodded. "I told her that day actually."

Sophie let out a harsh breath. "Laura just wants to hear the puncture story. Tell her the puncture story then we're stopping all this nonsense."

☁

"Isn't this beautiful," said Jazz, waving at the green fields on either side of the path. "Imagine being on one of those old trains as you travelled through this countryside."

"What are you talking about? I can't see anything; your backpack's right in my face."

"Oh, Sophie, we've been going for ten minutes now; can't you sit up? You're not holding the bottom bit of the racing handles are you?"

Sophie screeched. "Don't turn around! You just wobbled us!"

"Hold the top bit of the handlebars, or like I said, just let go; you're not the one steering."

"You made me wear these racing sunglasses so I'm down here in my position doing my bit."

Jazz stopped pedalling and the chain immediately went slack. "Do your legs only go around when mine do?"

"I think so."

"That means you're not pedalling."

"I'm just trying to cling on!"

"Look around you, Sophie. It's so picturesque. Did you know this whole trail used to be the track bed of the old railway line? That's what I was saying about the trains. It was an experimental scheme. The first one in the country. They took up the tracks and the track bed and turned it into this thirteen-mile trail for walkers, cyclists and horse riders, back in 1971 I think."

"What are you talking about? Please just concentrate on the steering."

"You're missing out on all the wild flowers and wildlife."

"What wildlife?"

"Sheep over there in that field and, look, is that a little cat in the long grass?"

"No clue. I'll take your word for it."

"Oh it is, look!"

"Why are you slowing down? Don't slow down, we'll never get started again!"

"Oh bless, it's following us. Sophie, look at the cat."

"I'm not looking at the cat."

"Oh, it wants to play! Come on, little cat, I'm going slowly so you can catch us up."

"Jazz!"

"Can you see it? It's right next to you."

"I don't care about a little cat!" snapped Sophie, suddenly gasping. "It's at my wheel! It looks feral! Quick! Pedal faster!"

"No, it's a cutie."

"Jazz! It's jumping up! It might have diseases!"

Jazz felt the front of the bike wobble at the sudden surge from Sophie's pedals. "Steady!"

"No! I don't like it! It's snapping at my heels!"

"It's a cat!"

"And it's chasing us! You encouraged it! It's literally right by my wheel!"

Jazz gasped as the bike lunged to the side. "What are you doing?!"

"Turning!"

"You can't turn! Stop leaning! You'll send us into the grass."

"I'm up off my saddle doing that fast pedalling the professionals do!"

"You're wobbling us!" said Jazz as the bike veered into the verge.

"It's foaming at the mouth!"

"The cat?"

"Yes, the cat!"

"Oh for goodness sake, Sophie," said Jazz, pressing hard into the pedals. "It's only a cat."

"It's a feral racing cat with diseases."

"And it's gone," said Jazz after a short burst, steadying her pedalling back to a normal pace.

"Keep going fast for a bit, just to be sure."

"Are you pedalling too?"

"Yes."

Jazz let the chain go slack. "You're not."

"I am."

Jazz let the chain go slack again. "You're not."

"It's hard work. I may need to suck on your pipe."

"You'll have to sit up and reach around. That's it. Oh well done, Sophie. Now look at the scenery; isn't this all so beautiful?"

Sophie spoke between sucks. "Wonderful."

"Are you looking? Look how huge that field is. It's just a massive expanse of green for as far as the eye can see. Now close your eyes and feel the gentle wind on your face. Isn't it just magica—"

"STOP!" screeched Sophie.

"What?!"

"JUST STOP!"

Jazz slammed on the brakes, skidding the bike to a juddering halt.

"THERE!" Sophie was hitting Jazz's arm. "By the gate! In the soil! The corner of the field!"

"What?!"

"I was peeping past the pipe and I saw it! The corner of the field! There! In that bit of soil!"

Jazz stared in the direction of Sophie's pointing finger. "What?"

"A human skull!"

"Oh, don't be so ridiculous," said Jazz, clambering off the bike and kicking the stand down.

"It's a human skull! Look!"

"Get off the bike, Sophie. The stand can't support the bike and you."

"No, that cat might get me. You go and look." Sophie gingerly lowered one foot to support the bike.

"And if the cat comes back what are you going to do? Ride the bike from the back with handlebars that don't steer and no one on the front?"

"I'll call you if I see it. Please, Jazz, go and have a look."

Jazz shook her head as she stepped across the grass verge towards a five-bar gate. "It's not a skull."

"It's a skull!" came the shout from the bike.

"There's a ditch here."

"You'll be okay. Just jump the gate. The skull's right there. Can't you see it?"

Jazz looked towards the chalky coloured object, half hidden by the soil. "I'm going over the gate," she said as she swung herself over the top bar and dropped into the field.

"Have you got it?" shouted Sophie. "That's it! Pull it up! It's a skull! A human skull!"

Jazz growled as she turned, holding the object up like a grim executioner. "It's a BLOODY turnip!" she shouted.

"A what?"

"A TURNIP! Now look at me! I'm all muddy!" She lifted each foot in turn and tutted.

"Can I see it?"

"You still think it's a skull? For god's sake, Sophie, it's a turnip."

"Jazz, I think we've got a bit of a problem."

"Too right we have. I'm standing in a muddy field holding a turnip that you insist is a skull so if that feral cat's caught up with us, I don't care; you'll have to fend for yourself."

Sophie pointed at the front wheel. "I think that cat's given us a puncture."

Sophie's hands were in the air but not in surrender. "It *was* the cat! It was jumping up and its claws were right at the tyres!"

Jazz shook her head. "We either got that puncture when you veered us into the grass to get away from the cat, or when we screeched to a stop to see the turnip you said was a skull."

Laura spoke up. "So Jazz rightly got angry? You had a row? She told you off for being silly? You didn't handle the criticism well so moaned some more and she told you to fuck off?"

Both Sophie and Jazz turned to smile at each other.

Laura frowned. "What? What am I missing?"

Jazz spoke first. "We actually made really wild love under a bridge a little further along the trail."

Sophie nodded. "It was so hot."

"Oh, you know what, you two?" said Laura, gasping. "You're as bad as each other. My diagnosis? You're like Eminem and Kim."

Sophie laughed. "Who?"

"I think she means we're like Elizabeth Taylor and Richard Burton, don't you, Laura?"

"I just know I'm done. Life coaching's not for me. Maybe if you two actually answered the questions when I asked them we might be getting somewhere, but we're not. I still have no clue why you actually like each other or what keeps going wrong."

Sophie sat beside her and squeezed Jazz's hand. "I think we *are* getting somewhere. It's been good for me to hear things from Jazz's point of view and I will, consciously, from this point on try to be less snappy and moany."

"And I'd love to hear things from Sophie's point of view," said Jazz, "as I want to get things right and I want to understand why she sometimes behaves the way that she does."

Sophie took a sharp intake of breath. "See. New me. Not reacting."

Jazz continued. "You have to admit you behaved very strangely at the end of what turned out to be a fantastic day."

"Me? You're the one who left me with Cheryl."

"You told me to go."

"Because you told me to fuck off!"

"Dammit," said Laura. "Last chance! Sophie, from your point of view, what the bloody hell happened?"

CHAPTER TWENTY ONE

Sitting on the grass verge watching Jazz tending to the upside-down tandem bike, Sophie was awash with pride. At least four male bikers had stopped to offer their assistance, with Jazz politely telling each one that she'd got this. Sophie smiled, because Jazz had got this. She'd first pulled a pump from her backpack to check the tyre wasn't just flat, which it wasn't as it deflated again almost immediately. Next, she'd decanted vitamin water from her camelback into a discarded bottle lid she'd found beside the path. She immersed the tyre's valve into the water before announcing there weren't any bubbles, so it wasn't a leaky valve. Now whether Jazz needed to do all this, or whether she was simply showing off, Sophie wasn't sure, but she liked the feeling of Jazz being in charge. Her knight in shining armour, once again making her feel safe.

"I'm going to have to take the wheel off," announced Jazz. "It'll take a little while."

"I think you should take your shirt off too. It looks like hot work to me."

"Are you just going to sit there and stare at me?"

"Do you need my help?"

"No."

"Exactly," said Sophie, smiling. "So take it off."

"I've only got a sports bra underneath."

"How many men have we seen with their tops off? Please? I want to see your muscles rippling as you work that spanner. Go on, work it, that's it. That wheel bolt looks tough."

Jazz laughed. "I see you've forgiven me, then?"

"I deserved it," said Sophie, sinking her chin on her knees and pulling on the short grass. "I didn't start this session in the most positive way."

"It's not a session, it's a day outing."

"I see that now and this is my favourite bit so far: the sun on my face, watching my woman be all manly; but your speed-shades and that all-action backpack threw me at first."

"Womanly," corrected Jazz. "Don't gender stereotype, but I did say we'd be stopping at pubs en-route and that we weren't in any rush. I want us to take our time and enjoy the whole day."

"We will," Sophie smiled. "We are. But I'd enjoy it even more if you took your top off."

Jazz looked up and down the path before pushing herself up on her knees as she teased the bottom of her shirt and started to sing: *"Du dee dhar, du duh dee dhar."*

"Mmm hmm," said Sophie. "My bitch is hot! Look at you! Wow! Take it off completely. That's it. Now rub a bit of that wheel grease across your bare shoulder. Amazing! Look at your boobs bulging. I love them so much."

"No!" Laura was out of her armchair. "I don't want to hear about bulging boobs!"

"I do," said Jazz, turning to Sophie. "You really thought I looked hot?"

Sophie smiled. "That image is etched into my memory. You, greased up in your sports bra having flung your shirt over your shoulder, your muscles working as you yanked that wheel off. Honestly, I'm so attracted to you that it sometimes makes me feel feral. I felt feral that day. I just wanted to stare at you and I knew I was going to come over and take you."

"That's how I felt last night. I just got lost in the moment."

"I know."

"And I'm so sorry I didn't stop, but I promise I didn't know you wanted me to stop."

"I know, and I'm so sorry I chose such a crap safe word and even more sorry that I nipped at your lips."

"I like it when you nip at my lips, but that was a full on bite—"

"Enough!" shouted Laura, jamming her fingers in her ears. "I don't want to hear this! And two minutes ago you were describing a stray cat with a frothy mouth as feral, so why are you now thinking it's a sexy way to describe yourself?"

"Wild then," said Sophie. "I watched Jazz fix that tyre and I was so turned on. My action man."

"Action woman," corrected Jazz.

"I just wanted to go over there and own her."

"I thought you did it under a bridge?" said Laura, frowning. "And why would you want to own her? Wouldn't you just give her a quick servicing to say thank you for fixing the tyre?"

Jazz and Sophie laughed together.

"What?"

Jazz cleared her throat and leant forward. She spoke conspiratorially. "That's the difference between lesbian sex and straight sex. A woman often gives the gift of herself to a man, like you say, when she wants to say thank you, or reward him, but lesbians are all about that power battle where they take the pleasure for themselves."

Laura grimaced. "So you didn't come then, Jazz?"

"Ha! I came like one of those steam trains on the track bed."

"Enough!"

Sophie smiled. "You don't want to hear it?"

"No!"

"You don't want to know how we wheeled the now-fixed bike under the old stone bridge?"

"No!"

"Or how most of the bikers were going too fast to notice us but we did have to smile and nod at the odd slow walker who passed through?"

"You could have been reported!"

Sophie smiled. "I was only massaging her."

"How's that even sex?!"

Sophie pointed to the armchair. "Sit down and let me explain."

☁

"Push the bike faster!" said Sophie, jogging along the path beside Jazz. "I need you under that bridge."

"Let's just jump on and ride it."

"No, we're almost there and I want your fingers to be the first thing that fucks into me, not the saddle."

☁

"Gross!" came the scream from the armchair. "You do *not* talk to each other like that!"

"Oh, we do," said Sophie. "We get really graphic."

"Spare me the graphics, just give me the logistics." Laura cleared her throat. "Billy's always saying you can have sex in places other than the bedroom, but I think it's too risky."

Sophie smiled. "It was risky, which made it even more frantic and feral."

☁

"Just leave it on the grass."

Jazz kicked again at the piece of metal. "I'm struggling with the stand."

"Sod the stand," said Sophie, dashing at the bike and pushing it over as she grabbed Jazz by the hand. "In here, it's dark."

"Careful! You'll give us another puncture! And what am I meant to do with my backpack?"

"Leave it out there. It'll be fine. I need you here in the shadows."

Jazz gasped loudly as Sophie pulled her into the darkness, forcing her bare back against the chilly stone of the bridge. "Steady!"

"No, I want to kiss you. I want to kiss you for the rest of your life." Sophie ploughed her tongue straight into Jazz's mouth as she spread Jazz's legs with her hand.

Jazz cried out. "The stone's so cold on my back."

"Good, because your tits are going to take it." Sophie spun Jazz around and pulled up her sports bra, forcing Jazz's bare breasts into the wall. "That's it, now feel my fingers inside you."

🖤

"What?!" Laura was out of the armchair and squealing. "Why's it so aggressive?! You shoved her tits against a cold stone wall?"

"I loved that bit," said Jazz. "She took me from behind and I came so quickly."

Laura was shaking her head. "And that's you owning her, is it, Sophie?"

"I just needed to get the arousal I was feeling out of me and onto her, I guess."

"And then what?"

"Well then some bikers whizzed past, but I think they thought we were hands-up admiring the old stonework of the bridge."

Jazz laughed. "But then when I was pleasuring you we could see that couple walking in the distance and it was a race against time to get you to come before they got to the tunnel."

"Tunnel? I thought it was a bridge?"

"There are loads of them along the trail. High arching bridges."

"So it's not a tunnel then, you're both just pretty much having sex out in the open."

Sophie laughed. "It was shadowy. We were in a sort of niche in the stonework. The couple couldn't see us."

Jazz nodded. "Until they could."

"But you had me bent over from behind and told them you'd just done the Heimlich manoeuvre on me."

"Which worked well because you'd just orgasmed and your cheeks were all red."

"Which sold the story of a stuck sweet just perfectly."

Laura tutted. "Look at the two of you, lost in your little memories of debauchery."

Sophie smiled. "It was a good day. We got back on the bike and I finally managed to sit upright so I could see all the views and we stopped at a couple of pubs and made it to High Peak at the end."

"But then you got a bit cross that we had to turn around and do the whole thing all over again."

"I thought it was a circuit."

"It's not."

"Anyway," said Sophie, re-focusing. "It was quite amazing really because, of course, it all looked different going the other way. We made it back to the cycle shack and that's where it all went wrong."

Laura nodded. "Did Cheryl flirt with Jazz again?"

"No, we gave the bike back, dropped the backpack in the car and climbed this little slope at the start of the trail."

Jazz smiled. "I wanted to show Sophie the view."

"You'd just biked twenty-six miles, I bet she'd had enough of the view."

"But I wanted to tell her something and I wanted to pick the perfect spot and right there, on top of that hill, you get the most incredible panorama."

"What did she tell you, Sophie?" said Laura, nodding her head in a way that was supposed to look encouraging.

💭

Gazing out across the expanse of beautiful countryside, Sophie felt that she could be in heaven. The sun was still shining, highlighting the long trail they'd just cycled and glinting off the trees in their full summer leaves. "It's more obvious as an old train line from up here.

The arched bridges look so impressive. You can't even see where it finishes."

"And you did that, Sophie." Jazz was smiling. "I'm really proud of you. Whoever was in charge of your cycling proficiency test robbed you."

"They did."

Jazz paused. "Did you mean what you said back there in the tunnel? That you want to kiss me forever?"

🌩

Laura gasped. "Oh my good god, she proposed to you! You rightly said no and she said fuck off!"

"Of course I didn't propose!" said Jazz. "And please stop interrupting, I want to hear Sophie's side of things."

🌩

Sophie nodded. "I do feel like I want to kiss you forever. I'm in love with you, Jazz. You make me so happy. Today's been the very best of days and I just want to shout it from the rooftops." Jumping up, Sophie hollered out across the landscape. "Teddington Trail, I'm in love with this woman!" In the next field, a cow stopped munching and peered at them for a moment.

"You're so sweet, Sophie. But just sit down here with me for a minute."

"This sounds serious."

"I want more," said Jazz.

Sophie smiled. "I know and I'm going to give you more. I want you to meet my parents and I want you to meet my friends and I'm going to just let go and go with whatever this thing is that's happening between us."

"Really?" said Jazz.

"Really. You make me happy and I know we have our moments but I think that's because I've been holding back. I've been holding onto this fear that it can't ever be real between us, but I think it can. I think I'm ready now and I just want to say thank you for bearing with me and not putting any pressure on me."

Jazz's wide smile was dazzling. "This is perfect timing because I've got some news that I want to celebrate with you." She took a deep breath. "I haven't really talked about it before, but I wasn't always a comedian. I was an actress first and I loved it. I worked a lot at the Grand Theatre but then some stupid teenagers burnt it down and ruined everything for me. My life pretty much ended, and I know it sounds melodramatic, but my hopes and dreams, and my whole future really, went up in smoke." Jazz turned to Sophie. "But they've almost finished the rebuild and they're making plans for another in-house production company. *The Sound of Music* is the first show on the slate and they want me to be Maria. They also want me to play a big part in the official opening. There'll be so much press with loads of articles and features about who I was then before the fire and who I am now, and I want you by my side through it all. You can give me the courage to do this, Sophie. To be that person again."

"No."

Jazz laughed, then didn't. "What do you mean, no? I think I forced myself to forget what a passion acting is for me. That door closed and I pretended I didn't care, but I do and I'm excited and I want you there. There's talk of a line up and a royal handshake. It'll only be low-level royalty like Anne or someone, but the coverage it'll get will be huge because it had so much when it burnt down and—"

"No."

"Stop saying no." Jazz laughed again. "What are you saying no for?"

Sophie shook her head. "I can't."

"Can't what?"

"Any of this. I want to go home."

"What? What are you talking about?"

"I can't do this, Jazz."

"Can't do what?"

Sophie stood up. "Just take me home, please."

"No, I'm not going to just take you home. What's going on?"

"Take me home."

"No! You can't just switch from wanting to shout about me to suddenly going all cold with no explanation whatsoever. Is it the photos? I know you don't like photos but you can get help with that."

"You're saying I need help? You're calling me weird?"

"I'm calling you selfish!"

"How dare you?"

"How dare I?! Where's your congratulations, where's your pride in me, where's you thinking about anyone other than your goddamn self for once, Sophie?"

"Oh, just get lost, Jazz."

"No, you just fuck off. Seriously, fuck off. I've been so excited about telling you."

"You're telling me to fuck off?"

"You're not interested are you?"

"Jazz, are you telling me to fuck off?"

"Yes, I'm telling you to fuck off!"

"Forever?"

"Yes, forever! I'm finally done with all this bollocks." Jazz stood up. "I'll take you home."

"And you don't want to see me again?"

"I don't give a shit, Sophie."

"Say you don't want to see me again."

"I don't want to see you again! You're a game player, Sophie, and I have no clue what's going on with you."

"Say it once more."

"Say what once more?"

"Fuck off."

Jazz pointed her finger towards the car park. "Fuck off."

Sophie nodded. "Will do."

"Wait, where are you going? Let me take you home."

"You just told me to fuck off so I'm fucking off."

"Only to make a stand against all of this bollocks!"

"I'll call a lift from the shack."

Jazz shouted. "If you keep walking away then honestly, Sophie, I'm done. Sophie?! Sophie, wait!"

"Goodbye Jazz."

"What in god's name is wrong with you, Sophie!?" Laura was open-mouthed. "You forced her into saying that. You pushed her away! That was the big bust up? The big fuck off?! Just more of your nonsense? Goddamn it, Jazz, I feel sorry for you."

Jazz shrugged as she reached out to Sophie's knee. "I don't care, we're here now and it feels different this time."

Sophie shook her head. "It's not different and I can't believe I've let it get back to this point. It's like I keep forgetting."

"Forgetting what?"

"It's over, Jazz," said Sophie, standing up.

"No!" snapped Laura. "You don't get to do this to us!"

"What do you mean, to us?" Jazz was laughing. "I've been dealing with this shit since day one."

"See, you don't really care, do you, Jazz?" Sophie started to cry. "I'm just one big joke to you."

"Stop playing the victim!" Jazz flung her hands in the air. "No matter whose point of view you look at it from, you're the one with the issues! You told the story! You admitted that you forced us into that break up!"

"Coo-ee," chirped Maureen from the doorway. "I'm terribly sorry, but I think someone should stand up for Sophie."

"Mother! What are you doing?"

"Look at her crying. I've been listening at the door."

"Mother!"

"It's all rather obvious. Let me grab us some malt loaf and I'll sit down and go over the evidence."

"You're not Poirot!"

"But I know what happened."

"What happened?" said Laura and Jazz in unison.

The older woman shrugged. "Well she started the fire, didn't she?"

CHAPTER TWENTY TWO

Maureen was nodding. "Sophie's had to keep this awful secret for the past five years, haven't you, my darling? It's forced her to change her appearance and essentially disappear, and whilst one may think the sensible option would be moving away with the orchestra, Sophie didn't want the fame and attention that would bring. What if someone recognised her? Yes, you may think there'd be a greater chance of someone recognising her if she stayed in the vicinity of the crime, but just remember how you picture people. Think of an old school friend you haven't seen since your school days. You see them as they were. Now think about Sophie. You picture her how she is now. Mouse-like and school marm-y. Hidden in plain sight, but hidden. Sophie's clever. She knew this. She chose to front things out from where she was instead of having people speculate that the culprit might just be the girl who ran away."

The Agatha Christie-style monologue continued in the stunned silence. "Sophie's stayed here but worked hard to avoid any additional exposure. Photos. Social media. Getting close to people inevitably leads to more exposure – new friends, that person's family, more people who might know your secret. And what's worse in this case is Jazz's life in the public eye. Sophie's always known in the back of her mind she'd have to push her away. Silly blow ups so she wouldn't have to face the possibility of her misdemeanour ever coming to light. But love's strong and you two couldn't stay away from each other, could you? So you, Sophie, came to the conclusion that maybe you could ease up a bit. Five years have gone by after all and you've not been found out. Jazz was declaring her love on top of that pretty hill and you were declaring your love right back. You thought you could work through it, but then, up popped her links to the theatre and although she didn't say it or know it of course, how you'd ruined her career. And hearing yourself repeat that same story again today has made you realise you can't do this."

Laura burst out laughing. "Ha! Mother you're hilarious!"

Maureen laughed. "I know! I watch far too much *Murder She Wrote*! But your sessions are wonderfully entertaining. It's not good for my knees though. I think I should get a chair for the hallway and maybe a stethoscope because I'm missing bits."

"Sophie?" said Jazz. "Sophie? Turn around and look at me."

Sophie stayed still, staring out of the windows.

Jazz spoke louder. "Turn around and look at me, Sophie."

"She's probably laughing," said Laura.

Jazz screamed. "Look at me!" She went to Sophie and grabbed her shoulders.

"Hey!" Laura leapt to her feet. "What are you doing? Let go of her!"

Jazz kept hold of Sophie's shoulders. "Tell me!"

"Let go of her!" screamed Laura.

"Oh dear me, what have I started?" Maureen was bobbing from foot to foot around the three now entwined bodies. "I was only being silly. Can I help in any way? Would anyone like some malt loaf? Or what about an apricot jam tart? You could fight over that instead."

"Tell me, Sophie!"

Laura's scream was wild. "Let go of her!"

"Trust me, I'm letting go," said Jazz, finally dropping her grip of Sophie's shoulders and barrelling away across the room. She paused in the doorway. "You don't need me to fuck you, Sophie, because you're doing an absolutely splendid job of fucking yourself."

"Get lost!" shouted Laura. "Yeah, that's it, slam that door! No one liked you anyway! We all knew you had a violent streak in you! People always get found out in the end!"

"She's gone, darling," said Maureen.

Laura continued to yell. "And I know you made Sophie sound more moany than she actually is! Telling your side of the story like you're a saint! We're all wise to it, Jazz!"

"Darling, the door's shut."

"You must think we're all so stupid! I know Sophie! She's my friend! I know everything about her!"

"Laura, stop shouting, she's gone."

Laura ran out of breath. She stroked Sophie's shoulder. "Are you okay, Sophie? Why are you crying? Did she hurt you? Shall I call an ambulance? The police?"

Sophie stared at the floor.

"Talk to me. What's going on?" Laura turned to her mother in the silence. "Mum? What's going on? You made that up, right?"

Maureen laughed. "I was only having a bit of fun trying to piece it all together. But I do have form with these things. Remember when I got the three cards correct in Cluedo that time? Total guess. Miss Scarlett, in the ball room, with the lead piping. Your father couldn't believe it."

"Sophie didn't start that fire. You didn't start the fire, did you? The one in the theatre? The one Jazz was talking about?"

Sophie took a sharp breath and her face was a picture of misery.

"Sophie?"

Crossing her arms around her waist, Sophie finally raised her eyes to the room. "I started the fire."

****

Pulling her car to an abrupt halt, Jazz checked the time on the dashboard clock. Exactly midday. Unfastening her seatbelt, she stepped onto the pavement and slammed the door shut. Midday, Saturday 22 June. Fitting really. Almost five years to the day since The Grand Theatre burnt down. Shielding her eyes from the dazzling sun, Jazz marched across the road and pushed her way through the double doors, heading straight to the reception desk that she'd visited many times before. She stopped in front of the duty officer. "Sergeant John Strudwick, please."

****

"If she tells on you then she never truly loved you," said Laura, shoving another chunk of malt loaf into her mouth. "What am I doing?" she managed, between chews. "I don't even like this shit." She swallowed quickly. "It's nervous energy. Sophie, you haven't even touched yours."

"Would you like an apricot jam tart instead?" asked Maureen.

Sophie's gaze didn't waver from the windows.

"The fact is," said Laura, squashing more of the sticky brown loaf into her mouth. "This is the ultimate test of her true feelings. You couldn't have planned it better, Sophie. If she loves you, she won't tell. It's that simple."

"A-ha," said Maureen. "But what if Jazz follows the same line of reasoning. If Sophie truly loved her she'd have owned up."

"You didn't give her the chance, Mother!"

"She could have come clean on top of that hill after the bike ride. She could have reconnected with Jazz at any point after that and come clean with a confession. She could have come clean last night instead of doing the dirty." Maureen turned to Sophie. "That really was quite the sex session you had there, my dear."

Laura scooped crumbs from her plate. "I guess she could have come clean today when she was retelling the story."

"I am here," whispered Sophie.

"So say something!" gasped Laura.

Maureen rose from the sofa and walked to the French windows. "Was I right, dear? It honestly was a wild guess and I never usually win on things like spot the ball, or pin the tail on the donkey."

Laura wailed. "When did you last play pin the tail on the donkey, Mother?!"

"Let the poor girl speak, darling."

"Me?! You're the one who did a Poirot and laid everything out for everyone."

Maureen shrugged. "It's like when you're reading a book, I guess. You start to get a feel for the plot twist. The author drops in the odd strange reaction or mention." She lifted her arms to the room. "Every time I overheard anyone talking about the fire it got weird, but I never guessed I'd be right." She reached out and awkwardly patted

Sophie's arm. "Sophie here, an arsonist? Sounds silly." She turned back to her daughter. "But remember when I caught you, Laura, lighting a match and spraying a can of deodorant at the flame. Do you remember? You were out there in the garden and it caused a huge fireball."

Laura tutted. "The flame just got a bit bigger. And anyway, it was a science experiment."

"It was not a science experiment! I can't believe you're still telling that lie. It was like I'd walked into the middle of a fire-throwing display. The flame could have been sucked back into the can which would have exploded like a grenade in your hand."

Laura laughed. "I remember you showing me loads of pictures of people with body parts missing, telling me I'd end up like that if I played with fire."

"And you never played with fire again. Poor Sophie hasn't been blessed with parents like us."

"Mother."

"It's no secret. I've seen it with my own eyes. They're standoffish to others and they're somewhat indifferent to you, aren't they, Sophie? And I know I'm busy with all of my charity events and groups but I still ensure I know exactly what Laura's up to at all times."

"You do not, Mother! You never have any clue what's going on."

"I just solved your first life coaching case! And I used to wash the dogs before they arrived here for your pooch pampering business. Plus it was nearly all of my chiropodist's customers who signed up for your massage sessions."

"Don't say that, that's gross."

Maureen smiled. "There's a fine line between giving you space and independence and not knowing what's going on. I choose to pretend that I don't know what's going on, but deep down you know I do." She smiled again. "We both know I do." Before Laura could interrupt again she quickly went on. "But let's not do all of this in front of poor Sophie. She hasn't had the parental guidance you've been blessed with."

"You can't honestly believe that Sophie's been messing around with fire throughout her teenage years just because she has normal parents who go to work? I was nine-years-old when you caught me in the garden. Sophie was eighteen when the theatre burnt down."

"But she was never taught about the dangers of flammable liquids and open flames."

"I am still here," said Sophie again.

"So say something then!" shouted Laura. "Because my mum here's got you pegged as the next Guy Fawkes." Laura got up from her squeaky armchair. "Did you really start the fire, Sophie?"

Sophie kept her head bowed but did the smallest of nods.

"So why aren't you saying anything? Why aren't you defending yourself? Excusing yourself? Explaining yourself?"

"She's clearly in shock," said Maureen. "She's held onto this secret for five years and it's all just come tumbling out."

"Nothing's come tumbling out, Mother. You've put two and two together and made a great big bonfire."

"You think I'm wrong?"

"Of course you're wrong!"

"Poirot's never wrong."

"You're not Poirot! You're my mother!"

"Maybe so, but..." Maureen started to pace the room. "Wait. Sometimes Poirot does a double reveal. Not because he's wrong, but because there's more to the story. Oh goodness, it's coming to me." The pacing got faster. "I feel like Whoopi Goldberg in Ghost. Remember that psychic bit where she's dressed in gold and things just keep spilling out of her mouth?"

Laura snorted. "Even Patrick Swayze said that bit was a crock of shit."

"It's the same with books. If you guess the ending too soon you'll find there's another big plot twist. I know what the plot twist is here." She nodded at Sophie, triumph in her eyes. "Jazz recognised Sophie from the very start. I overheard her saying she'd seen the CCTV of the culprits. Who were the others, by the way?" The pause was short when it became clear that Sophie wasn't going to answer. "Anyway, Jazz was privy to the CCTV. And you said, Sophie, during your first session, that it was Jazz who approached you. Jazz who chased you down the aisle at the comedy club. What if she recognised you and has been playing you this whole time?"

"Mother! Don't make Sophie feel worse!" Laura stopped as her eyes widened. "But it does explain why Jazz went for a plain Jane as opposed to someone more alluring like me, maybe?"

Maureen nodded. "Jazz could be at the police station right now, having spent six months waiting for today's final confirmation."

Laura shook her head. "That would make their whole relationship a lie."

"Wasn't it a lie already? Sophie pretending to be someone she wasn't?"

"You're confusing me, Mum."

Maureen tapped Sophie on the shoulder. "You need to talk to us. You need to clear everything up."

The whisper came slowly. "I can't."

CHAPTER TWENTY THREE

Sophie pushed her key into the lock and twisted, but nothing moved. She tried again, more forcefully this time, before pulling the key back out. Wrong key. Fumbling with the choices, she put her hand on the front door of her family home and slumped against it, her head resting on her knuckles. There were only four keys on her key ring. Her house key, her car key and two music studio keys. All totally different and never before confused. She closed her eyes, surprised she'd even made it this far having walked back from Laura's into the path of two pushchair-pushing mothers, one bus, thankfully slowing for a stop, and one mobility scooter, slowing for no one.

"What are you doing out here?" asked her father, opening the door from the hallway, causing Sophie to stumble onto the doormat.

"Thanks, Dad."

"I wasn't letting you in, I was going out. Parish council meeting. It's in the calendar app."

"Right." Sophie called to her father who was already halfway to the car. "Is Mum home?" No answer. The car engine started and he was gone. Closing the door behind her, Sophie took off her shoes and placed them neatly on the rack.

"Shoes off, please, I've just cleaned."

Sophie followed the voice into the kitchen. "I always take my shoes off." She smiled at her mother who stood at the pristine sink and didn't look up from the saucepan she was scrubbing. "Have you got a minute?"

"Not really. I'm hosting the Mother's Union meeting this afternoon. It's in the calendar app."

"I should have checked. Sorry, I didn't log that I was out last night."

"Weren't you home?"

"I've only just got back."

"Log it next time. It only takes a second to update on your phone."

"What's the point if you didn't even notice I was out?"

"That's not the point. The family calendar's the best way of knowing what we're all up to."

"Can I tell you what I've been up to?"

"Oh, Sophie, I haven't got a second at the moment. Go and give your room a quick tidy? That would help."

Sophie stared for a minute at the unchanging scene of domestic busyness before turning away from the gleaming kitchen and making her way up the immaculate stairs to her bedroom. Everywhere was spotless, including that one space left in the house where she was allowed to show a bit of her personality: both parents of the mindset that minimal was favourable, seemingly in all things… including their interactions with their daughter. The changes in her appearance and behaviour five years before had been a welcome turn of events that clearly neither wanted to address for fear of reversal, but Sophie knew it was there. She'd spotted their nods of approval when her outfits became more subdued, and their whispers of congratulations when she'd explained to a friend that social media did more harm than good. The only thing they'd taken issue with was her decision to teach piano instead of join the London Symphony Orchestra – something they'd cooed about to their peers, having hosted a gathering to watch the news programme that ran a segment about their daughter being the youngest person to be offered a place in the prestigious ensemble, taking the 2014 record from trombonist Peter Moore.

Showing her parents an Excel spreadsheet that detailed how she'd be better off financially and more stable career-wise if she taught the piano and kept on the cello for fun maybe, had helped ease their disapproval. It also helped that they had decided to assume this was simply another mature decision by their recently level-headed only child, their loss of face among peers lessened by the fact that they could reference an *Independent On Sunday* article entitled *Playing For Peanuts*.

Closing her bedroom door and leaning against it, Sophie looked around. There was nothing to tidy. Everything had a place and everything was neatly in that place. She knelt down and pulled out the bottom drawer of her wardrobe, reaching into the secret space at the back for the scrapbook she pored over most evenings. Sitting against the bedroom door, she lifted the bottom of her duvet onto the mattress, just in case she had to shove the scrapbook out of sight under the bed at short notice. Relaxing a tiny bit, she turned to page one. She'd stuck her ticket for the *Whooping Wednesday* show in the middle of it and drawn a large red heart around it in thick felt tip pen. She smiled. It wasn't childish, it was just scrapbooking, something she'd done since she was a youngster, her parents insisting they log details of their sightseeing holidays just in case they ever returned, or someone asked what they'd recommend, or maybe just to serve as a record of their time together. Not that it was ever much fun, or nicely memorable. Sophie stopped that thought. That was wrong; her parents were fun, in their own way, and her childhood had been fine. They just liked order and routine and hadn't been prepared for a teenager who was loud, adventurous and sometimes quite challenging. The fact she'd suddenly gone into hiding was probably a blessing for them all. Who knows where she might be now? Abroad probably, with a vegan banjo player and two kids.

She turned the page and there was Jazz's smiling face on the flyer for the *Whooping Wednesdays* show. Sophie had printed it at home from the internet so the colours weren't quite right but she'd been unable to find one at Montel's when she'd returned the second time. What she did have from that evening with Jazz, however, was the receipt from the taxi that had driven them home. What would have happened if she'd just brought Jazz inside? Introduced her to her parents as a friend who was staying the night? Sophie laughed; her mum would probably have continued to clean and her dad would have been just as indifferent. She frowned. Would they though? She never had anyone around to the house apart from Laura; in fact, she didn't really have anyone in her life apart from Laura and as much as her parents liked to keep their home life rather detached, the fact that their daughter didn't appear to have friends was definitely a concern made evident by their constant suggestions for her to join their choral society or bell ringing club.

Sophie sighed as she turned the page before smiling once more. The petal page always made her smile. It was a petal from the very first rose Jazz ever bought her. A petal she'd secretly pressed in her mum's flower press before sticking it down and covering it with Sellotape so it didn't disintegrate. Admittedly, she couldn't smell it anymore, but it was there: a reminder of the moment her beautiful woman had given her a small, beautiful gift. Sophie smiled again. Jazz had given her so many gifts, something to do with most of them stuck in the scrapbook, including a cocktail stick from an olive that Jazz had seductively fed her over the table at one of their tapas meals. She flicked through the book, always sad that among the bits and bobs there were no photos of the two of them together. But how could she justify taking photos while not allowing others to take any? That would make her appear controlling, or a princess, as if she were so precious about her appearance that she only trusted the outcome of her own shots, or something. It was just easier to avoid the camera altogether and Jazz had understood. Or maybe she didn't understand, she simply accepted.

Sophie closed the scrapbook. Jazz had been so accepting of so much. Could she accept her secret? Would she accept her secret? She shook her head. The debate had changed. It wasn't a secret anymore. It was no longer something she could work up to discussing in the hope that Jazz might understand and forgive. It had been revealed by somebody else, and everything from here on in was damage control. Clambering to her feet, Sophie knew she had to control the damage.

"I knew you wouldn't go!" hissed the voice belonging to someone who had barged into the room, causing Sophie to fling the scrapbook towards her bed. Unfortunately, it hit the frame and bounced back, wide-open at Laura's feet. "Your mum let me in. What's this?"

"Give it here," snapped Sophie, too late.

"Oh my god, it's like a shrine. You've got Jazz's Comedy Show lanyard in here! Isn't that stealing?"

"She was going to throw it away, and it's not a shrine, it's a scrapbook."

"So you stole it and stuck it in here?"

Sophie shrugged. "It had been around her neck. I could smell her perfume on it."

Laura lifted the book and sniffed. "Smells of nothing now. This is too weird."

"A shrine would be weird. That scrapbook's just memories. Can I have it back please?"

"Your mum wouldn't let you have a shrine. She'd clear it up before you even built it."

"So be quiet and make sure she doesn't hear about this."

"It's fine, she's gone out to get some cleaning stuff. She said she'd put it in the calendar app."

Sophie heard the ping on cue and got her mobile from the dresser. She opened the family log and read: *Agnes – shopping*.

Laura sighed. "Why don't you make an entry: *Sophie – police station*. Oh, that's right, because you didn't go." Plonking herself on Sophie's bed, Laura tutted. "I've been sitting outside that bloody police station for the past twenty minutes waiting for you to arrive. Why didn't you answer my calls? My mum's really worried; she wanted to call my dad and tell him to go out looking for you but we agreed the fewer people that know about this the better. You've kept it quiet for five years, Sophie, so there's no reason why anyone else should find out."

"Jazz knows."

"And Jazz says she loves you."

"So?"

"So she won't tell. Which way did you walk home, by the way? Because I couldn't find you."

"I was in a daze and got lost. I will be going to the police station… I just wanted one last look at my scrapbook to remind me why I'm doing this."

"You're not doing this. Me and Mum have decided you're not doing this. You should have stayed at our house and talked it through instead of wandering off."

"I'm doing this. I love Jazz and it's the only way I can make things better."

"By admitting you're the reason her career went up in smoke?!"

"I am."

"You're not! I bet she was a crap actress anyway."

"It doesn't matter. I should have done this years ago."

"But you didn't."

"I was too scared."

"And now?"

"And now I can't live with it anymore."

"Because of her?"

"Because of everything. I've been living a lie, Laura, and it's made me so sad, sadder than you could ever imagine." The volume rose. "But that was my choice and I can't blame anyone but myself." Sophie nodded in commitment to her words. "What's inexcusable though, is the way I've treated other people. I've acted irrationally. I've deliberately been difficult so they'll push me away. But Jazz didn't push me away."

"Glutton for punishment."

Sophie shrugged. "Or maybe she saw me. The real me."

"So you pushed her away?"

"I've just found everything so hard. I've had no one to talk to and I know I've handled everything horrifically, but that's going to change, from today."

"You tell the police, you'll go to jail. Someone could have been killed, Sophie."

"It was an accident."

"So tell me! Mum's made me think you sauntered up there with a flame thrower!"

Sophie managed to laugh.

"You didn't?"

"I just... I was..."

"Oh for god's sake, spit it out!"

Sophie shook her head. "I need to go to the piano studio and tell Tessa and John the truth."

"Before I know the truth?!"

"They're the only people, aside from you, that I have in my life."
"Oh stop being so dramatic! You have loads of friends!"
"Acquaintances."
"People like you!"
"People don't know me."
Laura stuck her hands to her hips. "Well, if you're going to see Tessa and John first then I don't think I know you at all!"
"I know."
"Really? Really? That's where you're going with this?" Laura got up and entered Sophie's personal space. "I might not understand you, Sophie, but I do know you."
"Then you know I've got to do this."
"Oh, do what you want," said Laura, barging past her friend and out of the door. "See if I care."

****

Sitting on the bar stool at the back of Montel's basement room, Jazz gulped down her second tumbler of whisky.
"Steady," said Ben. "That's a lot more potent than the sherry you've been drinking."
"Don't talk to me about that woman!"
Ben raised his palms in self-defence.
"I didn't know her at all," continued Jazz.
"My lips are sealed."
"Hers have been sealed for the past five years."
Ben swung his glass-cleaning towel over his shoulder. "You didn't have sex then?"
"Not funny," said Jazz, shoving her empty tumbler along the counter towards him. "Fill me up."
"Watch it!" said Ben. "This isn't *Cocktail* and I'm not Tom Cruise."
"You caught it though."
"I'm not giving you another. We're not even open."
"I need another. I can't believe I went to the police station."
"You can't have it both ways, Jazz."

"Everything makes sense." She nodded for more as Ben gave in and poured the whisky. "Right to the top, please." Taking the offering, she swallowed quickly. "With Sophie's secret out in the open there's a chance she may become the person I saw. The person I knew was in there. The person I put up with the silly nonsense for."

"She won't be out in the open though, she'll be in jail."

Jazz dropped her head on the counter with a painful thud. "I'm so stupid."

"She'd never have told you."

"She wanted to tell me something the first time we went to her piano studio. I remember it, there was something on the tip of her tongue."

"Your lips?"

"Oh stop it, Ben. She sang about it and she was about to tell me, but I stopped her."

"*London's burning, London's burning, fetch the engines, fetch the engines.*"

Jazz ignored him. "It would have come out eventually. I'm sure of it."

"And then what?"

"I'd have behaved exactly as I have now." Jazz lifted her head. "I'd have been angry. I'd have gone to the police. I'd have…" She sighed. "I get it though. I stole a lip gloss from Superdrug once. I was thirteen, and I didn't actually mean to steal it, or at least I don't think I meant to steal it, or maybe I did, but then I convinced myself it was an accident. Anyway, I couldn't even walk past that shop for years afterwards. I'd always cross the road. And once my mum wanted to take me in there to buy some makeup for my birthday and I couldn't even do that and I loved makeup when I was a teenager. But I'd built up my crime into such a big deal that my only response was to shut off." She sighed, mournfully. "I shut off to Superdrug."

"Have you ever been back?"

"Into that store? No. Which is ridiculous, but I was so panicked and guilty. The idea of getting found out was overwhelmingly horrifying… and that was for a stupid stick of lip gloss. Imagine if you burnt down a two-hundred-year-old theatre." Jazz managed to laugh. "I get it completely."

"Jazz!" came the scream from above. "Thank god I've found you. She's going to the police! You're the only one who can stop her!"

Jazz turned and watched Laura who'd come running down the stairs into the basement room. "Who let you in?"

"The cleaner. Why does that matter? We have to stop Sophie. She says she's going to speak to Tessa and John first before going to the police station to confess. You're the only one who can stop her. Please stop her, Jazz?"

"Why should I?"

"Because you care. Because she's going to ruin her life."

"Like she ruined my life and all the lives of all the other people who had links with that place?"

"Oh, stop being so bitter. We're the ones in control of the paths our careers take. You could have been an actress if you really wanted it. Maybe you weren't good enough?"

Ben coughed. "Not the best way to get her onside." He clicked his fingers. "I know. Tell her you've seen an orb. Tell her it's a flashing red orb that's communicating danger." He slammed his towel onto the counter. "Danger if she gets mixed up in more of your shit."

Jazz straightened in her chair. "Thanks, Ben, I've got this."

"You haven't got this. I've lost count of the number of nights you've sat in here drowning your sorrows about one Sophie-related misdemeanour or another." He pointed at Laura. "These silly girls have hurt you."

Laura laughed. "And how old are you? Twenty-five?"

Ben leant over the counter and pointed at Laura. "It's too late. She's already been to the police."

"What?! You have not!" Laura gasped. "How could you, Jazz?! My mum was right! You knew who she was! This was all a trap!"

"What?"

"You never liked her at all, did you?!"

"I loved her." Jazz shook her head. "I love her."

"Well, get to the studio right now! Stop her from talking to Tessa and John! The fewer people that find out the better. Give her a heads-up! There's probably a warrant out for her arrest! How could you do this?!"

"I haven't done anything."
"YOU TOLD!"

CHAPTER TWENTY FOUR

John nodded his head. "It's okay, Sophie, we're listening. Just tell us what happened."

Falling off the kerb and in between two parked cars, Sophie whooped. "She's taken a fall!"
"Who's taken a fall?" wailed Laura.
"Me! I've taken a fall!" squealed Sophie, as she crawled back onto the pavement. "The night only gets going when someone takes a fall!"
"You took a fall on the dance floor; that's why we're out here!"
"Why's it called taking a fall? Where are we taking it?"
Laura dropped onto her knees next to Sophie. "I've taken a fall too! Let's take our falls to the kebab house! Crawl with me!" The laughter was loud. "We're crawling along the kerb! Look at us! We're so cool!"
Sophie cocked her leg to one of the cars. "I'm a dog! Wee-ing!"
"Hilarz!" squealed Laura. "Come here, let me mount you!"
"Get off!" said Sophie, falling flat on her front the second Laura clambered onto her back.
"You love it!"
"My face is on the pavement."
Laura rolled off. "You'd love it if it was Rebecca Lynch. I saw her watching you in there."

Sophie dusted herself off as she sat on the pavement. "Doesn't mean she wants to come and dry hump me in the doggy position on the pavement though."

"I think the rumour's true."

"Shut up!" laughed Sophie.

The voice was loud. "Move along please girls."

Laura reached out and slapped the steel toe caps of the bouncer who'd manhandled them out of the club. "You kicked us out! Ow, that hurt! What sort of shoes are those?"

"Seriously girls, you need to move along."

"We just finished our exams! Can't you let us back in?"

"You were rolling around on the dance floor."

"We were having a dance-off!"

"Dance-off somewhere else."

"What's that in my hair?" asked Sophie, using a car wheel and side mirror to haul herself up while ignoring the bouncer.

"Ha!" Laura pushed Sophie under a street lamp. "It's a cigarette butt! From the pavement!"

"Get it out, would you?"

Laura turned to the bouncer. "Look what you've done. She's got a cigarette butt in her hair. And that looks like chewing gum too!"

"Zhoosh me," said Sophie with a nod.

"Come here, Tina Turner." Laura moved her fingers up and down through Sophie's bouncing head of brown curls. "It's like I'm emptying a handbag; look at all this shit falling out."

"Ladies, can you please move along."

"We're going!" snapped Laura.

Sophie peered down the street. "Taxi to Hurricane's or Snooker After Dark?"

"Kebab shop."

"No. They cook rats in there."

"We need to refuel. This is the only time in our whole lives we're ever going to finish our exams."

"Unless we fail."

"As if you'll fail! You don't even need qualifications to ping your strings and clank your keys!"

"What?"

"Cello and piano. Kebabs, come on."

"I'm not going in there." Sophie pointed at the flashing lights and queue of people.

"I need my meat, and I'm going to miss you."

"In the kebab shop?"

"When you leave me here for that posh orchestra. Pleeeeeeease stay and do hypnotherapy with me!"

"It's rat meat. In the kebab shop."

"It's not rat meat. Fine, wait on the bench then, you deserting vegan."

"I like meat, and dessert."

"Not what Bobby said."

"I was never going to give Bobby a blow job; he's using me to get to you. I've told you he likes you."

Laura swung on the side of the shop's door frame. "Oh look, there's Rebecca Lynch. Go and eat her instead."

"Where?"

"Wait! I was joking! Sophie! Sit down. I didn't mean it!"

"They're smoking," said Sophie, as she crossed over the road.

Laura hollered even louder. "So you won't eat rat meat but you will suck on tar?!"

"I've just been face first on the pavement, it's no different."

"You're crossing the road for her! I knew the rumour was true!"

"It's not true," yelled Sophie, pointing back at the shop. "Your queue's massive. Meet you back at the bench in ten." Tottering up the other kerb towards the sixth former, Sophie smiled. "You're not going, are you? Who's this?"

The girl handed over a cigarette. "Tommy, my cousin."

"Has he finished his exams too?" asked Sophie, studying the small boy as she took the tiniest of sucks without inhaling.

The boy laughed. "As if. I'm fourteen, me."

Rebecca's sharp fringe flicked as she brought her head closer to Sophie's. "He's sorting us out. I'll be going back into the club in a minute."

"We've been kicked out. We're heading to Hurricane's if you fancy it? Where are you going now? What's he sorting you out with?"

Rebecca signalled Sophie into the alleyway. The boy followed. "Whatever you want." She took some crumpled notes from her purse. "I've got orders from half the sixth form."

"Drugs?"

"Do you want anything?"

"No, I do not! And you do sports, Rebecca!"

The boy huffed. "It's not like it's heroin or anything."

Sophie waved her cigarette in the air and pointed at the glowing embers. "You shouldn't even be smoking!" she said, as she threw the stub over the wrought iron gates at the end of the alley. "Goodbye!"

☁

John nodded. "So the gates led to one of the theatre's side entrances?"

Sophie sniffed back her tears. "I stormed off all dramatically and found Laura on the bench. She'd been thrown out of the kebab shop for telling people it was rat meat, so we got a taxi and went to Hurricane's."

"And then?"

"And then we carried on clubbing. Every single eighteen-year-old in town was out that night. It was the last night of our exams. It got messy, moving from place to place, staggering home, feeling ill the next day." Sophie shook her head. "But nothing compared to the sickness I felt when Rebecca confronted me the next morning. She had the local paper and made me turn on the radio. It was everywhere. She said if I kept quiet about her and Tommy and what they were up to, she'd keep quiet about my cigarette starting the fire. It was there on the front page: they said there were some old props from the theatre just behind the gates. Rebecca said she saw them catch light. Obviously she ran, but she promised me she never thought it would take hold and do what it did." Sophie sniffed into her sleeve. "And I promise I would have called someone if I'd seen it, but we'd already gone to Hurricane's by then. And I know it's all too little too late and I know I should have owned up straight away but I was scared. I was so scared."

"What's changed?"

"I just want to start again with no secrets. I want people to know who I really am. I'm not a bad person. Or maybe I don't want to be a bad person anymore."

****

"Stop!" squealed Laura, dashing up the music studio's stairs and into the reception area.

"Wait for me," panted Jazz. "I've had three whiskys and these stairs are like marble."

"They're not here," said Laura, eyes flashing from the empty bucket chairs to the water cooler.

"Try John's room. He practises his duets with Tessa in there. First on the left."

"Stop!" squealed Laura again, crashing her way into the small music room. "Don't tell anyone anything!"

John hastily threw his arms from Tessa's shoulders, knocking his knuckles onto the piano and causing an off-key plink. "Excuse me!" he gasped.

"Oh sorry." Laura looked at the ceiling. "I didn't realise you were…"

Jazz puffed her way into the room. "Oh John, yay! You made your move. At least you two have got your happy ending."

"Don't be so silly," gasped John again, his face as red as a prize Koi. "Isn't that silly, Tessa."

"So silly, John," said Tessa, clumsily removing herself from John's lap. "What's going on?"

"Sophie. Where is she?"

Tessa straightened her smock. "She's not here."

"She's been here though?"

"Not that I'm aware of. John, has Sophie been here?"

"No, Tessa, I don't think she has."

Laura turned to Jazz. "Dammit! She's gone straight to the station."

****

Sergeant John Strudwick spoke again. "Sophie, you need to tell me what time all of this happened."

CHAPTER TWENTY FIVE

"I can't do any more dashing," said Jazz, clambering out of Laura's car and struggling to keep up with her quick march to the police station.

"Hurry up!"

Jazz puffed. "We should have come straight here. Why would Sophie have gone to Tessa and John's anyway?"

Laura shouted over her shoulder. "She said she wanted to tell them the truth."

"Above us knowing the truth? Above her parents knowing the truth? She fooled you, Laura. She sent you on a wild goose chase. She was always going to come straight here; she just didn't want you following her."

"Hey! I stormed off! I wasn't going to do any of this."

"Yet here you are."

"And here you are too," said Laura, yanking the door wide open. "I'll follow you. You've been here already, after all."

"Touché," said Jazz, entering the building and scanning the waiting area. "She's not here."

"Oh no," gasped Laura. "We're too late. She'll be locked up already."

"It'll be fine. Come with me." Checking her breath in her cupped hand, Jazz walked as confidently as she could to the reception desk. "Sergeant John Strudwick, please."

"Oh, hello again. He phoned you back, didn't he? Yes, he did. I remember, he made the call right here. You said it was a false alarm. Or did he say it was a false alarm? Either way he told me to put 'actioned' next to your visit."

Laura turned to Jazz. "You didn't tell?"

"Tell what?" asked the duty officer.

Jazz cleared her throat. "Is he busy now?"

"Yes, sorry."

"She's here," hissed Laura.

"Who's here?" asked the woman, angling herself forward. "Have either of you ladies been drinking?"

"Sorry, another false alarm," said Jazz, putting her arm around Laura's shoulder and steering them back to the doors. "We can't do anything if she's in there already, especially with me stinking of whisky!"

Laura gawped at Jazz, clearly in shock. "You didn't tell! Oh god, it's like you're a modern-day Romeo and Juliet. She's in there killing herself with her confession when there's no need! She didn't have to tell! You'd never have told! My mum thought you knew it was Sophie all along but I said that was ridiculous." Laura looked back as they trotted down the station steps. "You could have stopped all this, Jazz. She's only confessed because she thought you'd tell. Gosh it's exactly like Romeo and Juliet!"

"It's nothing like Romeo and Juliet." Jazz shook her head. "And I hope that's not the reason she's in there."

"What other reason is there?"

"She wanted to do the right thing."

"Oh, don't be so stupid. It's been five years; she was never going to do the right thing. She's in there because she's been found out."

"What if she wanted to clear the air between us and start afresh with an open and honest playing field?"

"Starting with twenty years in prison? As if! She's just trying to save her own skin at the last minute."

"She's your friend, Laura."

"And she's your girlfriend."

"Where are you going?"

Laura looked both ways and began to cross the road. "Back to the car. Mum will know just what to do."

****

"Oh, it's just like Romeo and Juliet!" said Maureen, passing around a tray of cakes.

"That's exactly what I said, Mum!" laughed Laura, grabbing two jam tarts.

Jazz refused the offering, staring instead at the two women. "Why are you laughing?" She shook her head. "Why are you so excited? Sophie's committed a crime."

"But she's gone to confess so that makes it a crime of passion," said Maureen with a nod.

"This makes it all so commendable," agreed Laura.

Jazz gasped. "Nothing about this is commendable or passionate. Sophie's an arsonist."

Maureen placed the cake tray on the coffee table and gestured for Jazz to come and sit next to her on the sofa. "The fact you missed each other by moments at the police station, and the fact she decided to confess when you kept quiet, makes this all so bitter sweet. Our little Sophie's finally a woman."

"I'm proud of her," said Laura.

"Will you two just listen to yourselves?" said Jazz, staying exactly where she was. "It's no wonder she's been lost if this is the kind of advice she's been getting."

Laura ignored the jibe and shook her head. "She never spoke to us about any of this."

"That's exactly my point! I can't believe neither of you ever questioned her involvement."

"Of course not." Laura took a bite of jam tart. "We were each other's alibis." She swallowed quickly. "Not that we ever realised we needed alibis; it was more of a: Ooh, good job we weren't around."

"What?!" Jazz moved to the armchair. "You were with Sophie on the night of the fire?"

"It was the end of our exams. We went out. I've got some pictures. It was a hilarious night."

"It obviously wasn't!" gasped Jazz.

"Let me go and get my album. And sit down, would you? You're looking all intimidating again, looming over us both."

"You saw her do it?"

"Of course not. She must have doubled back or something. No clue why though. Do you think the police will issue details of her confession?" She paused in the doorway. "Hang on, what if we see the outline of a box of matches or a lighter in her pocket or something? Do you think the police will want the photographs as evidence, only I was going through a bad hair phase?"

Maureen clapped her hands. "Let me go and find my magnifying glass. The one I use for my 'spot the difference' puzzles. Have you seen it, Laura?"

Laura laughed. "Ha! Maybe Sophie's stolen it."

"Does she struggle with her eyesight as well?"

"To start another fire, Mum! Keep up, would you! And don't you dare magnify my mullet."

****

Sergeant Strudwick's female colleague entered the room and nodded.

"Is that the fire report?"

"Yes, Sarge." She handed over the file. "As you thought. Page four. Top paragraph. I checked the names too. Right again."

He flicked through the contents before nodding. "You burnt it to the ground," he shouted, slamming the folder onto the desk.

Sophie's eyes shot to the lino flooring. "I'll never forgive myself for the damage I caused."

"I don't think you have any clue about the damage you caused. You can't put a price on the loss of people's livelihoods, people's careers."

"I've learnt that."

"Too little, too late. I had the theatre people in here watching the CCTV over and over again, desperate for answers. Actors too. Anyone even remotely associated with that place saw the footage."

"So there was CCTV?" Sophie kept her head down but pulled her plait over her shoulder. "I knew it."

"We couldn't make it public. The boy was clearly a minor and we assumed you were one of the hundreds of sixth formers out and about that night and potentially still seventeen."

"I was eighteen."

"See, if we'd known that we could have plastered your mug shot everywhere." He nodded. "Would you like to see your mugshot?"

"Do I have to?"

"I think you should." The stern voice rose again. "You could have saved so much police time and money if only you'd had the courage to speak up."

Sophie shook her bowed head. "I was too afraid, and I know that makes me sound like such a coward but the idea of telling someone wasn't an option for me. I had to keep my head down, that was it."

"And how's that worked out for you?"

"Not great."

"So you kept quiet and prayed your little pals kept quiet too?"

Sophie started to sob. "I've spent the past five years of my life afraid of everything and everyone, and I don't expect anyone to feel sorry for me but I started my sentence the day after it happened."

"You should have confessed."

"I was too scared."

The sergeant slammed his hand on top of the folder. "You weren't too scared to break the padlock and gain access to the back of the theatre though, were you? And you weren't too scared to mess around with the theatre props, were you? And you weren't too scared when you threw your cigarette onto a pile of straw left over from *The Wizard Of Oz*, were you?"

"That's not how it happened!"

"Let's watch the CCTV shall we, Sophie?"

****

Kneeling in between Laura and Maureen, Jazz stared at the page of photos open on the coffee table. "Where's Sophie?" she asked.

Laura laughed. "There!"

"Where?"

Maureen handed over the magnifying glass. "Do you need this?"

"Don't be ridiculous, Mother, of course she doesn't." Laura tapped the photograph. "Look, she's here, and here, and here, and here."

Jazz shook her head. "That's not Sophie."

"Ummm, yes it is. It might not be the Sophie you know, but that's the real deal right there."

Jazz shook her head again. "It's not Sophie."

"Um, it is."

"No!" she shouted. "IT'S NOT SOPHIE!"

****

Sophie looked around the empty room. What was going on? Surely both police officers didn't need to go and get the CCTV footage? Unless they were playing it on one of those big TVs they used to have at school with a video player underneath that took at least two people to manoeuvre because of a missing wheel or wonky shelf. Or maybe they'd gone off to get handcuffs and a prison jumpsuit? Glancing around a bit more, Sophie rose from her seat and crept over to the door. She tried the handle and gasped. It was unlocked. She could run away if she wanted to. Shaking her head, she let go. She'd been running away for too long. Exhaling heavily, she felt free for the first time in five years. Bizarre given the fact she was in a police cell. Looking around again at her surrounding she realised she was being dramatic. She wasn't locked in and this wasn't a cell. This was more like a family liaison room with soft seating and posters on the wall. She wasn't in custody.

Sophie read one of the posters: *Parents, please don't tell your children that we will take them off to jail if they're bad. We want them to run to us if they are scared... NOT be scared of us. Thank you.* She huffed. Sergeant Strudwick had been very scary indeed and that was without the memory of her mother's threats to call the police every time she didn't want to eat her greens, or do up her seatbelt, or even that time she rode her bike too fast down a hill. Strange though how they hadn't hauled her into an interview room and started a tape recorder like they did on TV. She looked at another poster: *Lying to the police is a crime.* Maybe they were checking she wasn't a phoney before they started to document everything properly?

****

"It wasn't her!" gasped Jazz, leaning over the police station reception desk for the third time that day.

"Madam, I think you've been drinking," said the same duty officer, wrinkling her nose.

"I know! But I was drinking because of her, only it wasn't her all along!"

At that moment, Maureen was the second person to make it to the desk, throwing the page of photographs at the woman. She thrust over her magnifying glass. "Take a look!"

"Wait for me, would you! I had to park the car!" shouted Laura, bringing up the rear. "And don't you dare go magnifying my mullet!"

****

Sergeant Strudwick pressed play on the laptop. "Three thirty a.m. and the male and female suspects have broken through the gates and come into the CCTV's line of vision."

Sophie gasped. "Wait."

The sergeant continued. "The suspects proceed to mess around with the discarded props at the side of the theatre." He clicked the footage forward. "Particular highlights include this version of *Swan Lake* by the male who's now wearing angel wings." He clicked the footage forward once more. "And the female does quite a good Superman impression with that cape."

Sophie squinted. "Wait."

"Three forty-five and the suspects sit on the theatre's back step for a cigarette. Three forty-seven and the male flicks his cigarette towards a small mound of straw. Three forty-eight and you can see the first flickers of flame. It's black and white but you can see it, there." He pointed with his finger. "Three forty-nine and the female's trying to stamp out the flames. Three fifty it becomes obvious they need to run. Three fifty-one, they run."

"Wait!" gasped Sophie. "That's not me!"

"I know it's not you. I knew from the moment you told me you'd been in the alley at around ten p.m." Sergeant Strudwick folded his arms. "This is Rebecca Lynch and Tommy Gutteridge, right?"

Sophie squinted at the poor-quality footage. "I think so. The newspapers never said exactly what time the fire started, only that it took a while to take hold. It could have been my cigarette."

"It wasn't. You never broke through the gates. You weren't even there."

Sophie clapped her hand to her mouth. "It wasn't me?"

"It wasn't you. But your information could have saved the police an awful lot of time and money."

She started to sob. "It wasn't me."

"My colleague's informed me that Tommy Gutteridge is already inside on an aggravated burglary charge and an internet search appears to show that Rebecca Lynch is now a missionary in Cameroon."

"It wasn't me?"

"No, Sophie, it wasn't you, but I had to go in hard in the hope that you'd realise just how serious this is."

"I realise."

"Do you? Unfortunately it won't be in the public interest to prosecute you for perverting the course of justice so you'll have to leave here with the memory of my shouting at you as punishment. Remember the fear and learn to be honest in the future."

"Leave here?"

"Yes, leave here, Sophie. Why do you think we're still in this room? You haven't committed a crime. Someone will be in touch to take a formal written statement from you. Rebecca too." He huffed. "Who knows how we'll get in contact with her. Either way, your corroborating statements will add another crime to Gutteridge's ever-growing rap sheet. You may be required to give evidence in court but I doubt it'll get that far. We always knew it wasn't arson with intent, but it's nice to finally wrap it up."

"Will I be named?"

"You haven't done anything wrong in the eyes of the law, Sophie. You went down that alley for a cigarette five hours before the fire even started. More fool you for believing Rebecca's threats."

"She didn't threaten me, she was doing me a favour."

"Apparently not."

"It really wasn't me, then?"

"Goodness me, Sophie, it wasn't you! You might be silly and self-serving, but you're not a criminal."

"I'm not a criminal?"

"You're not a criminal."

"I can go?"

"You can go."

****

Slipping out of the room and racing down the corridor, Sophie saw the kerfuffle at the reception desk. "I'm not a criminal!" she shouted, bolting as fast as she could to the safety of the familiar group.

"I know!" wailed Jazz, pulling the photo album away from the duty officer and thrusting it towards Sophie. "Why didn't you tell me you had crazy Tina Turner hair? The girl I saw on the CCTV had a blunt fringe and bob! You looked like a pine cone from behind! A big bouncing fluffy pine cone! It wasn't you! You weren't even there!"

"I know!" said Sophie, throwing her arms around her girlfriend.

Maureen waved her magnifying glass. "We couldn't find the outline of anything in your pockets either, you know, like matches or a lighter. I'm ever-so sorry if I caused all of this?"

"I deserved it. I didn't realise but I knew who did it all along and I might have to testify, but I probably won't because he's already in jail."

"You knew who started the fire?" said Jazz, edging out of the embrace. "You knew five years ago?"

"I didn't know that I knew but if I'd been honest about my involvement he may have been found and charged, but the sergeant said it wasn't arson with intent and the fact no one was hurt makes it less of a crime, apparently."

Jazz frowned. "No one was hurt? I was hurt. I'm still hurting."

"Oh come on, Jazz," said Laura. "Today's a day for celebrating. We can finally get Sophie back. The real Sophie. The fun Sophie. The Sophie who wears her hair big and her tops low."

"I'm not sure I want to know her."

"Oh grow up, this isn't about you anymore. This is about Sophie and her fresh start."

Sophie reached out for her girlfriend. "A fresh start I'd like to have with you."

Jazz shook her head. "I'm not sure what I'm meant to be feeling right now."

The duty officer interrupted the gathering. "Whatever it is, can you feel it outside, please?"

Jazz nodded. "I think I'd rather feel it at home."

"With me?" asked Sophie.

"No," answered Jazz, turning to leave. "Not with you."

CHAPTER TWENTY SIX

Sitting down next to Tessa and John on the front row in Montel's basement room, Sophie handed over the glass of sherry and pint of stout. Ben hadn't been particularly friendly at the bar and there was a chance he might message Jazz to give her a heads-up that she was here, but there was a big queue to serve and the show was about to start, so hopefully her plan would run smoothly. She smiled at her colleagues. "Thanks so much for coming and, like I said, feel free to leave again if it all gets too much."

John reached out and patted Tessa's knee. "We'll try and see it through to the end this time. Tonight means something to you, Sophie, and your honesty means something to us, doesn't it, Tessa?"

"Yes, it does, John."

"We're just thrilled that you've decided to stay at the studio instead of jetting off to find fame and fortune with another orchestra, aren't we, Tessa?"

"That we are, John."

John continued. "And morally we both agreed that five years of worry is enough punishment." He nodded. "It took us a while to come to our conclusion, didn't it, Tessa? But we're happy."

"We are, John."

"Being honest about your involvement may have caught the criminals earlier, but the girl seems to be living a life of redemption and the boy's already serving time." John cleared his throat. "We did wrestle with the question of whether or not the boy would have committed his subsequent crimes if he'd been caught earlier, but overall we feel you've been punished enough, and essentially you didn't do anything wrong, aside from keep quiet, which isn't the nicest character trait to have, but then again we all have our faults, don't we, Tessa?"

"That we do, John."

John laughed. "You weren't meant to agree with me on that one, Tessa."

Tessa laughed. "Oh, you are a tease, John." She took a sip of her sherry. "Shush, it's starting."

Sophie slid down in her seat, a ridiculous thing to do given that she was on the front row, but she was nervous. She hadn't seen Jazz since she'd marched out of the police station a month ago, with all of her attempts at contact failing. Jazz continued to maintain she needed time alone to make sense of everything and Sophie just had to suck it up. She glanced at her colleagues. If Tessa and John could accept her inadequacy, then surely Jazz could? Her parents had been furious, but then quickly sympathetic when they realised it was the reason for her change in personality and toned-down appearance, suddenly concerned it might mean a return to her wild nights and raucous behaviour. Sophie sighed and looked at her simple jeans and t-shirt. There were some things she'd got used to over the past five years.

"Welcome, welcome, welcome," said the familiar voice from the stage. "You probably all know who I am. I'm Jazz and I'm your compère for the evening. Now, before I hand over to our first comedian, Deidre Dee, I need to make an announcement. This will be my last appearance at Montel's. I've decided I need a change. A fresh start. A new career." Jazz paused while boos and hoots from the crowd washed around the room. "Now, at the moment I'm torn between being a drug dealer and a hooker."

Tessa tutted.

"I mean they've both got their pros. But I think I'm edging towards hooker. At least then I'll be able to wash my crack and re-sell it."

The audience wailed with laughter.

"I guess I'll also know once and for all what's better oral or anal, because I've heard oral makes your day but anal makes your hole weak."

John turned to Sophie, his lips like string. "I'm sorry, Sophie, but we're going to have to leave."

"I agree, John," said Tessa, mirroring his expression perfectly.

"Please?" whispered Sophie. "She hasn't seen me yet, just a little longer. I want her to see me, to see us, to see our united front and to see how you've forgiven me. I want her to soften a bit before I approach her. I need her to see us all laughing together."

"I'll give it another minute," said John.

Jazz's monologue continued. "Do you know what's the best thing about fingering a fortune teller on her period? You get your palm red for free."

"That's it," said John, standing up. "Tessa, we're going."

"That we are, John."

"And what do we have here?" whooped Jazz, squinting through the lights to the aisle. "Cinderella making her escape!" She laughed. "Do you know what Cinderella did when she got to the ball?" Jazz nodded. "She gagged."

Sophie stared at the stage. Why wasn't Jazz looking at her? It was obviously Tessa and John clumsily making their way to the safety of the stairs, but she'd not glanced down once to see who they'd been with. There was only one thing for it. "If you really want a new career, I know what you could be," yelled Sophie, standing up and waving her arms. "You could be my girlfriend."

Jazz kept her eyes on the audience. "Right, where was I? What do you call—"

"She's pretty!" came a cry from the crowd.

"What do you call a..." Jazz lost her rhythm.

"Give her a chance!" came another cry.

Jazz dared to glance at Sophie who was still standing. "She is rather beautiful."

"I'm sorry too," shouted Sophie.

The whistles turned to cheers.

"Beautiful and sorry," said Jazz, smiling. "Fine. I'll give you three chances to make me laugh. I laugh, we talk."

Sophie blinked into the spotlight that suddenly lit her position. She waved nervously at the crowd before speaking in a strong voice.

"Okay. Um. What does Jazz put behind her ears to attract the women?" She paused as a fair bit of the crowd cackled. "Her ankles."

"Not funny," said Jazz, her voice rising above the hubbub.

Sophie grinned. "The audience liked it."

"You didn't like it, did you, audience?" asked Jazz, nodding in triumph as the laughs retreated back to their owners. "Thank you. Try again."

Sophie took a deep breath. "How do you tell if Jazz is hungry or horny?" She pointed at the stage. "You see where she sticks the cucumber."

"Not funny and not endearing me to talk to you."

"Fine. What do you do if an old lady at a cashpoint asks you to check her balance?" Sophie waited as Jazz shrugged and someone in the crowd yelled encouragement. Sophie smiled. "You push her over."

Jazz tightened her lips and turned her head away from the crowd.

"She's laughing!" shouted someone in a seat behind Sophie.

"I'm not," said Jazz, her shoulders betraying her.

"Look! She's laughing!"

Jazz raised her hands in surrender. "Fine, you've got five minutes. Deidre Dee, it's over to you."

Dashing around to the side of the stage, Sophie climbed the steps behind the curtain and pushed open the door to the broom cupboard.

"You push her over?" said Jazz, sitting in an arms crossed position on her stool. "You push her over? Where did you get that from?"

"The joke book I gave you."

"And the others?"

"Just some burns I came up with when I was angry at you."

"When you were angry at me? Sophie, you've got no right to be angry at me."

"And you've got no right to be so cold in front of your audience."

Jazz sighed. "I was being an idiot. I'm sorry."

"And I'm sorry for the jokes. Although a few people liked them." She smiled. "I think I did quite well since stand-up wasn't my plan for the evening."

"What was your plan?"

"For you to spot me."

"Well, here you are."

Sophie closed the door behind her, sealing them both into the small space. "I had this plan to recreate our first meeting, only this time I'd do things differently; I'd do things the way they should have been. I wouldn't walk out with Tessa and John; we'd meet at the bar and start afresh from there."

"You staged their walk-out tonight?"

"No, your gags were too much for them."

"I was only getting started."

"I want us to get started. Properly this time."

"Oh, Sophie, there's too much history and heartache."

"One chance, Jazz. Please just give me one chance."

"To do what?"

"To do things the way they should have been done in the first place." Sophie stood in front of Jazz and knelt down. "I should have made you come on that stool the first night."

"I'm due out in a minute!"

"So let me warm you up?" said Sophie, her hands on Jazz's legs. She grabbed her thighs and moved to kiss her neck where a pulse was beating rapidly.

"Don't tempt me, Sophie."

"Why not?" Sophie continued to kiss the fluttering skin. "We'll always have this fire."

Jazz pulled away. "Are you serious?!"

"Yes, and I should have used that word from the start. This is the new old me, Jazz, the real me and we do have a fire." She returned her lips to Jazz's neck. "We have a roaring, hungry inferno that devours us both whether we like it or not."

Jazz arched her neck, enjoying the embrace. "Fires are dangerous. They do lots of damage."

Sophie groaned as she felt Jazz's fingers ride under her t-shirt. "I want you to damage me, Jazz, right here in this room. I want you to fuck me so hard."

"You're fucking me," whispered Jazz, "with your face, in five minutes when I'm back from the stage."

Sophie watched as Jazz jumped up. They were back. They still had it. And Laura was right; the way they talked to each other was sexually aggressive, but it was a consequence of their desire, of the searing passion that engulfed them every single time they were close. Pulling the bobble from the end of her plait, Sophie ran her fingers through her hair and watched in the mirror as the curls she'd once loved bounced up around her face. Pulling her t-shirt over her head she hung it on one of the wall hooks, quickly doing the same with her bra and belt. Unbuttoning the top of her jeans, she fingered the material. Inviting, she thought as she looked at her reflection, still enjoying the novelty of being able to see herself as she'd been on that night; not braless obviously, just with big hair and boobs out… the worry of being identified no longer a concern. The whole world could see her like this for all she cared.

"Two sherries," said Ben, pushing open the cupboard door before gasping at what greeted him. "Sophie!"

"Shut the door!" wailed Sophie. "I don't want the whole world seeing me like this!"

"Sorry, here are your drinks, I'm going, she's coming, not like that, but she will be won't she, oh dear, look there's an orb, it's a purple one, purple for... I should piss off."

"Wait, I'm sorry about all that, Ben," said Sophie, arms wrapped around herself in a vain attempt to protect her modesty. "I didn't know what Laura was doing."

Ben gallantly spoke to the ceiling. "But you knew what you were doing, and by the looks of it you know what you're doing right now. Just don't hurt her again." Ben continued to stare everywhere but at Sophie. "Right, I'm going," he said, shuffling his way back out of the tiny space.

Sophie turned to the mirror and noticed a flash of blue dance around the room as the door was closed. She smiled. A reflection from the stage? Or a blue orb? Laura had said that blue orbs signalled courage. She smiled again and looked down at her open fly button.

"In for a penny, in for a pound," she whispered, sliding her jeans to the ground.

CHAPTER TWENTY SEVEN

"I can't believe you were stark bollock naked when I walked back in there," said Jazz between heated kisses in the back of the taxi. "And I love your hair like this."

Sophie pulled away for a second. "I'm so sorry about what happened on top of the piano, but I'd kept it plaited for five years." She shrugged. "I was hysterical about it being seen because my hair's so distinctive."

"Shall we leave all that in the past?"

"Like we do the talk of your exes?"

Jazz laughed. "Do you know what? I'm not sure how much of our relationship will actually change. You'll still be petulant."

"I call it snap-back banter."

"It's quarrelsome. It's the only child in you. Laura was right about that."

"Can you forgive Laura?"

"I haven't said I've forgiven you, yet."

Sophie smiled. "You looked pretty forgiving when I made you come on that stool." She smiled again as she checked the angle of the driver's mirror before popping open the top button of Jazz's jeans. "I've always regretted not finishing you off that first night… but I've rectified that now. I also regretted not making you come in the taxi on the way home." She slipped her fingers into the warmth and stroked gently. "You've given me a second chance to start again. To do this properly." Leaning forward to get a better angle and plunging her fingers deep inside, Sophie whispered. "So I'm doing things properly."

Jazz's moan was guttural as she let her head drop onto her chest. "Don't make me loud," she managed, gasping in pleasure under her breath. "We have to be careful."

"I don't want to be careful, I want to jump straight in."

"I'm talking about now," she whispered. "In the taxi."

"It's my new philosophy."

"Old you or new you?" Jazz parted her legs wider. "Maybe I don't know you at all."

"Good, because we're starting again and the real me never shies away from people or experiences or adventure. I feel like I have a new lease of life, Jazz."

Jazz moaned softly. "That you want to spend with me?"

"Yes."

"This is so good. You're so good. Keep going."

"My philosophy or my sex moves?"

Jazz adjusted her position on the back seat, making it easier to open her legs. "All of it."

Sophie smiled as she worked her fingers faster. "And I don't feel like I've got five years of mayhem to make up for." She pressed hard on Jazz's clit. "More like five years of fun to enjoy. This is who I am, Jazz. I'm carefree."

"You're fucking me. I'm so close. I'm in the back of a taxi getting fucked." Jazz dropped further in on herself. "Your arm's moving too much, Sophie."

"It's dark. Are you going to be the conservative one now?" Sophie slid her other hand under Jazz's top and found her nipple.

"No, I just..." Jazz groaned. "Fuck it, I'm coming."

"Come on my fingers," said Sophie, feeling Jazz's whole body begin to clench up in pleasure.

"Fuck, I'm coming."

Sophie kissed Jazz full on the lips, tasting the waves of her orgasm for herself.

"Yes!" cried Jazz.

The taxi pulled a sharp left. "I'm not homophobic," said the driver, not turning around, "and I don't care who's kissing who in the back of my cab. But you're taking it too far. You have to get out. I don't want paying, I've seen where your hands have been. I just want you out."

Sophie tried to remove her fingers from between Jazz's legs.

"Now, thank you," said the driver, nodding to the door. "You're on a main road and there are street lamps. I'm not leaving you in the lurch and as I said this isn't homophobic so don't start filming anything on your mobile phones."

"Sorry," whispered Sophie, hands out of Jazz's pants, trying to edge her towards the door. "We were just…"

"I know what you were doing, but you took it too far."

"Sorry," said Jazz, trying to open the door and step out without making it obvious her jeans were halfway down her legs.

"Here, have my bag," said Sophie trying to cover Jazz's modesty.

Both women bowed their heads as the cab pulled sharply away. "What if he has CCTV," whispered Jazz. "I'm going back into acting. Footage like that can't get out."

"Oh, don't you start," laughed Sophie.

"I'm serious; that was my last night at Montel's and I'm winding down my other gigs as well."

"Well, if you're planning on being a hooker you've made a good start."

"You're not funny, Sophie."

"The audience thought I was."

Jazz quickly did up her jeans. "We're between both our houses, aren't we? Shall we walk our separate ways?"

"No way! You're coming back to mine. You're meeting my parents. We're doing this properly, Jazz."

"Are we?"

"Yes! I was serious about everything! This is the start of our future."

"Lots of sex?"

"Lots of proud sex and public displays of affection. Now link my arm and walk me home like a gentleman."

"Like a woman. I see your gendering still needs work."

Sophie smiled. "I need work. My pussy needs work. I want you to work my pussy so hard."

Jazz upped their pace. "I've missed your body. Will your parents let us go straight up to bed?"

"I'd be surprised if they even realise I'm home."

****

"And here we all are," said Sophie's mother to the now seated group around the dining room table. "Who's for some fish-rice?"

"It's gone midnight, Agnes," said Sophie's father.

"Tighten your dressing gown, Robert; we have guests."

"Mum, honestly, it's fine," said Sophie. "We didn't even want to sit down."

"Nonsense. We can't have your friend here thinking we're not hospitable."

"Mum, she's called Jazz, and she's my girlfriend."

"Yes, you did say. Right, fish-rice, Robert?"

"Agnes, sit down."

"I'm fine," said Agnes. "Will someone please just have some of my fish-rice?"

Jazz lifted her plate. "Lovely, what is it?"

"Fish and rice," said Agnes, thumping a huge dollop onto Jazz's plate.

"Careful," said Sophie.

Agnes clutched the bowl into her chest, her bottom lip beginning to quiver. "I just don't know what's happening anymore. First you tell me you were involved with that fire, then you bring home a girlfriend."

"Put the fish-rice down," said Robert.

Agnes remained standing. She didn't let go of the bowl. "It's our bell ringing night tonight. We're always up late on our bell ringing night. It's in the family calendar app."

"I didn't check."

"No, you didn't and now I'm facing this latest bombshell in my dressing gown."

Sophie smiled. "There's nothing to face, Mum. I've been out with my girlfriend and I've brought her back for the night. That's okay, isn't it?"

"That's fine, Sophie," said her father.

"Is it, Robert?" said Agnes, finally setting the bowl down in the centre of the table. "Are we just going to bury our heads in the sand like we've done for the past five years?"

Jazz swallowed a forkful of food. "Must run in the family."

Sophie nodded. "Jazz is a stand-up comedian."

"Retired stand-up comedian. I've decided to go back into acting."

"Oh, tell us a joke," said Robert happily.

Jazz cleared her throat. "So, there's an elderly couple in church and the wife leans over and whispers to her husband: I just let out a long, silent fart. What should I do? And the husband replies: First off, replace the batteries in your hearing aid."

Robert laughed uproariously.

"Robert! Will you please tighten your dressing gown!"

"Only if you sit down and smile. This is nice. I'm enjoying myself."

"I'm not," said Jazz.

Robert laughed again.

Agnes turned to her daughter. "What else have you been hiding from us, Sophie?"

Sophie shrugged. "The fact that I've felt all alone. The fact that I hate not having a proper relationship with you both."

"But you've been so distant."

"So have you, Mum."

Robert got up and guided his wife into her seat. "Your mother and I were just thrown by your change in behaviour. We felt it was a change for the better and we haven't wanted to rock the boat."

Agnes stood back up. "And here you are immediately rocking the boat again."

"Mum, I'm introducing you to my girlfriend, that's all."

"Well, you should have built up to it. I could have done us a nice Sunday lunch or something."

"The fish-rice is good," said Jazz. "Is no one else eating?"

"Is it serious between you two?" asked Agnes.

Sophie smiled. "I love her. I love her with all of my heart." She reached out and took Jazz's hand. "I've loved her from the moment I met her and I've always been hers, even when she hasn't wanted me."

"Oh Sophie, that's beautiful," said Robert.

"You're not just acting out?" asked Agnes.

"Of course not. I came clean about what I thought was my involvement in the fire because of Jazz."

Jazz moved her head from side-to-side. "Slight grey area as to whether it was me, or the fact I found out."

Robert laughed loudly. "Oh, you are funny!"

Jazz returned her fork to her plate and smiled at Sophie's parents. "I love your daughter, and I'm not just here for the pretty parts, or the fish-rice. I'm here no matter what."

"You forgive me?" said Sophie.

"I'm not sure there was anything to forgive. We've all been through enough and we all need to move on. Me. You. Your parents."

"Wise," said Robert.

Jazz nodded. "Can I stop eating this now?"

Agnes laid her napkin neatly beside her place, went around to Sophie and knelt down beside her. She reached for her daughter's hand. "I'm so sorry you couldn't talk to me, and I'm so sorry your father and I have selfishly kept our heads in the sand. It was just so much easier for us both."

"I missed you, Mum."

"And I missed your nonsense."

"Did you?"

Agnes nodded.

"Good, because there may be some sex noises coming from my bedroom tonight."

"Oh Sophie," said Agnes, playfully slapping her daughter on the leg.

Robert clapped his hands. "Tell us another joke, Jazz."

Jazz put her arm around Sophie. "Knock-knock."

"Who's there," said Sophie.

"Leena."

"Leena who?"

"Leena little closer so I can kiss you."

Robert cheered as the pair embraced.

"Robert! Do up your dressing gown!"

"Oh, isn't this lovely," he said, as the kiss continued.

Agnes coughed. "Girls. Would anyone like any more fish-rice?"

"Let's leave them be," said Robert, rising from his seat. "I think I'm in the mood for something more filling," he said with a chortle.

"Don't be getting any ideas," said Agnes, as a small smile crept over her face for the first time that evening.

"Night, girls," said Robert.

"They're not listening. They're still kissing."

"I know a joke about kissing," said Robert, leading his wife by the hand. "Kiss a geologist and feel the earthquake."

"You're an accountant, Robert."

"So account on me to give you a good time," he said, patting her bottom and chivvying her out of the room.

Sophie peeped with one eye. "Have they gone yet?"

"Keep kissing me just in case," said Jazz, "I think we turned your dad on."

"That's gross. They're gross."

Jazz dared to peep as well. "They're not gross, they're actually quite lovely. The only gross thing is that bowl of fish-rice. Seriously. What the fuck is it?"

Sophie laughed. "Fish and rice."

"Just mixed together and left to go cold?"

"That's the one."

"And you all sit around and eat this together."

"Not usually, but I have a warm feeling in my tummy that we might start."

"You haven't eaten it. The feeling won't be warm."

"You know what I mean."

"I do," said Jazz, smiling. "And I'm happy for you."

"I'm happy for us," said Sophie, "because I'm taking you upstairs."

"I'm not having a gang bang with your parents."
"No, you're having a gang bang with me."

CHAPTER TWENTY EIGHT

"We're not really going to have sex, are we?" asked Jazz, shimmying herself under the covers and snuggling up close to Sophie.

"No, we're going to make love," whispered Sophie, reaching out to turn off the bedside light.

"Does love making require total darkness?"

"Yes, and total silence." Sophie smiled as she locked her fingers between Jazz's. "Until the end, that is."

"Won't they hear us then?"

"They'll be asleep, because this is going to go on for hours." Sophie let her lips brush gently against Jazz's shoulder. "Making love is never a quick wham bam, thank you ma'am."

"You need to tell your dad that, because it sounds like they've finished already."

Sophie bit gently on the smooth shoulder. "Love making's always romantic, so if you can't say anything romantic don't say anything at all."

"What am I allowed to do?"

"Lie there and enjoy it."

"What if I want to pleasure you? Is that why you're holding my hands? To keep me locked in position?"

Sophie used her lips to shush Jazz softly. "This is pleasuring me too, so just relax... but not too much."

"You'll never let that go, will you?"

"Let's see how we get on tonight, shall we?" said Sophie, moving her lips to Jazz's ear. She whispered softly. "I'm going to tease you. And I'm going to take my time."

"But you're not using your hands, you're holding mine."

"Exactly, my lips are all we need right now." Sophie brushed them gently down Jazz's neck. "People forget how erotic kissing can be. The build up to kissing. The wait for the moment my lips press hard against yours." Sophie smiled as she saw Jazz's mouth open slightly. "You want to kiss me right now, but I'm in control. I want your neck first," she said, letting her tongue dance lightly across the velvety skin. "You want me to bite you and suck you, but I'm being gentle and sweet." She took Jazz's earlobe between her teeth.

Jazz groaned.

"See, the tenderness is turning you on. You're getting wet and I haven't even moved my fingers from yours. Imagine how you'll feel when I push them right inside you."

Jazz groaned even louder, turning her head as she tried to bring Sophie's lips into a kiss.

Sophie shifted higher in the bed, pressing her nipple deep into Jazz's mouth instead. "Kiss this," she gasped, using her weight to force Jazz's head back onto the pillow, but keeping their hands locked. She parted her own legs and thrust herself up and down Jazz's thigh.

Jazz moaned. "You're so wet. Bring your boob back here."

"I'm making love to you, Jazz," said Sophie, moving all of her weight onto her girlfriend and kissing her hard on her neck. "My wet nipple's pushing into your nipple. The nipple you just made hard. The nipple I just shoved into your mouth."

"Give me your tongue," said Jazz, desperately trying to raise her head from the pillow.

"You want that, don't you? You want me to kiss you, but I want to feel you first. My body on yours. My weight on yours. Feel this closeness and enjoy it, Jazz, because I haven't even started yet." She brought her lips back to Jazz's cheek. "We haven't even started yet," she said, kissing back down the jaw line and neck.

"I need your tongue," gasped Jazz again, trying to open her legs so Sophie's would slot in between hers.

Sophie pinned the thighs closed with her knees. "My tongue's the first thing your clit's going to feel." She brought her mouth back down to Jazz's ear. "This tongue," she said, sucking gently on the lobe before trailing down to Jazz's chin.

"Kiss me," urged Jazz.

Sophie hovered agonisingly close to Jazz's mouth before taking Jazz's bottom lip between her teeth. She tugged gently.

Jazz pulled out of Sophie's grip and threw her hand to the back of Sophie's head, yanking her hard into her mouth.

Sophie groaned as Jazz's tongue devoured her own. "You really want this," she said between deep kisses.

"I want to turn you over and fuck you."

Sophie took control of her hands once more, pinning them back to the pillow. "Slow," she said, kissing the lips more gently this time. "You're wet, and you want me, but you're waiting."

Jazz moaned, returning the kiss slowly, tenderly.

"That's it, now imagine me kissing your nipples. Exactly like this. My lips working around the outside as my tongue flicks gently over the top."

"Now," said Jazz. "Please, I need you right now."

"You have me," said Sophie. "We're making love. This is our moment."

Jazz lifted her lips back to Sophie's. "I love you, Sophie."

Sophie smiled in the darkness as she returned the kiss. "I know you do," she said happily, "but your nipples are going to love me even more." Keeping hold of Jazz's hands, she moved down Jazz's body, blowing gently across her nipples.

"Just fucking bite them, would you?"

Sophie laughed. "You're never going to change, are you?"

"It's not my fault you're so fucking hot all I want to do is bend you over and spank you as I thrust my face right into your pussy."

"Shush," said Sophie. "Romantic." She smiled as she brushed around Jazz's breasts with her cheeks, darting her tongue out ever so slightly every time she passed over her nipples.

"This is agony," said Jazz. "I'm literally dripping."

"Be romantic," continued Sophie. "I'm being romantic with your nipples. I'm blowing them little kisses. Oops, I might just have grazed my lips against them that time."

Jazz moaned. "Do it again."

Sophie used her teeth, catching the nipples ever so slightly. "They're so hard," she whispered. "They want my lips, don't they? They want me to encase them in my warm mouth. They want my teeth to bite down." Sophie moved herself onto Jazz's right thigh, making sure she kept Jazz's legs together. She spread her own legs and started to move up and down as she worked Jazz's nipples in her mouth.

Jazz cried out in pleasure.

Sophie moaned at the gratification she was giving herself. "Your nipples are hard in my mouth and it's making my clit hard. Can you feel it rubbing against your thigh?"

"Yes," gasped Jazz.

Sophie moved from breast to breast, pulling the nipples between her teeth before kissing them deeply and sucking them hard.

"Fuck, I'm so close," said Jazz.

"This is just the beginning," said Sophie, finally releasing Jazz's right hand and moving her fingers straight to Jazz's breasts. She squeezed hard.

Jazz cried out.

"You like that, don't you? My teeth drawing out one nipple while my fingers pull on the other." Sophie gasped as Jazz's free hand went to her waist. "Yes," she gasped, as she worked herself harder on Jazz's thigh. "Oh, Jazz, that's so nice."

"Let me use both hands, let me push my fingers inside you."

"No," said Sophie, slowing it down once again and taking Jazz's fingers back in her own. "Open your legs," she whispered, moving her weight to one side.

Jazz groaned. "Freedom."

"Imagine how it'll feel with my mouth down there." She kissed Jazz's stomach, lingering just below her belly button. "My tongue touching your clit."

"Please, Sophie."

Sophie moved her head between the trembling legs and blew gently.

"Yes," said Jazz. "Do that again."

Sophie blew once more, this time directing it straight at the clit before taking Jazz completely in her mouth.

Jazz's wail was guttural. "I'm coming," she gasped.

"Not yet," said Sophie, kissing the area softly.

"I am," she said. "This is amazing. I'm so close."

"We'll come together," said Sophie, working Jazz's clit with her tongue.

"I'm going to come."

"No, you're going to come with my fingers inside you, your fingers inside me, my tongue in your mouth and my breasts pushed hard against yours."

"Get here then," gasped Jazz, hauling Sophie back up the bed and kissing her hard as she freed their hands and parted their legs.

Sophie pushed her fingers deep inside Jazz, her palm still working her clit.

Jazz did the same, using her other hand to force their bodies even closer. "I'm coming," she cried.

"And I'm coming too," said Sophie, pressing their mouths back together.

"I love you," wailed Jazz through the embrace as her body began to shudder. "I love you, I love you, I love you!"

Sophie held on tight as her own orgasm erupted. "Again! Say it again!"

Jazz gasped. "This is our beginning, Sophie, this moment right here."

Sophie screamed out in pleasure. "It's the end of our start," she managed, locked tight into Jazz, "and the start of our end."

"What?" groaned Jazz, laughing. "I've just come. Explosively. I'm in no fit shape to decipher what that means."

"No need, just feel it."

Jazz smiled. "I feel it."

CHAPTER TWENTY NINE

Holding hands as they entered the health club, both Jazz and Sophie smiled at the odd glances that came their way. Sophie was used to it now, having adopted Jazz's advice on the subject: always lift your head higher and smile. Never look away. Never look down. Just smile at the person in question and if the person drops their gaze then smile at yourself because they clearly want a slice of the action having stared, then despaired.

The elderly woman in brightly-coloured gym gear and headband smiled even wider at Sophie. Jazz had also noted that people who continue to smile too enthusiastically want a piece of the action as well, so you should tone down your smile to ensure it's not misinterpreted. Sophie lowered her eyes slightly. The old woman winked.

"She's a cracker, isn't she?" said Jazz, pausing in the plush entrance.

"Rock on the lezzas!" said the wobbly voice, as the old woman made the victory sign.

Jazz laughed. "Are you...?"

"Jealous!" came the reply.

Sophie ushered Jazz towards the waiting area beside the reception desk. "Stop it; this place is posh."

"She started it. Look at her go. She's got a right little wiggle in her step."

"Seriously, Jazz, it's members only."

"So what are we doing here?"

"You said you'd be on your best behaviour. Now sit down."

"Oooh, deep sofas." Jazz pulled Sophie into a cuddle. "Sorry. I'm just excited. This is the last piece of the puzzle. Meeting your friends."

"About that."

"No." Jazz released her grip. "You're not changing your mind again. We've spent the past three weeks breaking every boundary that needed to be broken. Both sets of parents love us. Both sets of parents love each other." She smiled. "We've even learnt how to make love."

"Pushing it."

"Hey! You said I was getting better! I only asked you to spank me like a dusty rug once last night."

"Shush, would you! And I'm talking about our parents."

"What? They can't get enough of each other. Didn't you hear my mum asking your mum for her fish-rice recipe."

"She did not!"

"She did. Your mum said it was fish and rice."

"Oh, Jazz, listen."

"What? We're not turning around. This place looks gorgeous. Is that a Michelin star restaurant through there? You must have some pretty exclusive friends."

"That's just it," Sophie shrugged, "I don't."

"It's a members only health club. You do."

"We're meeting Tessa and John. They're the members."

Jazz laughed.

"No, seriously we are."

"Why?"

"They're my only real friends."

"They're your colleagues."

"Who I go out with on a monthly basis."

"You go out with other people too."

"Not really. Laura drags me to the odd party, but I don't have any real friends of my own."

Wrapping her arms around her girlfriend, Jazz sighed. "Oh, Sophie."

"I know, this makes me sound like a right saddo and I did try and arrange that coffee last week with some of the old girls from school, but it felt wrong, so I cancelled. They wouldn't have been able to tell you anything about me because they don't really know me."

"And Tessa and John do?"

"They know who I've been for the past five years. Hard working. Good with the students. Good with the students' parents."

"But there's so much more to you, Sophie."

"There isn't. Or there hasn't been. Honestly, Jazz, I've kept myself to myself."

"And now?"

"And now I'm rebuilding with the people who matter."

"So we sit in a sauna with Tessa and John, and then what?"

Sophie laughed. "I think it's quite cool to have friends who invite us to places like this."

"We're going to get jiggy with them in the Jacuzzi, aren't we?"

"That says more about your attitude to your friends than anything Tessa and John might try."

Jazz laughed. "They might try something? What? Stroke us up in the steam room? Make a pass in the pool?"

"It's not that sort of club, Jazz."

"Damn."

Sophie squeezed her girlfriend's hand. "Seriously though, you're okay with it?"

"That the love of my life is a billy-no-mates?"

"I guess."

"I'm joking! I've always liked Tessa and John and I actually envy the fact that you can start afresh with your friendship groups. I'm constantly being invited to all sorts of stuff and I never know if I'm just there to make up the numbers or because people genuinely value me."

"Your friends are lovely."

"Which ones? Who exactly?"

"All of them. That gang from the club the other night and the first set of girls we met at that comedy thing."

"See?"

"What?"

"I don't have any particular group of go-to girls. I socialise with so many people and it's fab and it's fun, but sometimes I question if any of it's real."

"Of course it's real."

"But do those friendships add value?"

"Like you said, they're fun."

"Maybe I'm ready for something more than just fun."

"You want to be stroked up in the sauna, don't you?"

Jazz laughed. "I just want you to know that we're not that different."

"Oh, bless you." Sophie smiled as she dropped her head onto Jazz's shoulder. "You always have a way of making me feel better about myself."

"It's my job. I'm your girlfriend."

"And I'm your girlfriend too."

"So tilt your head up and kiss me."

Sophie straightened in her seat. "We're in a posh members only health club."

"I thought you'd learnt this too? Kiss wherever you want, whenever you want."

"Your pussy?"

"Stop deflecting."

"I don't want to make other people uncomfortable."

"Is it that? Or is it because you're uncomfortable?"

Sophie glanced around the area. There were a couple of people helping themselves to coffee and cakes from the complimentary refreshments stand, one man reading a newspaper and an elderly couple who looked as if they were asleep on the high-backed chairs near the floor-to-ceiling window. "I guess I'm not used to drawing attention."

"Says you flirting up a storm with that old bird on the way in here." Jazz smiled. "Seriously though, I understand this too, but you're at the beginning of a new life, Sophie. You can be whoever you want to be."

"I want to be brave."

"So kiss me."

Sophie didn't hesitate this time; she took Jazz's face in her hands and drew her in for a gentle kiss."

"See," said Jazz with a smile. "There's nothing more beautiful."

Sophie laughed. "Your pussy?"

"I can show it to you in the showers if you like?"

"Tessa and John have to sign us in."

Jazz feigned shocked concern. "Oh no. What if they've decided they don't want to be our friends? What if they've had second thoughts?"

Sophie shook her head. "They've been trying to get me here for years but the idea of seeing them both in the showers never appealed."

"And what's changed?"

"You can't have it both ways. Either you're making me brave or you're not."

Jazz grimaced. "We're not really going to see them in the showers, are we?"

Sophie laughed. "Of course not."

****

Jazz shuddered from her position next to Sophie in the warm Jacuzzi. "I can see them in the showers!"

"You don't have to look," said Sophie.

"How can I not? Tessa's using her breast ledge to keep the button for the water pressed in."

"No, she's not!"

"She is! Look! And John looks like a sperm! Why's he wearing a white swimming cap?"

"Stop it."

"Look! He's got a big round body and skinny little legs," Jazz laughed, "and a really tight swimming cap."

"Don't be mean."

"I'm not, but would you please just have a look?"

Sophie twisted around and followed Jazz's gaze before gasping. "Wowzers."

"Right?! That's why I hurried us in. Tessa's strip tease in the changing room was getting too much."

"So you didn't want to steal a moment with me in the bubbles all by yourself?"

Jazz nodded at the group of suave looking men emerging from the sauna. "That's never going to happen in a posh place like this. We should have gone to Waterworld. All sorts of shenanigans go on in that lazy river."

"You're right. This place is all businessmen and retirees."

"Stop gendering."

"Well, have you seen any business women?"

"Yes, there's one in the shower right now, pressing the knob with her tits."

"Tessa's not a business woman."

"She is, and so are you."

"I like it when you get all fierce about equal ops, but I'm not a business woman, Jazz, and I'm only here because of the free invite."

Jazz found Sophie's hand under the water and lifted it out of the bubbles. "In life we manifest what we believe, what we think; and so many women have this horrible habit of putting themselves down. Whatever you focus on, Sophie, it grows." Jazz paused. "What are you doing?"

"Focusing on your boobs."

"They're not big enough for you?" asked Jazz, playfully releasing Sophie's hand as she covered her own cleavage with a splash of water. "You've always liked my ample bust."

"Your bust is nothing, I repeat, nothing, compared with what's about to enter this Jacuzzi." Sophie lowered her voice. "Could you imagine getting a tit slap from one of those."

Jazz looked at Tessa and John who were walking their way. "That's my mission: by the end of the day I want to have been on the receiving end of a tit slap from one of Tessa's boobs."

"You always said my tit slaps were more than enough."

"Oh, Sophie, there's a tit slap and there's a TIT SLAP."

"Shush!" Sophie stood up, welcoming her colleagues into the bubbling pool. "Thank you so much for inviting us. This is lovely. I love your costume, Tessa."

Tessa edged her way down into the water "I like these costumes. The ones with the skirts. They're wonderful aren't they, John? They cover a multitude of sins."

"How many times, Tessa? I'm happy in my trunks."

Tessa laughed. "Oh, you are funny, John."

"And you're wonderfully beautiful, Tessa, multitude of sins or not."

Jazz laughed as she shifted around to make space. "John! You can't say that to your lady."

"It's fine, Jasmine. He was giving me a compliment, weren't you, John?"

"Of course I was. You look wonderful, my dear."

All eyes turned to Tessa, now seated in the Jacuzzi, struggling to see over the top of her floating bosom. "Should I turn the bubbles down a bit?" asked Sophie.

"Oh no, we like the tickling jets, don't we, John?"

"That we do, Tessa." John lowered his voice. "We spend most of our time in here getting tickled by the jets, don't we, Tessa?"

"That we do, John."

Jazz reached out and notched up the pressure before arching her back and lifting her bottom slightly. "Oooh, I see what you mean. I've got it firing right between my legs."

"Bad backs," said John. "It helps."

"Oh," said Jazz, sliding back into her original position.

Tessa giggled. "I'll admit I like to partake in that sometimes, Jasmine. This membership costs a fortune and it's always good to get your money's worth."

Jazz whooped. "Yes! I knew it! You're a devil, aren't you, Tessa?"

"That she is," said John.

"I'm so happy for you." Jazz was smiling.

"Me too," said Sophie, not wanting to get left behind as she had in every other interaction between Jazz and her colleagues. Moving slightly to the left, she felt the jet blast hit her back. "Oooh, I've got one."

"Let me notch it up again," said Jazz.

Sophie giggled before lifting her bottom. "Stop!" she gasped.

"What?" said Jazz, laughing.

Sophie went pale.

"Are you okay?" asked Jazz.

Sophie lowered her voice and angled herself away from her colleagues. "It shot right up there!"

"What did?" said Jazz. "Where?"

Sophie hissed. "The water."

"Just relax, it'll come out."

"No! Up my bottom!"

John spoke up. "Share with the group, ladies. Tessa's already shared more than I was expecting this morning."

Tessa tried to push down on her floating bosom. "Are you talking about my breasts, John?"

"Dear me, no, Tessa. I'm just asking the girls to share their secrets."

Sophie hissed to Jazz. "I can't share this. The pool will go brown."

Jazz laughed. "It will not."

"That jet just blasted right up my backside! Like an anal enema! Trust me, I'm not unclenching."

"So go to the toilet."

"I will," said Sophie, rapidly getting up and climbing the steps with her knees clasped firmly together.

"Is Sophie okay?" asked Tessa, concerned.

The group of three watched as Sophie waddled towards the changing rooms. "She took a jet blast up the arse," said Jazz matter of factly.

"Well for goodness sake, why didn't she tell us? She's always keeping things to herself, isn't she, John?"

"That she is, Tessa, but I'm glad she kept that to herself. Or else... you know..."

Jazz laughed. "That's exactly what Sophie said. You guys have much more in common than she thinks."

"We never quite know where we are with Sophie, do we, John?"

"No, we don't, Tessa, but we hope things will change now she's not holding on to that nasty old secret anymore."

"She's sure holding on to something," said Tessa, nodding at Sophie who was now clasping her bottom with one hand as she pushed open the changing room door with the other.

"She's just been a bit lost," said Jazz. "It'll take her a while to find her feet."

"You're good for her, Jasmine," said Tessa. "Isn't she good for her, John?"

"That she is, Tessa," said John. "And thank you for encouraging her to come here today. We really appreciate it."

Jazz shook her head. "Nope, that was all Sophie. She really does value you both as colleagues and friends."

"And you think she'll stay at the studio?"

"I do. She's been offered slots with touring music groups but those opportunities have been coming in for the past five years, ever since she refused the symphony orchestra place and she's never looked at them before."

"But wasn't that because she was hiding from public attention?" asked Tessa, her eyes anxious.

Jazz leaned towards them and whispered. "Why don't you change the plaque outside the studio."

Tessa giggled. "What a good idea! We've wanted to do it before, haven't we, John? But Sophie's always said no. Let's do it as a surprise."

Jazz smiled. "You should. It'll mean a lot to her. Shush, she's coming back."

"What are you three whispering about?" asked Sophie, now with slightly more colour in her cheeks.

"Oh, just the anal enema you gave yourself from that jet."

Sophie gasped. "Jazz!"

"What? Tessa and John want you to share more with them."

"Really? You want to hear how I arched my bottom up and the jet blasted all the way in there?"

John wiggled in his seat. "Oh, Sophie, you're making me feel all tingly. Is it making you feel tingly too, Tessa?"

"No, John, it's not. I think you should go for a cold shower."

"Oh, Tessa, you are a tease. She's such a tease is my Tessa." John smiled. "Isn't this wonderful. Four friends having fun."

"With jets blasting up Sophie's bum," sang Jazz.

Sophie couldn't help but smile. "This is ridiculous." She smiled again. "In a good way, I mean." Settling back into her seat, she swirled the bubbly water with her fingers. "Now seems like a good time to thank you all for the way you've been there for me. You've supported me and you've made me believe that just being me is enough."

Jazz reached out to cuddle her girlfriend. "Oh, Sophie, you're so sweet. Isn't she so sweet, Tessa and John?"

"That she is, Jasmine. That she is."

Sophie smiled. "We've all got our happy endings."

Tessa cleared her throat. "I'm not a hundred percent there."

John spoke up. "Tessa, we've debated the moral side of the conundrum, we've—"

"My bosom, John."

"Pardon me, Tessa."

"I'm not happy with my bosom. Look, I can barely see the three of you." Tessa tried to press her breasts down under the water but they immediately pinged back up. "I have a buoyant bosom."

Jazz laughed. "I'd love a buoyant bosom. I'd fire things at people. I'd pull them down, put something on top and release."

"Jazz! You can't say that," said Sophie, with a gasp.

"It's all very well," said Tessa, "but you try doing the breaststroke."

"I think they already have," chuckled John.

"Oh, I like that one, John. That was a funny one."

Sophie smiled at the trio. "Happiness was here all along, wasn't it?"

"What was that, dear?" asked Tessa, over the top of her floating bosom.

"It's fine," said Jazz. "She gets like this sometimes. Profound in the most awkward of moments. The other night we'd just had really hot se—"

"I'm happy," interrupted Sophie. "That's all I'm saying. For the first time in a very long time I'm genuinely happy."

"Oh come here, dear," said Tessa, pushing herself off her Jacuzzi seat only to plunge into the deeper middle section. Momentarily she submerged but shot back up spluttering. "It's okay!" she yelped, over her buoyancy aids. "They've got me!"

Sophie didn't know what to do to help. Tessa was clearly trying to make her way across for a hug, but all you could see was her floating bosom. "Shall I give you a hand?"

"That's my job," said John, pushing himself off and plunging straight under the water next to Tessa.

Jazz laughed. "Let's get out and leave them to it."

"Oh, I love this," said Sophie, laughing at the scene.

"And we love you more," said Jazz, pulling her girlfriend in for a cuddle before plunging them both into the bubbling melee.

CHAPTER THIRTY

Knocking on the door to Laura's house, Sophie giggled again. "I cannot believe you got the tit slap."

"I got THE tit slap," said Jazz with a satisfied nod.

Sophie knocked louder. "I feel bad that we laughed at them in the showers at the start."

"We weren't laughing at them, we were laughing with them. Tessa's fully aware of her breast ledge. It just floated there all afternoon, her own personal buoyancy aid."

"Did you really have to try and sink it?"

"How else was I meant to get a tit slap? Anyway, she started it by saying she couldn't get them underwater."

"She couldn't!"

"That's why I dunked them, or tried to, until I went face first into them, getting the tit slap of all tit slaps."

"You're so naughty."

"I'm not. I was doing her a favour."

Sophie turned to her girlfriend. "You really think they like me?"

"They love you, Sophie, and this is the last piece of closure you need."

"I don't need this closure."

"You didn't think you needed friends and look at the fun we've just had."

Sophie smiled. "Are you right about everything?"

Jazz nodded. "Mostly. I trust my gut and my gut says they're good people. My gut also says you're a good person and you need to accept that Laura's not that great."

"I'm not dumping her. She's the only friend I've had for the past five years."

"And how good's she been to you?"

"Please don't cause any trouble, Jazz."

"I won't. But we need to draw a line under all of this."

Sophie knocked one final time. "Strange. Laura's car's on the drive, so's her mum's."

Jazz jumped over one flower bed and leaned over another, craning her neck at the lounge window. "They're in here," she said, tapping her fingers on the glass and waving.

"What are they doing?"

"Hunched over a laptop with headphones on. They're coming now."

****

Holding Jazz's hand on the sofa in Laura's life coaching room, Sophie nodded at both Laura, who was sitting uncomfortably in her armchair, and Maureen, who was standing uncomfortably by the French windows. "I just want to make it clear that I forgive you both."

Laura huffed. "You're the criminal."

Jazz spoke immediately. "She's not, actually. The police say Tommy Gutteridge has admitted he accidentally started the fire and Rebecca Lynch has been reprimanded for not reporting it."

Maureen tutted. "Reprimanded? So now she's dedicated her life to the Africans she's a saint?"

Jazz continued. "There's no legal requirement to report a crime."

"She was there. She had a moral duty to call the fire brigade."

Laura huffed again. "Just like Sophie had a moral duty to say she was there too."

"I wasn't there." Sophie shook her head. "Not when it started. And anyway, you two were the ones telling me to stay quiet when I wanted to speak up. Why are you so angry with me now?"

Jazz squeezed Sophie's hand. "Because you've called them out on their behaviour."

"Listen, Jazz," snapped Laura. "I was doing Sophie a favour when I came to find you in the club. It's because of me that you two are back together and everything's now out in the open."

Maureen cleared her throat. "I think I'm the saviour here. I put it all together."

"You had a wild stab in the dark, Mother, and somehow you hit the jackpot."

"This is what I'm talking about," said Sophie. "I forgive you both for this. This is my life and I've been struggling with it all for so long now. I just want you to know that I don't think it's particularly cool how you handled it and treated me."

"Wait. You don't get to play the victim, Sophie." Laura propelled herself forward in her armchair. "You chose not to talk about any of this. You can't blame us for not being there for you."

"I'm just asking for a fresh start."

"You're not," said Jazz. "You're telling them you need closure."

Sophie shrugged. "I have closure."

"Lovely," said Maureen. "That's all sorted then. Shall I get us some jam tarts? Or do you fancy a bit of malt loaf?"

"Oooh, a cup of tea as well please, Mum. I want to tell Sophie all about my next venture."

"Jazz? Tea, coffee, juice?"

Jazz stood up, shaking her head. "Thanks, but I've got rehearsals to get to."

"That's not for another hour," said Sophie.

"It's fine, I'll go early."

Laura rose from her armchair, engulfing Jazz in a huge hug. "Lovely of you to pop round." She tapped Jazz on the bottom. "And I'll always know Sophie better than you do."

Jazz looked down at her girlfriend still seated on the sofa. "You might just be right."

"Oh, Jazz, I was never coming to rehearsals," said Sophie, looking over her shoulder. "You never let me. And I've done well to stand my ground here today, and it'll actually be nice to get everything back to normal with Laura with us just waffling on about all sorts instead of everything being so heavy like it has been recently."

"Sure," said Jazz, shrugging her shoulders.

Laura patted Jazz's bottom once more. "See you soon."

Sophie jumped up. "Hands off the merchandise, she's mine." Whispering into Jazz's ear, she smiled. "Thank you. I did my best, and I love you."

"You should love yourself a little bit more," replied Jazz.

"I'll talk to you later," said Sophie, more loudly this time.

Maureen re-entered the room with a sandwich bag. "Here's a jam tart for your travels."

"She's only driving to the theatre, Mum." Laura smiled at Jazz. "It's fine. I'll drop Sophie back home."

****

"You didn't notice, did you?!" whispered Laura, conspiratorially on the sofa seat next to Sophie.

"Why aren't you in your armchair?" asked Sophie, shifting away slightly.

Laura edged herself closer. "Because I'm no longer a life coach."

"What are you now? A limpet?" said Sophie, standing up.

"I'm a private detective!" wailed Laura. "You didn't see me plant that tracker in Jazz's back pocket, did you?!"

Sophie stared down at her friend. "What?"

"A GPS tracker. eBay. Five pounds. Size of a thumbnail. We planted one in Dad's briefcase this morning. We've been tracking him on the laptop all day."

Maureen nodded. "And we're testing out a new listening device."

"eBay," said Laura again. "Twelve pounds. You can call it from 50 feet away and hear everything that's being said."

Maureen sat down in the armchair. "The woman from the corner shop's been fiddling the system."

"What are you talking about?" asked Sophie, her eyebrows knitting in utter confusion.

Maureen pointed in the general direction of outside. "Debbie from the corner shop. I went in to buy some malt loaf last week. Ninety-five pence. I gave her a pound. She apologised and said she didn't have any change. I said not to worry about it, but five pence is five pence and if she's doing that to every customer then she's making a tidy little sum every day."

Laura nodded. "So I went back in a couple of days ago and bought another malt loaf. Still ninety-five pence and, guess what, no change."

Sophie groaned. "So you decided to become a spy?"

Laura bounced in her seat. "I've had enough of life coaching. It's all so dreary having to listen to other people's problems and pretend you care."

"So now you listen to Debbie from the corner shop short-changing her customers?"

"She is! We had our headphones on before you arrived. Anyone who pays in cash and is owed less than ten pence change gets nothing."

"You stuck a listening device in the corner shop?"

"Yes, and a tracking device in your girlfriend's back pocket."

"Jazz isn't doing anything wrong."

"I know, I just wanted to test out my sleight-of-hand skills. There's a private investigator course starting next week. I found it on Groupon. I want to practise a bit before it begins."

Maureen stood up. "Let me go and get the laptop and show you," she said, patting her daughter's shoulder as she passed. "I'm so proud of Laura's initiative. We'll have to paint this room black though, this light-green's too life-coachy."

Sophie shook her head as Maureen left the room. "I can't believe I used to be jealous of the relationship you had with your mum. Jazz was right about everything."

"I knew she put you up to this!" said Laura. "Coming around here and standing up for yourself. That's not you. And it's not like the relationship you've got with your mum's anything to shout about."

"We're good now."

"Really?"

"We're getting better, and I've got Jazz to thank for that as well. She's made me realise what's important in life."

"And I'm not important?"

"Maybe your nonsense isn't?"

"Oh dear," said Maureen, re-entering the room with the laptop balanced on her arm. "She's not gone where she said she was going."

"Who?" said Laura. "Jazz?"

Maureen nodded as she placed the laptop on the coffee table. "She's gone home."

"For goodness sake, I'm going home too," said Sophie.

"But she said she was going to the theatre," said Laura. "She lied to you."

"Don't be ridiculous. Her rehearsal doesn't start for almost an hour. We were going to come here and then pop for a coffee or something."

"But she hasn't gone for a coffee," said Laura, studying the tracking report. "She went to… Baker Street for five minutes and then home. What's on Baker Street?" Opening Google, she typed quickly. "Wait, I can tell you."

Maureen nodded and smiled at her daughter. "I told you she was good."

"It's just houses." Laura looked up at Sophie. "Who does Jazz know on Baker Street?"

"How should I know?"

"Call her."

"No!"

"If you trusted her you'd call her."

Sophie laughed. "It doesn't work like that."

"And what does it work like?" asked Laura. "Jazz controlling where you go and who you see but you not knowing what she's up to?"

"She's at rehearsals. She goes at this time every week."

"And you've never been?"

"No! She's done it since I met her."

Laura frowned. "I thought she was rehearsing for her theatre comeback. I thought this acting thing was new. The theatre's only just been rebuilt."

"I don't know; she does some sort of stage presence practise or something."

"Where?"

"Tonight? At the theatre."

"But where was it before the theatre was open again for rehearsals?"

"I don't know. There are lots of rehearsals going on at lots of different places and at lots of different times."

"But this one you've never been to?"

"I've never been to any, just like she hasn't sat in on Billy Baxter playing the *Eye of the Tiger* for me on a Wednesday afternoon."

Laura exhaled heavily. "She's been pushing you towards Tessa and John. I didn't want to make a big deal out of it because I didn't want to seem jealous, but it's an issue."

"Why?"

"Good question. Aren't you questioning why? Aren't you questioning why she's trying to cause an issue between us?"

"What are you talking about, Laura?" Sophie looked perplexed.

"She's a controller. I knew it from the very first time I met her."

"You don't know anything about her."

"Nor do you by the looks of it. You think she's at the theatre but she's not." Laura tapped the laptop screen.

"She's gone home first, so what?"

"So she lied."

"No, she didn't!"

"Call her then."

Sophie pulled her mobile phone from her back pocket. "Fine," she said, clicking on Jazz's number. "But then I'm having closure from all of this nonsense." She continued to speak as the phone rang. "I'm happy. I want you to be happy for me too."

"There are always bumps in the road," said Laura sternly.

"I've had my bump," said Sophie. "Jazz and I have got over our issues." The ringing continued. "Some people do get their happy ever after, Laura. There doesn't always need to be a curve ball thrown in at the end." She stopped. "It's her answer phone."

"Text her then," said Laura.

Sophie flicked to the messaging app. "There," she said. "I've asked if she has time for a quick coffee."

The message tone pinged back almost instantly.

"And?" asked Laura.

Sophie coughed. "She says she's at the theatre."

"Oh dear," said Maureen, starting to pace in front of the windows. "Oh dear, oh dear, oh dear."

"She's probably just cross at me for not leaving with her."

Laura gasped. "Is that what she told you to do? See. Controlling."

Sophie typed again.

"What are you asking?" said Laura.

"If I can come and watch."

The message tone pinged.

"And?"

Sophie coughed again. "She's said no."

"What's she doing at home and who's she doing it with?" Laura snapped.

"Someone she picked up on Baker Street," said Maureen.

Sophie turned to leave. "You two are ridiculous."

"We were right about Debbie."

Sophie gasped. "Debbie's pinching a pound a day at most! What do you think Jazz is doing? Having a weekly rendezvous in the house she shares with her parents?"

Laura paused. "Didn't you say her mum and dad spend Tuesday evenings at salsa?"

"How can you remember that when you can't even remember simple common sense?" asked Sophie.

Maureen sighed. "Often in life the most logical explanations are the correct explanations."

"And what's the logical explanation here, Maureen?" said Sophie.

"All we know right now is that Jazz lied."

CHAPTER THIRTY ONE

Crouched on the backseat of Maureen's car with Laura half hidden under a blanket next to her, Sophie felt stupid. How had they talked her into this? Maybe Laura's shenanigans in the past had seemed quite exciting because she was leading such a dull life herself, but now she had Jazz and both their parents and Tessa and John and she didn't need any of this nonsense. "I'm not comfortable with this," she said.

"You said the same things when I was training to be a life model, yet you had no problem sneaking into all of those other life modelling classes so we could see what sort of poses they did." Laura suddenly put a huge pair of binoculars to her eyes and stared straight at Sophie. "I see it now! A sign of your sexuality! You loved looking at those women! Why didn't I notice it before?"

"Put those down, would you?" said Sophie, pushing the binoculars away.

Laura turned the lenses out the window and onto the driveway ahead of them. "Explain why her car's here."

"She sometimes walks to rehearsals."

"I thought you said you didn't know where they were."

"Some are at the theatre, some are at a youth group, others are at bars. She's back into her acting in a big way."

"That all sounds very sketchy to me."

Sophie shook her head. "You always see what you want to see, Laura."

Laura ignored her. "Mum, what's the tracker saying."

"She's still in her house."

"How do you explain that?" said Laura. "Her rehearsal should have started ages ago. Mum, you're going to have to pretend you're delivering an Avon catalogue or something and post a listening device through the letter box." She whipped the blanket from her knees. "Here, wrap this around your head."

"I'll look like a homeless woman. Someone will call the police. You do it, Laura, you're the spy."

"No one's doing it," said Sophie. "But it's fascinating to see how far you'll go."

Laura nodded. "A private detective has to be all in."

"I was being sarcastic! Hasn't it occurred to either of you that Jazz simply nipped home and got changed before walking to rehearsals?"

Maureen turned around to face her daughter in the back of the car. Laura started to say something but stopped.

"Exactly," continued Sophie. "That tracker will be in the back of her jeans pocket on the chair in the corner of her bedroom where she flings her clothes and I'm going to get it back before you two can do any more damage. Honestly, if she finds out about this she'll never let me see you again."

"Controlling," said Laura under her breath.

"Is that honestly all you've got to say for yourself? You've tried to put doubt in my mind and I don't want any part in it. Jazz is a good person. She makes me happy and I want you to be happy for me too." Sophie addressed Maureen. "And I know you're only being supportive of Laura and I get that but I want to move on with my life now. I have a job that I actually love and a person who's stuck by me. Jazz and I have overcome a huge obstacle together. If we can get through what we've got through then there's absolutely nothing that can stop us."

Maureen turned back to the steering wheel. "I'll start the engine just in case."

"Just in case of what? I'm going in, I'm getting the tracker back and I'm sending you both on your way."

Maureen looked in the rear-view mirror and spoke to her daughter. "Make sure the back door's unlocked in case of a quick getaway."

"A quick get-away?! What do you think's going to happen? I'm going to burst in there and catch her in the act with the mysterious person from Baker Street?"

Laura shrugged. "What do you know about her exes?"

Sophie was now the person who couldn't reply.

"Exactly," continued Laura.

"I'm calling her again."

"You've already tried twice; she's not answering."

"Because she's in rehearsals!"

"Is she?" asked Laura. "Or is she in that house shagging Mr and Mrs Baker Street?"

Sophie laughed. "Oh, so there are two of them now? This is beyond stupid. I'll be back in a minute."

"Don't damage the tracker," said Laura. "Five pounds from eBay."

Sophie slammed the car door. She didn't feel comfortable with any of this, but the idea of Jazz finding out that Laura and Maureen had tried to spy on her was worse than getting caught creeping into her house for all of two seconds. She'd seen Jazz do it loads of times before: grab the key from under the pot next to the door instead of fishing around in whatever bag she'd been carrying for her own. Sophie nodded to herself as she lifted the pot. They'd also spoken about getting keys cut for each other, again so that after nights out it would be easier to find the key for whichever house they were staying at. Slotting the key into the lock, Sophie inhaled. They'd even spoken about the possibility of moving in together, so this really wasn't that bad at all. Was it? She shouted loudly. "Jazz? Are you home?"

Laughing nervously to herself when there was no reply, Sophie dashed up the stairs two steps at a time before freezing in terror.

"You've made me so wet," screamed the voice. "I love being your little slut! How hard do you want to hit me?" The paddle sounded loudly. "That's it!" It was Jazz's voice. "Harder! I want it harder." The paddle sounded again.

Clinging onto the bannister, Sophie couldn't breathe. All she could hear were the clinking noises from the chains that had started to rattle in Jazz's bedroom.

"You're going to tie me up and you're going to fuck the life out of me!"

"AND YOU'RE GOING TO HELL, YOU ABSOLUTE ARSEHOLE," screamed Sophie, before dashing back down the stairs and slamming the door so hard it bounced open again. "Go!" she shouted to Laura and Maureen as she stumbled out onto the street, towards the car. "Just go!"

"Sophie!" shouted Jazz, from a now open upstairs window. "Sophie wait!"

Sophie dived through the open car door straight across Laura's lap as Maureen sped off with the blanket wrapped around her face like a head shawl. "Go!" she shouted again.

"I am!" said Maureen. "But I can't see much with this blanket all over me. Let me pull in for a second."

Sophie banged against the back of the driver's seat before hitting the floor in the footwell. "Help me up," she said to Laura.

"I can't!" gasped Laura. "I need to shut the door! Oh no!" she shouted, peering through her huge binoculars. "She's coming! Jazz is coming!"

"She was coming!" said Sophie trying to right herself, unsuccessfully. "Coming with somebody else!"

"And we're off again," said Maureen, now able to see.

Sophie was flung back out of the footwell, then again onto her knees. "She was with somebody else! She was having sex! They were paddling her! She was loving it!"

"I'm so sorry, Sophie," said Laura, before thumping the back of the passenger headrest with the palm of her hand. "But goddamn it, I'm good at my job!"

"I'm proud of you, Laura," said Maureen, now settling into a more stable driving rhythm. "How much will you charge people for your services?"

Laura sucked on her bottom lip. "I'll give Sophie this one for free, but I think the going rate's around twenty-five quid an hour for things like honey-trapping and surveillance."

"You'll need some more black clothes," said Maureen. "Some of your black jeans and tops have become a bit faded in the wash. What's that washing powder that keeps blacks black?"

"I think it's Ariel."

Maureen indicated left. "Actually, I think it's more about the temperature you wash your black clothes on. Sophie, what washing tabs does your mum use for your black clothes?"

"She's still in the footwell," laughed Laura.

"Don't worry about Jazz, dear, we've left her for dust."

"She's crying. Why are you crying, Sophie? Get up here, would you?"

Sophie stayed where she was, sobbing loudly in the foetal position.

"Have you hurt yourself?" asked Laura.

"My heart!" shouted Sophie, through the tears. "My heart's hurting!"

"Phew, as long as you've not broken anything." Laura nodded. "Are you staying down there?"

"She's broken my heart," said Sophie.

"What was that? I can't hear you over Mum revving the engine. Slow down would you, Mum? We're almost home."

"Should we stop at the corner shop?" asked Maureen. "Kill two birds with one stone?"

"Well, we've definitely got a wounded creature down here, so why not?"

Sophie hauled herself up and pointed her finger at her friend. "You have no clue, do you, Laura? And you honestly don't care!"

"Of course I care; that's why we're here. You're in shock. Put that finger down."

"How could you?!"

"How could I? How could she, more like?" Laura shrugged. "You do have to admit it's kind of apt that your story's ended this way."

"What are you talking about?"

"Cheating. No matter what hurdles you think you've overcome, like finding out you're the reason each other's careers went up in smoke, it's always the simple things like cheating that get you in the end."

"Our happy ever after was there. We had it."

"You didn't. You had horrific teething problems. Mismatched personas. A huge lie. And now different sexual appetites it seems."

"I did everything she wanted in bed."

"Controlling," said Maureen with a nod.

"Because I wanted to!" shouted Sophie.

"Please don't shout at my mother, Sophie."

"It's fine, Laura, she's in shock."

"I'm not in shock, I'm… I'm…" Sophie sobbed. "I'm being cheated on."

CHAPTER THIRTY TWO

The clock ticked quietly in the corner of the room. Steady. Stable. Safe.

Sophie had concluded over the course of the six weeks that the little mechanical heartbeat was as comforting as it was horrifying. The tick of the fleeting present, immediately knocked into the past by the tock.

Comforting that nothing lasted.

Horrifying that nothing stayed.

"The memories we have of events and experiences, and sometimes even people, are often better than the actual reality of those times," said the counsellor, sitting in the plastic chair opposite Sophie with his legs crossed. "Maybe the good times weren't quite as rosy as you've recounted them?"

Sophie sighed. "I know what I feel. What I felt. Jazz was my one."

"*Was*, not *is*?"

"I've already explained this. I guess I'm still struggling to let go of the hypocrisy of it all. I'm made to believe that I'm the worst person in the world for keeping a secret for so long, yet she was doing exactly the same thing."

"And your friend Laura and her mother?"

"Totally done with them."

"But you're not totally done with Jazz? Even though she cheated on you?"

Sophie's body stiffened at the remark.

The counsellor tilted his head to one side. "Tell me once more. I'm listening."

Pulling herself out of the car and dusting herself free from the bits of crap her jumper had picked up in the footwell, Sophie slammed the door and marched off.

"Where are you going?" shouted Laura. "Don't you want to confront Debbie?"

Sophie spun back around. "The only person I want to confront is you."

"Me?" laughed Laura. "What about Jazz?"

Maureen stepped between the pair. "Sophie, dear, you're projecting your upset and anger onto Laura. Laura, darling, Sophie's just letting off steam."

"I'm not," said Sophie, "I'm done."

"With me, or Jazz?"

"Both of you. All of you. I'm going to take one of those touring opportunities and do what I should have done five years ago."

"And what's that?" demanded Laura, hands on hips.

"Get the hell out of here!"

"Go on then, go."

"I am," said Sophie, turning around to march away. "Shit!" she gasped, seeing Jazz's car driving towards them. "Hide me, she's coming!"

"You were going, weren't you?" said Laura, smirking.

Sophie grabbed onto Maureen's arm. "Can you let me in the house? Please, Maureen? She's coming."

Maureen looked at her daughter before stepping away from the contact. "Sorry, Sophie, we're heading to the shop to catch Debbie in the act."

"Laters," said Laura, waving as she crossed the road before shouting "Sophie's right there" towards Jazz's open car window as she pointed at Sophie.

Sophie turned and ran, her feet hammering the pavement as she dashed down the street.

"Wait!" yelled Jazz, driving alongside Sophie and matching the speed of her now sprint. "I've got my clothes on!"

"Good for you," managed Sophie, in between breathy pants as she looked left and right, desperate for somewhere to hide.

"Didn't they tell you I had my clothes on?" shouted Jazz through the other open window now that Sophie had crossed the road. "Didn't you see that I had my clothes on?"

"You must have been spanking her then, big deal!" said Sophie, spotting the cutting through to the park up ahead. "Now leave me alone!"

With her hazard lights flashing, Jazz pulled onto the kerb. "Wait! I'm coming!" she shouted.

"I've heard that before," hollered Sophie, almost to the safety of the high hedges before realising that Jazz was on foot and had almost caught up. "You can't leave your car there!"

"Watch me," said Jazz, reaching out to stop Sophie.

"Get your hands off me!" she shouted, fully aware that anyone in the park would be looking their way. She turned around; the park was empty. "Go back to your woman from Baker Street."

Jazz dropped her grip. "I've got my clothes on."

"So fucking what!" said Sophie. "Just get away from me. I'm leaving."

"I've got a head set on. Didn't they tell you I had a headset on? You dived straight into the car; you didn't see me."

"I'm going to tour with an orchestra. I should have done it years ago."

"You're not listening to me."

"Leave me alone, Jazz."

Jazz's grip was back. "No. You need to look at me, Sophie. Look at my clothes." She bounced her shoulders up and down, drawing attention to the headset and mic now hanging around her neck. "I was on a call."

"With your bitch from Baker Street? I don't care, Jazz, just let go of me, I want to leave."

"I do it on the side."

"Yeah, you're telling me."

"I'm a phone actor."

Sophie laughed. "Is that what you call it?"

"Why are you talking about Baker Street?"

"You went there!"

"You had me followed?"

"Don't turn this around on me!"

"I was dropping off an invitation for Mum. Her friend Sue lives on Baker Street."

"So then you took Sue home and fucked her?"

"Listen to me, Sophie. I'm a phone actor. That's what the suitcase is for, mostly."

"You're an actor, that's for sure."

"The chains and the whips. They make noise."

"How dare you? How dare you say you need space from me because of my misdemeanours while all along you're the one cheating?"

"I'm not cheating, Sophie."

"I HEARD YOU!"

🌩️

The counsellor nodded. "We've been through this. Is phone acting cheating? What did we conclude?"

Sophie folded her arms. "Who calls it phone acting anyway? Sex lines. Sex chat. Prostitution of the voice. Making money talking dirty to dirty perverts."

The man lifted his pen to his notepad. "You're still very angry."

"I think I always will be"

"What about Jazz's explanation?"

"It's a lie that she kept from me."

"Everybody has secrets, Sophie."

"Not like that!"

"And you still feel that Jazz's secret was worse than your secret?"

"Yes!" Sophie paused. "Well, no. I don't know. I just know it hurt me."

The counsellor made another note. "And your secret hurt Jazz."

"You can't make that comparison! Jazz tried to make that comparison."

The head tilt was back. "Last session, last time, tell me once more."

⋆

Jazz was talking fast. "Mum knows, and I even think she's told Dad. She hauls him off to salsa every Tuesday so I can have the house to myself. I used to do it a lot more when I lost my job at the theatre but then the comedy slots took off and I dropped it down to twice a week. Now I only do Tuesdays."

"Oh, that's okay then as long as you only paddle yourself once a week for strangers."

"A yoga mat."

"What?"

"I paddle a yoga mat. It makes a nice slapping sound."

"That's horrible. I'm going."

Jazz followed the fast walk. "I only started because of the fire."

Sophie shouted. "The fire wasn't my fault!"

"I needed a bit of extra money when the acting work dried up. I still need a bit of extra money now."

"For what?"

"For a house. For me, for you."

"That's never going to happen, Jazz. You lied to me."

"I didn't. I just kept something from you like you kept something from me."

Sophie halted her march. "You cannot use that comparison!"

"Ultimately your involvement with the fire didn't hurt me at all and my involvement with this chatline shouldn't hurt you at all."

"You told a random stranger to fuck the life out of you!"

"That was Frank. He's a regular."

"I'm going. Get away from me, Jazz. I never want to see you again."

"Sophie?"

"I'm leaving. We're through."

"I was too ashamed to tell you," said Jazz, following past the swings and the see-saw. "A bit like you were too ashamed to tell me about the fire."

"Stop comparing the two! You choose to do this! You choose to cheat on me!"

"I don't choose to, I have to. Do you know how badly comedians get paid? Why do you think I'm still living at home?"

"Get a job in Tesco then, down the freezer aisle; you seem to know a lot about that." Sophie continued to march. "Or teach Spanish! Or teach primary school kids about homonyms! Or wash cars if you have to!"

"I don't want to wash cars."

Sophie spun around. "But you do want to tell Frank with the big dick to fuck the life out of you?!"

"I've never seen it, and I've never handled it, and I doubt it's very big."

"I bet he's described it to you, though. Honestly, Jazz, you're so disgusting and I don't want anything to do with you ever again."

"I keep the television on mute in the background. Sometimes I even tidy my room."

"And that makes it okay?!"

"Mum's okay with it. She came up with the idea of using two flip-flops."

"What are you talking about?"

"You bang them together and it sounds like I'm wet."

Sophie gasped. "Why are you even telling me this? You're making it worse!"

Jazz upped her pace. "You've just busted me, just like Maureen busted you, but now everything's out in the open we can start afresh properly."

"And what if I hadn't busted you?"

"What if Maureen hadn't busted you?"

"STOP comparing!"

"It's probably my slightly warped comedian's sense of humour but I think phone acting's quite funny. I do, however, completely understand that I should have spoken to you about it, even though it's just acting. It's always just acting."

"You need help, Jazz."

Jazz stopped walking. "Maybe we both do."

The counsellor closed his notepad and placed it on the floor. "And can I confirm what you originally hoped to get out of these sessions? I know we addressed it six weeks ago, but I wanted to check that your aim's still the same? That you haven't changed your mind now you've told me the whole story from all angles?"

"Closure," said Sophie, nodding. "I want closure."

"*We* want closure," added Jazz.

The counsellor double-checked. "Not closure of the relationship?"

Sophie and Jazz smiled at each other before Jazz spoke up again. "No, closure on the start of our story. Every couple goes through conflicts and bumps in the road, but we want to draw a line under ours."

"I think you've done that." The man stood up. "And thank you for clarifying the ending one final time."

"That's it?" said Sophie, looking at the door that was now open. "We don't need any more sessions? I thought you said I was still angry?"

"You processed your anger the moment you became aware of it."

Sophie stood up. "We just go?"

"You'll be fine," said the counsellor. "It's been nice working with you and I wish you both well."

Jazz paused in the doorway. "What if something like this happens again? If we have another bust up or misunderstanding?"

The counsellor smiled. "True love always finds a way. Out of interest, how long did it take from that episode in the park for you two to start talking again?"

Jazz smiled. "A day."

"And for you to decide to get proper counselling?"

Sophie laughed. "Another day."

"Exactly. And I'm sure a less reputable counsellor would try and find reasons to extend your sessions, but I'm happy. You've had no new misdemeanours occur over the past six weeks and your relationship's going from strength to strength." He paused. "I'm also very pleased that your friend's stopped life coaching. People like her give people like me a bad name."

"She's not my friend anymore." Sophie tried to ignore the way they were all standing awkwardly in the doorway. "Is this honestly it? Wait. I haven't told you about Jazz's mum yet. She helped bring us back together by convincing me she was fully supportive of Jazz's extra job and it made me feel slightly silly, like I was a prude or something. Should we have another session about that?"

"No, I think you'll be fine," said the man, smiling. "Thanks again."

Sophie nodded as the door started to shut. "Bye then," she said, craning her neck for one final look into the small room with the ticking clock in the corner.

"He always keeps to his schedule," said Jazz, throwing her arm around Sophie's shoulder and walking her down the corridor of the private building. "It's nothing personal."

"But that was our last session. I feel bereft. I think we should pay for more."

"I'm not taking more phone calls with Frank."

"You'd make the money in no time. We could sign up for another six sessions."

"There's nothing left to say, and we can't keep taking money out of our house fund." Jazz smiled. "It's actually been quite nice hearing our story laid out like that from the start. Your tears to Laura, my terrible jokes."

"It's pretty dramatic, isn't it?"

"Do you think he was properly listening?"

Sophie shrugged. "If I'm honest, I don't really care. Just telling the story's helped. It's made everything so much clearer." She smiled. "If love's real, it finds a way. And look at us, we've found our way."

"To the bedroom," said Jazz with a giggle. "Come on, let's nip back to yours. It's been all of four hours since we last had sex."

"We can't. Mum's preparing a posh dinner for tonight before the unveiling of the new plaque."

"That's right. The JTS Piano studio. Who's coming again?"

"Your parents, my parents, Tessa and John."

"And what are we having?"

"Fish-rice."

"We are not!"

Sophie smiled. "We are. And then we're all coming to watch you on stage."

"Again?"

"Yes again. Tessa and John can't get enough of your wholesome role as Maria."

Jazz sang loudly. *"The hills are alive, with the sound of music."* She smiled as they stepped out of the building and into the sunlight. "We're going to have that many children, you know?"

Sophie inhaled the fresh air. "One step at a time, Jazz, one step at a time."

CHAPTER THIRTY THREE

Standing in front of the gleaming silver plaque, Sophie smiled. *The JTS Piano Studio*. Admittedly, it looked a little lost next to the brightly coloured *Vets For Pets* sign and the huge *We Buy Any Car Dot Com* logo, but it was there and it meant that she was there too. "And on that final note," she said, continuing to address the small crowd, "I want to thank you one last time. You're the people who matter in my life and this means more to me than you could ever imagine. I know I never actually left home, but for the first time in my life I feel home. Back home."

"She does this," whispered Tessa to Jazz's parents in the small area at the bottom of the stairs next to the glass lift. "Gets profound. Jazz told us."

"Stop whispering, Tessa," said John.

"Sorry, John," replied Tessa.

Sophie continued. "And I know everyone keeps telling me to stop saying sorry, but I don't think I'll ever be able to apologise enough to the people I hurt and the lives I affected. Selfishly, I'm pleased though because all of this has changed me for the better. I know who I want to be. I want to be me. And I know I've always been me, it's just—"

"Time for some leftover fish-rice?" suggested Sophie's mum. "I brought some from the house. I thought we could have it in the theatre but this speech is going on somewhat longer than I anticipated."

"Let me finish, Mum."

"You have been talking for quite some time, darling," said Robert to his daughter.

"And I've got to get on stage," added Jazz before singing, "*The hills are alive with the sound of music.*"

"Have you heard enough, Tessa?" asked John.

"I think I have, John," replied Tessa.

Sophie smiled as she lifted her hands and conceded. "This. You've just put this feeling into words. This is what matters. This is what's real."

"We all love you, Sophie," said Sophie's mum. "I hope you know that?"

Sophie smiled. "And I love you all too."

"Finally!" said Jazz, starting the round of applause. "To Sophie and the JTS Piano Studio!"

"To Sophie and Jazz!" replied Sophie's father.

"To Tessa and John!" cheered Sophie.

"To Jazz's acting career!" whooped Tessa, her buoyant breasts bouncing.

Jazz shouted. "No one toast that bloody fish-rice, for god's sake!"

"To the fish-rice!" rang the laughter, between friends.

THE END

About the author:

Lambda Literary Award finalist and Polari First Book Prize judge, Kiki Archer is the UK-based author of ten best-selling, award-winning novels. Kiki ranked highly on the Guardian newspaper's Pride Power List and the Diva Pride Power List in 2017, 2018 and 2019.

Her debut novel *But She Is My Student* won the UK's 2012 SoSoGay Best Book Award. Its sequel *Instigations* took just 12 hours from its release to reach the top of the Amazon lesbian fiction chart.

Binding Devotion was a finalist in the 2013 Rainbow Awards.

One Foot Onto The Ice broke into the American Amazon contemporary fiction top 100 as well as achieving the lesbian fiction number ones. The sequel *When You Know* went straight to number one on the Amazon UK, Amazon America, and Amazon Australia lesbian fiction charts, as well as number one on the iTunes, Smashwords, and Lulu Gay and Lesbian chart.

Too Late... I Love You won the National Indie Excellence Award for Best LGBTQ Book, the Gold Global eBook Award for Best LGBT Fiction. It was a Rainbow Awards Finalist and received an Honourable Mention.

Lost In The Starlight was a finalist in the 2017 Lambda Literary Awards' Best Lesbian Romance category and was named a Distinguished Favourite in the Independent Press Awards.

A Fairytale Of Possibilities won Best Romance Novel at the 2017 Diva Literary Awards and was awarded a Distinguished Favourite in the New York Big Book Awards.

The Way You Smile was a finalist in the National Indie Excellence Awards for Best LGBTQ Book.

Kiki was crowned the Ultimate Planet's Independent Author of the Year in 2013 and she received an Honourable Mention in the 2014 Author of the Year category.

She won Best Independent Author and Best Book for *Too Late... I Love You* in the 2015 Lesbian Oscars and was a Finalist in the 2017 Diva250 Awards for Best Author.

In 2018 Kiki won Best Author at the Waldorf's star-studded Diva Awards.

Say You'll Love Me Again is Kiki's 10th and final novel.

Novels by Kiki Archer:

BUT SHE IS MY STUDENT - March 2012

INSTIGATIONS - August 2012

BINDING DEVOTION - February 2013

ONE FOOT ONTO THE ICE - September 2013

WHEN YOU KNOW - April 2014

TOO LATE... I LOVE YOU - June 2015

LOST IN THE STARLIGHT - September 2016

A FAIRYTALE OF POSSIBILITIES - June 2017

THE WAY YOU SMILE - November 2018

SAY YOU'LL LOVE ME AGAIN - June 2019

Connect with Kiki:

www.kikiarcherbooks.com
Twitter: @kikiarcherbooks
www.instagram.com/kikiarcherbooks
www.youtube.com/kikiarcherbooks